MINA'S MATCHBOX

ALSO BY YOKO OGAWA

Revenge

Hotel Iris

The Housekeeper and the Professor

The Diving Pool

The Memory Police

MINA'S MATCHBOX

Yoko Ogawa

Translated from the Japanese
by Stephen Snyder

Harvill *Secker*
LONDON

1 3 5 7 9 10 8 6 4 2

Harvill Secker, an imprint of Vintage, is part of the Penguin Random House group of companies whose addresses can be found at global.penguinrandomhouse.com

Penguin
Random House
UK

First published in Great Britain by Harvill Secker in 2024
First published in the United States of America by Pantheon Books, a division of
Penguin Random House LLC, New York, in 2024
First appeared in Japan in 2005 as a newspaper
serialization with the title "Mina no Koshin" by
Yomiuri Shimbun
First published in Japan in 2006 with the title *Mina no Koshin*
by Chuokoron-Shinsha, Inc.

Designed by Anna B. Knighton

penguin.co.uk/vintage

Printed and bound in Great Britain by Clays Ltd, Elcograf S.p.A.

The authorised representative in the EEA is Penguin Random House Ireland,
Morrison Chambers, 32 Nassau Street, Dublin D02 YH68

A CIP catalogue record for this book is available from the British Library

HB ISBN 9781787302761
TPB ISBN 9781787302778

Penguin Random House is committed to a sustainable future
for our business, our readers and our planet. This book is made
from Forest Stewardship Council® certified paper.

I

The first vehicle I ever rode in was a baby carriage that had been brought across the sea, all the way from Germany. It was fitted out in brass and draped all around with bunting. The body of the carriage was elegantly designed, and the interior was lined with handmade lace, soft as eiderdown. The metal handle, the frame for the sunshade, and even the spokes of the wheels all glittered brilliantly. The pillow was embroidered in pale pink with the characters for my name: Tomoko.

The carriage was a gift from my mother's sister. My aunt's husband had succeeded his father as the president of a beverage company, and his mother was German. None of our other relatives had any overseas connections or had even so much as flown in an airplane, so when my aunt's name came up in any context, she was always referred to as "the one who had married a foreigner"—as if the epithet were actually part of her name.

In those days, my parents and I were living in a rented house on the outskirts of Okayama City, and the carriage was more than likely the most valuable object among our possessions. A photograph from the period shows how out of place it looked in front of the old wooden house. It was far too large for the tiny garden, and it was far more eye-catching than the baby herself, presumably the subject of the picture. I'm told that when my mother pushed the carriage in the neighborhood, passersby turned to look at it. If they were acquaintances, they'd invariably come up to touch it, commenting ecstatically on how beautiful it was before moving on, without any mention of the baby inside.

Unfortunately, I have no memory of riding in the carriage. By the time I became aware of what was happening around me, that is, by the time I'd grown too big to ride in the carriage myself, it had already been relegated to the storage shed. Still, though the lace had yellowed a bit and was spotted with milk I had spit up on it, the carriage had lost none of its former elegance. Even surrounded by kerosene jugs and tattered blinds, it still gave off the aroma of foreign places.

Breathing in that smell, I'd let my imagination stray in my childhood. I'd daydream that I was, in reality, a princess from a distant land, abducted by a treacherous servant who had subsequently abandoned me, along with the carriage, deep in a forest. If you unstitched the embroidered *Tomoko* on the cushion, you would no doubt find some trace of my real name—Elizabeth, or perhaps Angela . . . The carriage always played a starring role whenever I invented these sorts of stories.

∿∿∿

The next vehicle that transported me was my father's bicycle. Jet black and featureless, it emitted a sad squeaking sound. It was, admittedly, quite plain in comparison with the German carriage. Each morning, my father would tie his briefcase to the rack and ride off to his office. On holidays, he would set me on the rack and ride to the park.

I can still recall the sensations associated with this bicycle.
The strong hands that lifted me so easily, the smell of tobacco coming from the broad back, the breeze from the spinning tires.

"Hold on tight! Don't let go!"

My father would turn to make sure that I was gripping his sweater, and then he would start pedaling. The bicycle flew along, easily negotiating steep slopes and sharp turns, and I held tight to his back, convinced that simply by doing so I could be taken anywhere in the world.

Though I was true to my word and never let go of him, he left me without warning, going alone to a distant place. Stomach cancer, discovered too late. In 1966, soon after I'd started elementary school.

〰〰

On the fifteenth of March, 1972, the day I graduated from that school, the Sanyo Shinkansen link between Osaka and Okayama was inaugurated. The next day, at the age of twelve, I boarded the train alone, seen off by my mother from the Okayama Station, which was still decorated for the opening ceremony.

This vehicle was different from any I had ridden in before. It was sturdy but cold, full of life, but without anything I could find to hold on to.

As we made our way to the platform, my mother kept repeating the same bits of advice—"don't miss your stop, don't lose your ticket, ask the conductor if you need help"—but once I'd finally boarded the train, she suddenly fell silent, her voice reduced to sobs. She cried a good deal more that day than when my father had died, large tears dropping from the false eyelashes that were starting to pull away from her face.

After my father died, she'd supported us by working in a textile factory while doing some dressmaking on the side. But as I was about to enter middle school, she'd apparently started thinking about her future. She'd decided to pursue a year's course of study at a school in Tokyo to improve her skills as a dressmaker, with the goal of securing more stable work. After discussing it with me, we'd agreed that she would move into the school dormitory, and I would go to live with my aunt's family in Ashiya. We had no money for an apartment for the two of us in Tokyo, so we would simply have to accept my aunt's generosity.

The decision clearly worried my mother a great deal, but I was less anxious about the move. After all, this aunt was the one who had sent the baby carriage on the occasion of my birth.

At the time, my uncle was already president of the beverage company. He and my aunt had two children, a boy of eighteen and a girl a year younger than me who was still in elementary school. The boy was not living at home when I arrived, having recently left to study in Switzerland. But there was one other resident: the German grandmother who had come to live with the family. My uncle was thus half-German, my cousins one-quarter.

I had never met them, but as the most remarkable household among our relations, I had decided I liked them and believed I knew all about them, down to the smallest details. Without any cause for thinking so, I was convinced that my new life with them would go well even without my mother, a decision I'd come to based solely on the fact that they'd given me such an extraordinary carriage.

"Go on then."

Even though there was still some time before the train would leave, Mother hurried me aboard. Once I'd reached my seat, she continued to give me her final instructions from outside the window—"put your luggage in the rack; if you get warm, take off your sweater; check one more time for your ticket." As the train began to move, she wiped her tears away with one hand as she waved over and over with the other.

∿∿∿

The moment I got off at Shin-Kobe Station, I was convinced that my premonitions had been correct. I knew without any sort of sign that the man waiting there was my uncle. He stood, totally relaxed, legs crossed, leaning against the hood of his car, in a perfectly pressed gray suit and elegant tie. His hair was brown, with soft curls, he was taller than anyone else around, and the spring sunshine lit the deep recesses around his eyes. When he saw me, he raised his hand and called out, a warm smile spreading over his face.

Having difficulty believing that a man so handsome would be smiling for me alone, I could only manage an awkward bow.

"Welcome," he said. "How was your trip on the new Shinkansen?"

My uncle bent over to look at me, then took my bag and opened the car door, as though I were a princess.

"Please," he said. His voice was deep and calm, his manner refined, his eyes the same chestnut color as his hair. My heart was pounding.

"Thank you," I managed to say at last.

As I sat down in the middle of the back seat, I realized I was in an elegant vehicle, as big as a small room and filled with an indescribable odor. The leather seats had been shined to a high gloss, and there were buttons everywhere, not only in front of the driver's seat but under the windows as well— all attesting to the vehicle's careful design. The engine was so quiet I hardly noticed that it had started before the car glided away, responding perfectly to my uncle's touch. It was only much later that I learned it was a Mercedes-Benz.

No doubt, in order to help me relax, my uncle asked me questions about Okayama and told me about the middle school where I would be going. But I was so absorbed in studying his profile that I could manage no more than monosyllables in response. A mere touch of the gearshift or the button on the heater turned them into objects of desire. Parting with my mother in tears on the station platform seemed like a scene from the distant past.

After about half an hour, the car turned off the highway and headed along a river in the direction of the mountains. The Rokko Mountain Range loomed over us. We passed under the train tracks and crossed a bridge. Soon, the road started uphill and began to narrow. Trees closed in around us, birds could be heard among the leaves. Stone walls lined the road, tracing gentle turns. The roofs of houses peeked out between the trees. My uncle calmly maneuvered up a steep road barely wide enough for two cars to pass. Finally, he glided through a gate that had been left open, made a half-turn, and came to a stop under a porch.

"Here we are," he announced, opening my door and taking my hand.

"Is this your . . . house?" I asked. "Is this really your house?"

2

I will never forget the house in Ashiya, where I lived from 1972 to 1973. The shape of the shadow under the arched entry porch, the cream-colored walls against the green of the mountains, the pattern of grapes on the railings of the veranda, the two towers with their ornamental windows. Every inch of it is etched in my memory, from the grand sight of the exterior to the particular odor in each of the seventeen rooms, from the quality of the light in the garden to the cool touch of the doorknobs.

Now, after thirty years have passed, there is no trace of the house. The sturdy palm trees that grew at either side of the door, as though keeping guard over the family, have withered and been uprooted, and the pond at the southern end of the garden has been filled in with earth. The land long ago passed into other hands and was divided up, and is now home to strangers, the residents of a nondescript apartment block and a dormitory for the employees of a chemical company.

But perhaps because they are now so completely removed from reality, nothing in the world can dim my memories. My uncle's house still stands in my mind, and the members of his family, those who have grown old as well as those who have died, live on there as they once did. Whenever I return there in my memory, their voices are as lively as ever, their smiling faces full of warmth.

Grandmother Rosa, seated before the makeup mirror she brought from Germany as part of her trousseau, carefully rubbing her face with beauty cream. My aunt in the smoking room, tirelessly hunting for typographical errors. My uncle, impeccably dressed, even at home, endlessly tossing off his quips and jokes. The staff, Yoneda-san and Kobayashi-san, working hard in their respective domains; the family pet, Pochiko, relaxing in the garden. And my cousin Mina reading a book. We always knew when she was about from the rustling of the box of matches she kept in her pocket. The matchboxes were her precious possessions, her talismans.

I wander quietly among them, careful to avoid being a nuisance. But someone invariably notices me, and, as if thirty years have vanished in a moment, calls out a greeting.

"Tomoko, is that you?"

"Yes, it's me," I answer to the family in my memories.

〰〰〰

It was my uncle's father who built this residence in the hills some two hundred meters above sea level to the northwest of Ashiya Station on the Hankyu Railway, along the Kōza tributary of the Ashiya River. The second in the family to serve as president of the beverage company, he had gone off in his midtwenties to study at the University of Berlin, specializing in pharmacology. It was there that he met and married Grandmother Rosa. After returning home, he had expanded the company by developing Fressy, a radium-fortified soft drink that was said to be beneficial to the digestion. And it was he who acquired fifteen hundred *tsubo* of land at the foot of Ashiya Mountain, where a residential area was being developed after the Hankyu Line came through, and there he built a mansion in the Spanish Colonial style. That was in 1927, the second year of the Showa period.

With its arched porte cochere and terrasse, semicircular sunroom on the southeast corner, and orange-tiled roof, the house gave an impression of cheerful graciousness rather than opulence. Great care had been taken with even the smallest details, and the balance of the whole had a special elegance. Though the exterior was in the Spanish style, the furnishings, dishes, and linens were all German made, to ensure that Grandmother Rosa would not be homesick. The garden to the south sloped gently toward the sea, in order to take advantage of the sunlight. Few cars passed along the road to the north, and trees grew all around. The bustle of the city was far away.

Protected from the seasonal winds by the Rokko Mountains, the winters were mild and the summers made bearable by the breezes from the sea. Perhaps it was due to this favorable environment that my grandparents were blessed with a child in the twelfth year of their marriage, almost as soon as they moved to this house. That child was my uncle.

My uncle's life unfolded along nearly the same lines as his father's. After studying in Germany, he had returned to work on improvements to Fressy, the company's key product. He also updated the packaging and ultimately achieved a substantial improvement in sales. The only difference was the fact that he did not find a wife in Germany. My uncle married my aunt, who was working in the company laboratory, washing beakers and testing new products.

This couple, who lived the early years of their married life in the healthy environment of the house in Ashiya, did not have to wait twelve years to conceive a child. On the contrary, just seven months after their wedding, they had a son, Ryūichi.

As if to counterbalance this precipitous first birth, it was seven more years until the next one. Mina, who gave me so much and asked nothing in return, was born in the winter of 1960. Mina, the darling of the whole family, whose body was too weak to travel but whose soul never stopped voyaging to the ends of the earth.

〜〜〜

They were all assembled in the hall to greet me when I followed my uncle through the door, and they all seemed more nervous than I felt. Grandmother Rosa, leaning on her cane, gave an awkward smile, and my aunt was apparently too disconcerted by this first meeting with her niece to find the right words to say. Mina's look was serious, as though she was determined to discover the true nature of this newcomer.

In addition to the family, there were two old people I could not identify. It wasn't long before I discovered that the man, who appeared to be the younger of the two, was the gardener, Kobayashi-san, who lived elsewhere, and the woman was Yoneda-san, the maid who lived in the house. Since the characters for Kobayashi, who took care of the trees, meant "little forest," and those for Yoneda, who prepared our meals, meant "rice paddy," I soon memorized their names.

"Please take your bags upstairs." It was Yoneda-san who spoke up first. "Your room is the second one in the wing just at the top of the stairs. The boxes that arrived from Okayama are already there. You can take your time arranging things to your liking. Mina, please give her a tour of the house. The location of the bathrooms, how to get hot water, everything she needs to know. Tea is at three o'clock, so come down to the parlor then. I've made a fruitcake for this afternoon."

As she spoke, the smile with which my uncle had greeted me at the station never left his face. Then we all left the hall in obedience to Yoneda-san's instructions.

My first impression of this family was that the group had a great deal of variety. The color of their hair, for example, ranged from white (Grandmother Rosa and Yoneda-san) to gray (Kobayashi-san) to light brown (my uncle) to dark brown (Mina) to black (my aunt). Nor was that the only way they differed. Their names freely mixed Chinese characters with foreign ones (my uncle's full name was Eric-Ken, Mina's was Minako), and they all spoke somewhat different languages. Yoneda-san, Kobayashi-san, and Mina spoke a very natural version of Kansai dialect, while my aunt and uncle spoke the standard dialect but with a large inflection from Kansai. Grandmother Rosa spoke a peculiar sort of Japanese that was, at times, difficult to understand.

But there was nothing negative about all these differences. On the contrary, compared to my small family, just my mother and me, it provided room for a lost girl to wander in and find her place.

〰〰

Mina followed Yoneda-san's instructions and gave me a thorough tour of the house. There were many doors to open, and each room they revealed was more attractive than the last.

A reception hall with a dazzling chandelier and a fireplace of black marble. A silent study illuminated by a ray of light through a stained-glass window. A guest room with a canopy bed of the sort I'd seen only in picture books. The excitement I had felt as I'd stepped from the car continued to grow.

But Mina, apparently unaware of what I was feeling, and apparently without a hint of vanity, continued the tour.

"This is where Mama hides to have a drink without Grandmother seeing. That's why the carpet is covered with cigarette burns." "I wish someone could explain to me why they chose such hideous curtains." "This is Yoneda-san's workroom. The spot on the wall is where she threw the iron one day when she was hysterical."

She went on and on like this. But I was barely listening; I was so taken in by this palatial house and thoughts of Yoneda-san's three o'clock fruitcake.

〰〰

The room they had prepared for me had been Ryūichi's before he went to study in Switzerland. It was next to Mina's, sunny, south-facing, with a balcony and a fine view of the garden. Since it had been a boy's room, it was a bit lacking in romance—nor was there a canopy on the bed—but still, how could I complain?

Mina and I went out on the balcony. Even the handle on the door, which had to be turned at a right angle to open, seemed strange to my eyes. It was then that I finally looked about the garden. It was so large that it seemed to stretch down to the sea, and at the far end was thick vegetation and a pond. Something was moving in the tall grass. A black, unidentifiable mass.

"Did something move down there?" I asked, pointing at
the spot.

"Oh, that's Pochiko," said Mina, her tone softening. "Our hippopotamus."

And that's how I learned of the final, and equally important, inhabitant of the house.

3

"A . . . hippopotamus?" I murmured. The question seemed natural enough, but Mina answered in a tone that implied she couldn't understand why anyone would ask about something so self-evident.

"She lives here," she said.

"A hippopotamus?"

"That's right."

"Here?"

"Yes, here." There had been no sign of arrogance when she showed me the chandeliers or the canopied beds, but for the first time a look of pride crept over her face. "It was a present from Grandfather to my father on his tenth birthday," she added.

"A hippopotamus . . . as a present?"

"A pygmy hippopotamus to be exact. From the order Artiodactyla in the Hippopotamidae family, common name pygmy hippopotamus. They're way smaller and much cuter than a regular hippopotamus. Grandfather bought her in Liberia, before any Japanese zoo even had one, and it cost more than ten cars."

"Did your father ask for it?"

"Not exactly, but I think Grandfather liked to spoil him."

Mina rested her elbows on the balcony railing without taking her eyes from the tuft of grass. Pochiko was still no more than a black lump.

Perhaps it was because she'd inherited it from Grandmother Rosa, or maybe it was due to her chronic asthma, but for whatever reason, Mina's skin was as white and transparent as tissue paper, revealing not only her blood vessels but the blood that flowed through them—or so it seemed. She was so beautiful that any girl would have wanted to look like her, but small for someone about to enter the sixth grade; there was no sign that her breasts had started to develop. To be honest, she looked more like a second grader. Her fingers and ankles were so delicate they almost made you want to reach out and touch them.

But the most remarkable thing about her was her hair. Soft and curly from the roots, it fell almost to the middle of her back. The sunlight brought out the delicate chestnut color, and it fluttered in the slightest breeze.

"Papa wasn't the only one who loved having her around. His friends from school and the neighbors—they all wanted to see Pochiko. Which got Grandfather even more excited, and in the end he turned the garden into a zoo. He bought peacocks and Taiwanese macaques, goats and monitor lizards, and he founded the Fressy Zoological Garden, open weekends only. But of course, Pochiko was always the main attraction."

"A zoo?" I murmured, more surprised than ever.

"But the war started soon after, and I think the zoo only lasted a couple of years. Grandfather died before I was born, and Pochiko was the only animal that survived."

I tried picturing the Fressy Zoological Garden spreading out in front of me. And it was very difficult to imagine, with plenty of space, a pond, a little hill, shade trees—all sorts of

16   places that animals might like. The children could laugh and shout to their hearts' content, the macaques scream as loud as they could, and still the trees on the hillside would easily absorb all the noise.

How had I gotten so lucky as to come to live in a house that had once been a zoo? I was sure it must have been a peaceful, wonderful place, though, truth be told, I had never in my life set foot in a zoo.

〰〰

We went to meet Pochiko straightaway.

"Is it really okay? She won't attack us?"

I cowered behind Mina, advancing ever so carefully. There was no cage or fence, and the black lump was moving toward us little by little.

"Pochiko would never do anything like that. She's very well-behaved, aren't you, Pochiko?" From her tone, Mina might have been talking to a kitten. She leaned forward and rubbed her cheek against the lump, and it was only then I realized we were facing the animal's hindquarters. As proof, Pochiko's tail began to swing back and forth in time with the movement of Mina's hand. A tail like a rounded ball of clay stuck onto the cleft in the animal's rear end.

"Tomoko, come and pet her."

"Me?" I said, taking a step back.

The front half of Pochiko's body was still buried in the tall grass. She stood perfectly still, except for her tail, and I had no idea whether she was sleeping, waiting for a pat, or simply a bit shy. But it was clear that she didn't seem at all dangerous. There was, in fact, something charming about the curve of her stout bottom. Her rear legs, planted carelessly one behind

the other, seemed absurd, so short you might have wondered
whether they served any purpose at all.

"Come," Mina said, beckoning me forward. Realizing that I
would have to be brave if we were to be friends, I made up my
mind. Tapping my finger near the base of Pochiko's tail, I let
my hand slide along the curve of her bottom.

It wasn't as rough as I had imagined. The surface of her
skin was covered with little bumps and wrinkles, but it was
smooth to the touch, warm, and covered with something
damp and sticky, like perspiration. In response to my greeting, Pochiko's tail began to move back and forth once again.

"Well? What did I tell you? She isn't a bit scary." Mina
stared into my eyes, anxious to know what I was thinking.
"Isn't she the smartest hippopotamus in the whole world?"

"I'm sure you're right. The smartest." Though I knew nothing about any other hippopotamuses, I agreed with Mina,
gingerly giving Pochiko another pat on the bottom.

Suddenly, without any warning, there was an eruption
from the base of her tail, which she'd been waving so vigorously, and her feces went flying in every direction. I cried out,
stumbling as I tried to get out of the way.

"Pochiko!" Mina laughed. "Is that any way to say hello to
someone you're meeting for the first time?" I was frantically
checking to see whether it had landed on my hands or my
dress, but Mina didn't seem to care at all. Rather than trying
to avoid the mess, she walked right through it as she came
even closer to Pochiko.

At that moment, there was a rustling sound in the grass,
and Pochiko finally emerged in her entirety. I thought she
would turn to look at us, but instead she simply took a few
steps backward, freeing her head from the undergrowth, and

then fell completely still again, seemingly uninterested in either a dip in the pond or a rest on the grass. Apparently, her very short legs were not designed for any sort of quick movement.

As Mina had said, Pochiko was quite different from an ordinary hippopotamus. First of all, she was not enormously large. From head to tail, her length was approximately the height of an average man, and her head came more or less to my waist. The skin on her back, which I'd imagined to be completely black, had flecks of green depending on the light, and the flesh under her chin and down to her belly was pale pink.

The part of her that least resembled a regular hippopotamus was her face, which was simple and neat, with none of the rough, doltish quality you might associate with a hippo. Her nostrils and mouth were small, and her eyes and ears, in particular, were so tiny as to be almost invisible. In other words, you might say that her existence amounted to this round lump of a body onto which a tail, little legs, and a face had been stuck.

"Pochiko, say hello to my cousin Tomoko who will be living with us from now on."

Mina brushed the dried grass from around Pochiko's mouth and ran her finger along the folds of her ear. Pochiko's eyes rolled up in her head in apparent annoyance and her nostrils flared. That was the extent of her greeting.

〰〰〰

Mina and I sat down in the grass at the edge of the pond, which was lined with stones and large and deep enough for Pochiko to swim at her leisure. The water was a bit cloudy, but if you looked carefully, you could see grasses waving gently at the bottom. From a shed shielded by the bushes came the constant hum of the filtration system.

Since it was clear that Pochiko was the most important thing in Mina's life, I made a point of questioning her closely about the hippo. Her daily diet (two kilos of kibble, seven kilos of compacted dry silage, and a few fruits and nuts), her weight (160 kilograms), her age (approximately thirty-five years), her bed (a hollow she had dug for herself in the garden hillock), her vocalizations (husky but somehow almost shy), her special talent (pretending not to hear) . . .

Mina seemed delighted to be able to answer my questions, and so to please her I asked every single one I could think of—and all the while the topic of our conversation remained absolutely still, staring off into space, seemingly unaware of all the attention she was receiving.

"Young ladies, your snack is ready." It was my uncle.

Of course! "Fruitcake!" Did that mean there was fruit on top of the cake? Or were they baked into the cake itself? I rubbed my palms, which were perhaps still a bit soiled from Pochiko, on the grass, brushed off my skirt, and ran with Mina toward the terrace.

4

My next surprise, discovered not long after I met Pochiko, was that the person who wielded real power in the household was neither Grandmother Rosa nor my aunt, but Yoneda-san.

Yoneda-san had been keeping house here since Grandmother Rosa arrived to marry my grandfather in 1916, the fifth year of the Taisho period. Fully fifty-six years—a length of time that seemed unimaginable to my twelve-year-old self.

To watch her work was to realize how completely she was convinced that no one else understood the house as thoroughly as she did, down to the last corner. She had no qualms at all about offering advice or the occasional rebuke to any of the other residents, often imbued with thick layers of irony. No one in the family minded, though; everyone saw it as her due. If a dispute arose, it was generally Yoneda-san who had the last word, and most arguments ended with the phrase "If Yoneda-san says so, then that's how it has to be."

Though Yoneda-san and Grandmother Rosa were both eighty-three years old, their personalities, their tastes, and even their appearances were completely different. Grandmother Rosa was short and plump, her back somewhat bent, and her knees riddled with arthritis, while Yoneda-san resembled a stork, without an ounce of excess fat on her body, as she moved restlessly about the house. It seemed that one of them had been defeated by old age while the other rebelled against it, refusing to give in.

Still, they were the best of friends. Their rooms were next to each other on the ground floor at the western end of the house, with a door connecting them to avoid the need to go out into the corridor. They sat next to one another at the table as well. They could often be seen with their heads together, trading secrets, and Grandmother Rosa never left the house unless accompanied by Yoneda-san. I can still see Grandmother Rosa perched on a stool at the counter as preparations for dinner were getting underway, finding something useful to do—peeling potatoes or garlic—while taking care not to bother Yoneda-san as she whirled about the kitchen.

I suspect it was Yoneda-san who had welcomed and encouraged my grandmother when she came all alone to Japan, a country whose language she did not understand and where she had no friends. Yoneda-san was an older sister, teacher, and friend to Grandmother Rosa.

〰〰〰

The quietest members of the household were my aunt and Kobayashi-san. Kobayashi-san was nominally the gardener, but his daily duties consisted mainly of caring for Pochiko, a job he had inherited from his father, who had been the first keeper at the Fressy Zoological Garden. In silence, he brought Pochiko her food, cleaned up after her messes, and scrubbed her body with a deck brush. Together they made quite a pair. Though Kobayashi-san spoke little, they managed to communicate their feelings with gestures and tail-wagging, waves and flaring nostrils.

My aunt's silence was deeper. She preferred to listen to others rather than talk herself. Whenever she had to speak, she would pause for a long while before saying anything, as if she were thinking about how best to express herself using the fewest words possible, or perhaps waiting for someone else to speak up in her place.

I knew it wasn't because she was ill-tempered, but rather that she was always listening attentively, not wanting to miss the slightest murmur from anyone.

And I knew one other thing—that she was the one who smiled most readily whenever my uncle told one of his jokes. A little smile, eyes lowered, accompanied by a tiny sound, so slight as to be indistinguishable from a sigh.

It was true, my uncle had a genius for making other people happy. And in turn, everyone loved my uncle. Even Yoneda-san had long since taken to referring to him affectionately as "Little Ken." Everyone wanted to hear his stories and tell him theirs. In any gathering, he could immediately sense who was bored or feeling weary, and he would find the right topic to cheer them up. He had a talent for turning any mishap into an amusing story, or adding a bit of fiction to a small happiness to make it a great joy. A simple conversation with him made you feel as though you were somehow very special.

〰〰

Three days after I arrived in Ashiya, I went with my uncle to a clothing store in Nishinomiya to get my middle-school uniform. Since I would be entering Y Public Middle School in Ashiya, it seemed odd that we would need to go to a store so far away, but it turned out that Nishinomiya was much closer than I'd realized. When we left the house, we headed south on

the national highway along the Ashiya River, passed under the
expressway, and in less than five minutes we'd arrived in the
neighboring town. I'd been looking forward to the time in the car
with my uncle, so I was a bit disappointed.

As we descended the mountain, the city spread out in front
of us, and I could feel the presence of the sea even through
the car windows. Holding the wheel with one hand, my uncle
sketched an imaginary map with the other, outlining the
long, narrow shape of Ashiya, running north to south. The
train lines, Hankyu, Kokutetsu, and Hanshin, he explained,
ran parallel to one another through the city. The store was
in the central commercial district around the Nishinomiya
Hanshin Station.

"We need a pretty school uniform for the young lady," my
uncle told the shop attendant, his hand resting on my shoulder.

"Yes, of course," the clerk replied. "I'm sure we have just
the thing."

The attendant was a middle-aged woman, but it was obvious that she was completely captivated by my uncle's manner
and appearance.

She must think we're father and daughter. That I was very
lucky to be out shopping with such a handsome father. That
it would be wonderful if her own husband were as elegant as
him. She must be very jealous. Or so I proudly told myself in
secret.

The store seemed to specialize in school uniforms, and the
racks were full of fancy ones with name tags from famous
schools like Konan Girls College, Shukugawa Institute, or
Nigawa Academy. But the design of the uniform for Y Middle
School, which I would be attending, was less interesting, with
a jumper skirt, matching vest, and formless blazer. As I stud-

ied myself in the mirror, I felt I had somehow brought my countrified upbringing along with me from Okayama.

My mother would have prioritized the practical over appearances and chosen a uniform that was large enough to last for the three years of middle school, but my uncle would have none of that. He had them take my measurements and instructed the attendant to adjust the sleeves on the blazer, shorten the skirt, and take in the vest.

"How does this look?" the woman asked, standing with pins in hand. My uncle took a few steps back and studied me, offering his opinion, a little longer or shorter, with great precision.

After a bit more of this back and forth, he put his hand to his chin and made a final check.

"It suits you perfectly," he said.

At that moment, my uniform became fashionable and quite citified, unlike anything you could find in Okayama.

〰〰〰

On our way home, we stopped at a patisserie near Hanshin Ashiya Station. The spring sun shone in through large windows facing the street to the south. In the light, the great array of cakes and pastries lined up in the window glittered like jewels. Everything sparkled—the creams, the strawberries, the sponge cakes, the paper napkins and ribbons they were wrapped in—even the cash register.

"Order whatever you like," my uncle said, folding his long legs under the table.

"Tea, please . . ." I murmured, eyes lowered, unable to meet his gaze now that he was so close.

"That's all?" he said, sounding terribly disappointed. "Don't you like sweets? These are the best pastries in Ashiya."

"Of course I like them," I added as quickly as I could, nodding vigorously to show him I had no intention of disappointing him. "But I thought it wouldn't be fair to Mina."

"Is that all?" he said. "Then don't worry. We'll get some madeleines to take home for her. She and Yoneda-san are crazy about the madeleines here." He looked out at me from the chestnut-colored spots deep in his eyes. "I think you might enjoy the crêpes Suzette," he added.

I had no idea what that might be, but I agreed immediately. "Yes, please," I said.

The crêpes Suzette arrived on a serving cart. Three rounds of dough, as thin as a handkerchief, had been folded like fans and lined up on a plate. The effect was less impressive than I had been expecting. The waiter bowed and then lifted a silver pot with both hands. I held my breath and waited, motionless, for what would come next. From the pot came a generous stream of liquid flowing onto the handkerchiefs. When the pot was empty, the waiter produced a match and set fire to the plate.

Blue flames shot up. They were faint, as though they might go out at any moment, yet they continued to burn there between my uncle and me, casting a pure blue light on the scene.

5

My uncle left the house the next day and did not return that night. For the first day of his absence, and then the second, I thought little of it, assuming he had gone somewhere for business. As president of a company, I reasoned, it was normal that he would be busy. But when on the fourth and fifth days there was no sign of him, I began to worry.

The soft drink factory that made Fressy was located by the sea to the south of Osaka, and my uncle drove himself back and forth from the house each day. I found myself looking out at the garage every morning as soon as I woke up, but the Mercedes-Benz was missing, and his parking place was empty.

〰〰〰

Though my uncle was the only one missing from the house, the atmosphere became strangely gloomy. In place of laughter, there were sighs from Grandmother Rosa, who complained of arthritis, and more frequent warnings from Yoneda-san to Mina and me about our behavior. Though normally everyone would have lingered in the parlor after dinner in order to spend as much time as possible with my uncle, now they excused themselves from the table and immediately retreated to their own rooms. Grandmother Rosa to her bedroom, Yoneda-san to the kitchen, and Mina to a chaise lounge in the sunroom.

Even Pochiko seemed somehow dispirited. As a nocturnal animal, she would go out to the edge of the pond to eat the food that Kobayashi-san had prepared for her after sundown. Though she had been slow and lumbering to begin with, now she seemed to eat even more wearily.

And my aunt became even quieter. She was either smoking a cigarette or sipping a glass of whiskey whenever I saw her.

We all pretended not to notice that there was an empty place at the table, as though it had never been occupied in the first place. Yoneda-san stopped putting a place setting in front of his chair and made sure there were no leftovers after the meal.

"Where is my uncle?" I asked at last, unable to restrain myself.

But as soon as the words were out of my mouth, I regretted them, feeling it was a question that should not have been asked. There was a silence, as they all stopped eating at once. Mina had been taking a bite of hamburger, Yoneda-san serving more rice, my aunt sitting quietly as always.

"When is Papa coming home? He doesn't even know himself." Grandmother Rosa finally spoke up to answer, near the end of the meal, but by then I'd nearly forgotten what it was I'd asked.

〰〰

That night, Mina had an asthma attack. At first, when I woke up, I didn't realize that the sound coming through the walls from her room was coughing. It was a quiet, diffident noise, like a mouse grinding its teeth near the ceiling or scratching its claws on the floor. But it grew little by little, becoming more distinct and painful sounding. I heard footsteps and adults whispering in the hallway.

Worried, I came out of my room just as my aunt was starting down the stairs with Mina clinging to her back. On either side were Yoneda-san and Grandmother Rosa, patting Mina as they went.

"Tomoko, there's nothing to worry about," said Grandmother Rosa, turning to look at me. "Go back to bed. It will be all right."

Headlights shone through the frosted glass in the windows of the entrance hall downstairs, and a car could be heard pulling up in the driveway. Kobayashi-san appeared, a jacket thrown on over his pajamas. He gathered Mina gently in his arms, taking care to avoid increasing her suffering, and carried her to the van. My aunt slipped her insurance card and wallet into her handbag as she whispered a few words to Yoneda-san, while Grandmother Rosa took off her own shawl and wrapped it around my aunt's shoulders.

Everyone played their appointed parts. I could tell that this was not the first time that something like this had happened, that this group had overcome similar crises many times in the past. With no more than a few glances between them, they agreed on what had to be done and set about doing it without any unnecessary fuss. Nevertheless, it was clear from the way they went about their duties just how worried they were about Mina. I was the only one who had nothing to do.

Mina coughed continuously, a painful little cry escaping from her chest each time she tried to take a breath, to the point

that I began to feel I was suffocating myself. In Kobayashi-
san's arms, she seemed thinner and more fragile than ever.

I lined up with Grandmother Rosa and Yoneda-san under the porch outside the front door and watched the van disappear, as if sucked into the darkness. As it went, the sound of Mina's cough went with it, at last fading away as well. Though it was nearing the end of March, the night air was chilly, and without quite realizing it we had drawn ourselves into a close little group. I could feel Yoneda-san's rough, bony hands, and the softness of Grandmother Rosa's ample chest. The only light that fell on us came from the lamp on the porch and the moon rising above the top of the tower.

"Now then, young lady, time for bed." It was the first time I'd heard Yoneda-san use such a gentle tone of voice.

It proved difficult to get back to sleep. The light on the stairs filtered under the door, having been left on in case Mina and the others returned. The two old women had apparently gone back to their rooms, and there was no sound coming from below. After tossing and turning for a time, I slipped out of bed and went to wander barefoot around the second floor. No matter how carefully I moved, the floorboards creaked ever so slightly. The moon filtering in through the skylight and the round window on the landing cast muddy pools of light here and there on the floor. Mina's door, my aunt's, and all the others were shut tight.

∿∿∿

When I reached the door of the guest bathroom at the western corner of the house, I discovered that there was one more small door beyond it, a place that, evidently, Mina had neglected to show me. Turning the doorknob, I discovered not another room but a narrow, dusty staircase leading straight up to the level above. At the top was storage room tucked under the eaves.

Boxes of various sizes and shapes, damaged furniture, skis, broken electrical devices, toys, stacks of magazines—all abandoned in random heaps. But even the junk here had a certain air of refinement, nothing like the stuff in our storage room in Okayama. The only thing the two spaces had in common was the most conspicuous bit of detritus stored in each: the baby carriage.

From the mark on the side, I knew it was the same German-made brand that had been sent to me. But this one was more like a jewel box than anything that could be accounted for by a name as simple as "baby carriage."

Mine had been lined with cotton lace, but this one was fitted out in silk from end to end, with luxurious draping all around, decorated with several layers of frills and satin ribbons. The down pillow had been sweetly embroidered with images of a monkey, a goat, a peacock, and Pochiko herself, as if to make it plain that the carriage belonged to the baby of the Fressy Zoological Garden. The metal fittings were gilded in gold rather than brass, right down to the hook that held the pacifier, and it was clear even in the moonlight that they had lost none of their glitter.

Near the base of the handle, there was a small wooden box with a key. I gave it a turn and the Schubert lullaby came wafting through the attic, dissolving slowly, note by note into the darkness, until it stopped somewhere in the third phrase.

It was then that my tears began to flow, which upset me as I had not been expecting them. I quickly wiped them away with my sleeve, but they continued unabated.

It wasn't that I was jealous of Mina's much more luxurious carriage. I knew for certain that the appearance of this one, with its eighteen-karat gold fittings, silk drapes, and music box, could not ever have seemed any grander than my own, could not diminish my memories of it in the slightest.

No, rather than jealousy, it was anger that had taken hold of me. Why was my uncle absent at a moment like this? His daughter, who was so precious that she'd been kept in this jewel box, was in crisis—so where was this uncle who was so important to her? Was Mina all right? Was she still breathing? If my uncle had been here, there would have been no need to call Kobayashi-san in the middle of the night. He could have taken her to the hospital straightaway, in the Mercedes he was so proud of. That was much more important than taking me to get my uniform. The woman at the store must have secretly thought that we made an odd pair. She must have known that a man as handsome as my uncle would never have a daughter with a face as plain as mine. And the waiter who'd brought the crêpes Suzette had been polite on the surface, but what had he really been thinking deep down?

It all made me terribly sad. I ran down the stairs and crawled into bed. Recalling how my mother had cried on the platform at Okayama Station, I found myself weeping as well and longed to see her again.

6

Mina came home early the next morning, just as she had left the night before, in the arms of Kobayashi-san. Her cough was gone, but she was still terribly pale and seemed exhausted. She went straight to bed and slept without a peep until the afternoon. Everyone took great care not to wake her. Grandmother Rosa walking with her cane, Yoneda-san hanging out the laundry, and Kobayashi-san calling Pochiko—all did so as quietly as possible.

My aunt sat for a long time in her usual chair on the terrace, slowly drinking her coffee, Grandmother Rosa's shawl still around her shoulders. She looked even more exhausted than Mina. It was a sunless morning, with a cold wind that stirred the branches of the trees, but my aunt showed no sign of moving from her place.

"I'm sorry for all the fuss last night. I doubt you were able to sleep," she said, when she caught sight of me.

"Not at all," I told her. "How is Mina?"

"She'll be fine. These emergencies happen all the time." She bent over and took a sip of coffee.

"You'll catch cold," I told her.

"Thank you, Tomoko. You're very kind."

At that moment, for the first time, I realized that her profile resembled my mother's.

I stayed with her on the terrace until she had finished her
coffee. We watched the smoke from her cigarette float up
between us and disappear into the distance. What was left of
the tears from the previous evening at last began to dry, bit
by bit.

〰

There was something extraordinary about the attention
everyone in the house at Ashiya paid to Mina's health. Preventing these emergencies was their top priority. At the
slightest cough, all the adults came running to bring her a
sweater or a scarf, a pocket warmer, or something to gargle.
Simply by clearing her throat, she set off an alarm that put
everyone on high alert. At least that was how it felt.

Compared to the luxury of the house itself, the daily
meals were somewhat plain, though thoughtfully planned in
terms of nutrition. In particular, the kitchen was always well
supplied with foods thought to be good for the respiratory
system—daikon, honey, yams, Chinese wolfberry, leaves of
the chameleon plant, and all types of unidentifiable herbs and
medicinals.

Furthermore, Yoneda-san took great care to use only the
freshest ingredients. She was of the opinion that nothing was
worse for the body than food that had begun to get old, and she
mercilessly discarded anything that gave the slightest indica-
tion of having discolored, gone limp, anything that seemed
suspicious in any way. Her nose, which had a few small white
hairs protruding from it, never failed to detect the slightest

odor of decay, though it might have eluded everyone else. Her most serious expression was reserved for standing in front of the refrigerator and bringing a dish of leftovers or a nearly empty bottle of milk close to her nose to examine.

Needless to say, the medicine cabinet was well stocked too. Liquid aerosol and powdered medicines for asthma supplied by the hospital, but also Asada's tablets, Ryukakusan, throat lozenges, iodine gargle, Kyushin and Seirogan tablets, Biofermin pills, Ohta's stomach powder, Ichijiku enema preparation, Kakkonto, Konjisui toothache remedy, Travelmin for motion sickness, Hiya's pills, Oronine ointment, mercurochrome, hydrogen peroxide, cod liver oil—it was all there.

But the thing they undoubtedly trusted most as treatment for any ailment was Fressy. If you had a headache or a stomachache, if you were feeling depressed—Fressy was the answer. A sip of Fressy and everything would be better—without it you'd never be cured. They all believed that emphatically. The advertisements claimed it was a "refreshing drink and aid to the digestion, made with radium-fortified spring water from Mount Rokko," but in the end it was nothing more than a sweet soft drink. Still, it occupied the most important place in their household, above every other remedy in the medicine cabinet. Since it was the company's trademark product, developed by my grandfather, I understood why it was that they felt this way, and yet somehow their faith in the efficacy of Fressy struck me as a bit naïve.

There was a special refrigerator in the kitchen that they used to chill a large supply of Fressy, newly bottled and delivered directly from the factory every week on the same day. The children—meaning Mina and I—were forbidden from taking food from the kitchen without permission, with the

exception of Fressy. We could take one whenever we wanted,
pop the cap off with the bottle opener that sat on top of the
refrigerator (shaped like a star, the symbol for Fressy, a complimentary gift for any customers who ordered a case), and
gulp it down.

When I thought back to my life in Okayama, where my
mother's fear of cavities had meant that I was allowed to drink
Fressy only on my birthday, I considered that the unfettered
access I had to this special refrigerator was one of the greatest luxuries I'd now been given, second only to life in that
enormous house itself.

〰〰

Yet another peculiarity of the house in Ashiya, insofar as
health was concerned, was the "light-bath room." It was a
small, windowless cabinet on the second floor, in the east
corner of the house, covered from floor to ceiling in Islamic
tiles. In the center of the room were two lounge chairs draped
in sheets. An oil lamp sat in one corner, and there were two
chandeliers, oddly shaped, as though two copper pots had
been suspended upside down from the ceiling. Other than
that, the room was empty. The pots hung from the ceiling
by cords wrapped in a rainbow of fireproof cloth—deep red,
navy blue, forest green—and they were each lined around the
edge with eight lightbulbs. When the switch was thrown, the
bulbs cast a beautiful orange glow and the chandeliers began
slowly to rotate.

Bathing in this light was thought to have health benefits.
The device must have been the height of scientific progress
when Mina's grandfather first brought it from Germany
before the war, and still, even now, Mina invariably returned

to the light-bath room after a health crisis, to rest and regain her strength.

The bulbs must have consumed a great deal of electricity, which may be why the room was otherwise lit only by the oil lamp. The day Mina brought me there, the day after she was rushed to the hospital, she took a box of matches out of her skirt pocket and, before I'd had time to think how odd it was for a child to have matches, she struck one with her dainty little fingers. The next instant, light glowed from the wick of the lamp. The faint smell of phosphorus, a slight whispering noise in my ears. A thin plume of smoke rose from the tips of Mina's fingers.

I climbed awkwardly onto one of the lounge chairs.

"It's really pretty simple," Mina said. "You lie here and every once in a while turn a little, so that the exposure is even all over. Just don't look right at the light since it can hurt your eyes, like an eclipse."

Then, with a practiced hand, she threw the switch next to one of the chandeliers and twisted the dial on the timer. Next, she stripped off her clothes, down to her slip and her underwear, and stretched out on the chair. She seemed more or less recovered since she'd come home that morning.

"Does it really work?" I asked a bit doubtfully.

"Hmm . . ." she murmured, eyes closed.

The rays of orange light, so dense they might almost have dripped from your fingertips if you touched them, suddenly illuminated the dim room and reflected the geometric patterns from the ceiling onto our white underwear. The metal fixtures made a terrible grinding noise, as though they had rusted in place, but still the lightbulbs continued to turn, and before long I began to feel a faint warmth on my belly.

"What's it like when you have an attack?" I asked, unbearably curious about how such terrible suffering could resolve
itself in one night.

"It's like having the exit blocked so you can't get out," Mina
said without opening her eyes. "The air can't go out, but it
can't get in either. Like being trapped in a tight space and
you're about to explode into a million pieces."

"Oh," I murmured. Mina's chest was flat, as I'd imagined it
would be; it was exactly as you'd have expected after seeing
the faint mounds of her nipples under her slip, with no trace of
swelling breasts at all. Only the knobby knees interrupted her
smooth, slender legs splayed out in front of her. The bleached
white underpants, visible beneath the hem of her slip, were
loose and baggy, too large for her tiny backside.

"The worst is when the air pressure is low outside," she said,
her chest rising and falling with the rhythm of her speech. "I
know right away when there's a mass of foul air forming in
the lower atmosphere. I can pretty much tell the barometric
pressure by the movement of the cilia in my lungs."

"What's a cilia?"

"Little hairs that grow in your bronchial tubes. They wave
back and forth like seaweed and push out the phlegm." Her
lips were lovely, childlike still, and yet nonetheless able to
tell me about bronchial tubes in great detail. "When I realize
that I can't breathe, my field of vision suddenly narrows and
things start to appear there that shouldn't be—things with
real colors and shapes, blinking and whirling in front of my
eyes. As I stare at them, I start to worry that I've gone off
somewhere really far away, but then pretty soon I realize it's
just the opposite; I'm not someplace far away, but someplace
much too close. I'm right inside my own heart."

At this, Mina turned over and folded her hands under her chin. I followed suit, and now the patterns spun about on our backs.

"Does it hurt?" I asked.

"No, when it gets to that point, it doesn't really. Actually, that's when I start to think that it feels good. But mother's voice always brings me back, and I suddenly realize where I am. I usually try blinking really hard, but it's too late," she said. "I'll already have lost sight of that too-close place."

7

"No," I said. Still on my stomach, I lifted my head to look at her. "You have to come back, quickly, before your mother calls. If you hang around in a place like that, you won't be able to come back at all. And then it will be truly too late."

Mina grunted noncommittally and flipped her hands so that they were still supporting her chin.

"But it's really pretty there," she said, and at that moment there was a little noise, like the popping of an elastic band. The timer went to zero and the orange light was extinguished. The chandelier trembled as the lightbulbs stopped turning. I smelled a slight burning odor, but everything began to flow along normally again. Mina got up, turning her head and taking a deep breath, as if assessing the effects of the light rays.

〰〰

Still in our slips, we sat facing one another on the couches, eating the snack that we'd prepared beforehand. Milk Bolos, and Fressy to drink, of course. I had not had Bolos for a long time, not since I was a baby, but at the house in Ashiya, they were considered a nutrient-rich food that aided the digestion. Odd as it seemed, it was taken as common knowledge by the family that eating them with a bottle of Fressy would enhance the effects of the light bath.

But even stranger was the fact that they called them "Milk" Bolos. No one in Okayama had called them that. We'd called them Egg Bolos. But everyone here, Yoneda-san and Mina and even Kobayashi-san, repeated the name again and again without a hint of embarrassment.

To my ears, the sound of the word "milk," *chichi*, recalled the word for breasts, and really their round, flesh-colored form, impossible not to roll in your palms, would remind anyone of exactly that. So I was more than a little embarrassed by the sound of that silly word.

We divided up the plateful of Bolos. Mina pinched them between her fingers and brought them to her pursed lips, eating them one after another with a pleasant crunching sound. Her legs, bare below her too-short slip, swung idly back and forth above the floor.

Mina's face appeared even lovelier and fresher when seen from so close, so vivid it seemed to bear down on me, seemed almost frightening to look at. Her eyes were wide, and a light shone from deep within her pupils. The bridge of her nose cast a rich shadow on her face. Her cheeks, full in proportion to her slender body, were flawless. Her brow had an air of intelligence, her lips of complete innocence. It was enough to cause anyone to wonder how such a beautiful girl could ever have been born.

Still, this perfect face seemed completely out of keeping with her immature body. Perhaps because she'd suffered from these attacks since she was very young, her back was bent—to allow her to cough more easily?—and her ribs seemed sunken. Even when she was relatively healthy, if you listened carefully, you could hear a sound like the winter wind blowing at the back of her throat—a troubled sound, as though her body were bewildered at the prospect of having to support such a beautiful face.

"What's it like having such a handsome father?" I asked her. Considering how plain my aunt, my mother, and I were, it was clear that Mina had inherited her looks from her father.

"I'm not sure what you mean . . ."

What I'd found so enviable was of no importance to Mina.

"If I were you, I'd brag about him to everyone."

"It would seem strange to brag about your own father." Mina tilted the bottle back and took a drink of Fressy. The wintry sound in her throat was quiet only when she was drinking. "Anyway, you can't choose your father. He's just there when you're born. How can you brag about something you had no part in? Now, a boyfriend you chose yourself, that you could brag about."

I was shocked; I'd never expected a word like "boyfriend" to come out of her mouth.

"Do you have a boyfriend?"

"No," she said, giving her head a light shake.

The final few Bolos rattled at the bottom of the plate as I took it in my hands. I'm not sure why, but I suddenly had the feeling that I was eating Mina's breasts. Perhaps because I imagined that they were the same eggshell color as the Bolos, soft enough to melt in your mouth. They gave no sign that they would be swelling, but rather, it seemed clear that they would remain quietly where they were, just little ornaments—or so it seemed to me.

Not that I had anything to boast of myself. Only a few girls were wearing bras in the sixth grade, and I was definitely not one of them. My mother had slipped one into my luggage as I left for Ashiya, to be worn at the opening ceremony at my middle school, but there was little chance that my breasts would have developed enough by then to need it.

"Oh," said Mina, giving her legs a kick. "I do know one reason I'm glad Papa's handsome: his nose. It's long and perfect to pinch." She tossed the last Bolo into her mouth.

We were still warm from the light bath, even though we hadn't gotten dressed. The afterglow lingered behind my eyelids; no matter how much I blinked, I could still see the orange light.

The light bath became the most important place for Mina and me after that day. No matter how much time we spent locked away in there, the adults left us alone, never worried about us at all. Mina struck a match and, in an instant, the room was ours.

〰〰

At the beginning of April, before the opening ceremony for my middle school, they held a ceremony for Mina's elementary school. She was entering the sixth grade, her final year.

In the morning, before they left the house, Yoneda-san tied up her hair and Mina added a blue velvet ribbon. Since the school would be holding the ceremony that day but no classes, Mina packed only her hall slippers and a dust cloth in her bag.

I went to the foyer to see her off—and who should I discover but Pochiko. She must have come around from the garden at some point and now was waiting in front of the door. Kobayashi-san was with her.

Pochiko looked quite different that morning. Her sleepy eyes and lumbering movements were the same, but she had some sort of collar around her neck and a small wooden seat on her back, secured by two leather belts around her fat little belly. Kobayashi-san stood beside her, holding a cord that was attached to her collar and decorated with a ribbon of the same blue velvet as Mina's.

You might wonder whether this was really a suitable getup for a pygmy hippopotamus, but everything seemed to be properly broken in and perfectly fitted to Pochiko's neck and back and belly. The collar nestled neatly between one of the deep creases under her throat, and the little seat seemed securely fastened, the belts not unduly tight around her middle. On the contrary, the color of the belts was so similar to Pochiko's skin that it was difficult to tell them apart.

But still it was hard to accept that the bright ribbon could possibly be a good match for Pochiko's round body, stubby legs, and somewhat distracted features. It seemed more like someone had tied it there by mistake, like they'd had nowhere else to put it.

"Well then, young lady, shall we go?" said Kobayashi-san. He placed an empty Fressy case upside down on the driveway, and Pochiko, as though that were her cue, lowered her head and bent her front legs. Using the box as a stairstep, Mina climbed into the seat.

This was all accomplished quite easily and naturally, with an air of confidence that seemed to surround the three of them.

"See you later," said Mina, settling her bag on her lap.

"Yes, see you soon," said my aunt, Grandmother Rosa, and Yoneda-san.

Kobayashi-san took hold of the tassel at the end of the cord, Mina sat up quite properly, Pochiko gave a few shakes of her tail, and they were off. They passed in front of the palm trees, descended the sloping driveway, and disappeared out the gate.

8

Every day Mina went back and forth to Y Elementary school on Pochiko's back.

Because of her health, she went to this local public school rather than the private elementary school in Kobe that her brother, Ryūichi, had attended. Exhaust fumes, be they from the school bus or the Mercedes, tended to set off her asthma and Y School was the closest school with the easiest commute. It took about twenty minutes to get there, after crossing the Kaimori Bridge over the Ashiya River; the only challenge was the steeply sloping road down to the school.

My uncle had met with the principal before Mina had started there and received permission for her to commute on Pochiko. It seems that the principal had taken a ride himself to make sure that the hippo wouldn't harm anyone. He had intentionally called out while riding Pochiko, tossed bread rolls from the cafeteria, had even pulled on her ears, but Pochiko had remained calm, responding with nothing more than a skeptical snort. She had passed the test.

It was my uncle who, through repeated trial and error, had devised the apparatus that turned Pochiko into a mode of transportation. He had cut the legs off of a high chair to use as the saddle, a belt became the collar, and a tassel from some curtains the reins—and with that, he had managed to create the world's first contraption for riding a pygmy hippopotamus. In the morning, Kobayashi-san would put Mina on Pochiko's back and deliver her to school, and in the afternoon he would lead her back to meet Mina at the gate. This had become their custom.

At first, I thought it was a shame, since they had such a magnificent Mercedes they might have used, but it didn't take long for my opinion to change—after all, Pochiko had cost more than ten Mercedes, so Mina was using the most expensive vehicle in the house.

∧∧∧

The march of Mina, Kobayashi-san, and Pochiko was nothing if not dignified. Mina looked straight ahead, Kobayashi-san held firm to the reins, and Pochiko made her way carefully, step by step, up and down the sloping road. The people cleaning outside the gate, the crowds hurrying to and from Hankyu Ashiya River Station, the children who attended Mina's school—everyone who met them on the road would stop and let them pass. Kobayashi-san would nod in greeting and adjust their course with a distinctive tug on the reins.

"Ah, Miss Mina, off to school?" a neighborhood lady would ask.

"Good morning!" Mina would call out politely from her perch on Pochiko's back.

Very rarely, someone who was not familiar with their march would cast a curious glance in their direction, but it never troubled them in the least. Mina kept her eyes straight ahead, and Pochiko plodded along more diligently than ever.

Though Pochiko might at times have appeared a bit distracted, she was actually quite aware of her job. She kept her head down to avoid bending backward and causing the seat to slip, and she would slow her pace whenever Mina started to squirm. Perhaps to keep Mina from worrying, Pochiko never appeared to be bothered by her task, no matter how steep the slope. On the contrary, she walked along as though there were no one on her back at all, as though the outings were exclusively for her own purposes, done under her own conditions.

The morning sun shone down on them as they went, illuminating Mina's backpack and Pochiko's rear end. The soft clicking of hippo hooves on the asphalt, making their way around the final curve, and then there was the school gate. Their matching ribbons swayed gently in the sun.

〜〜〜

For my part, the only time I'd spent at my desk before the opening ceremony for my middle school was when I wrote letters to my mother. She'd put practice books for math and Chinese characters in my luggage, believing that city students would be more advanced, but I hadn't opened either of them.

"Ashiya is close to Kobe and Osaka, so you'll have plenty of interesting places to see," my mother had written. "Has your aunt taken you anywhere yet? I've heard that the old site of Expo '70 in Osaka has been turned into a public park. We didn't make it to the Expo, but you should at least get to see the Tower of the Sun. Take advantage of your time there and see as much as you can. That's what I've been trying to do ever since I came to Tokyo. The next time I have a day off, I'm going to the department stores to buy you something useful. And something for Mina . . ."

I'd only been out of the house once since I'd arrived in Ashiya, when I'd gone to the store to have measurements taken

for my uniform. I hadn't been anywhere with my aunt, who
rarely went anywhere—but then, most of the residents of the
Ashiya house seemed to be homebodies. They liked nothing
better than to stay put and considered the things that they
might need to go out for to be either annoying or unpleasant.
Only my uncle and Kobayashi-san had driver's licenses, and
most of the food and other necessities were delivered from the
shops in town, so it was quite rare that anyone left the property.

My uncle, on the other hand, was extremely fond of going
out—and not returning home—so it could be said that over-
all things were balanced.

I felt no dissatisfaction with my situation. Just two years
earlier, when I'd found out that we couldn't go to Expo '70
because of my mother's work, I'd screamed and cried. I was
devastated to learn that only three children in the class,
including me, would not be going. But now I was completely
indifferent to the Expo, the Tower of the Sun, and everything
else about it. The house in Ashiya seemed to hold treasures
even more wondrous than American moon rocks.

〰〰〰

The part of the house that interested me above all was Grandmother Rosa's room. When Mina was busy reading, I would
often knock on Grandmother Rosa's door, and she would
always welcome me warmly.

Her room was larger than the other bedrooms, but it was
also filled with more possessions, so it seemed almost cramped.
The magnificent furniture she had brought with her when she
came from Germany—wardrobes, cabinets, a writing desk—
was covered with bisque dolls, bonbon dishes, a tea service,
vases, perfume bottles, music boxes, evening bags, hats, a doll-

house . . . But most impressive of all was the bed, with its four posts taller than me and a headboard covered in carved wooden roses. The quilt, always perfectly smoothed thanks to Yoneda-san, was embroidered with the initial *R*. Because she had problems with her legs, chairs had been placed around the room to allow her to sit every few steps if necessary, and each of these had a different and marvelous design.

The walls were thickly covered with worn, yellowed photographs of people I didn't know—as though Grandmother Rosa's life had accumulated in the room like the layers in a geological formation.

When I first walked in, I felt like an archaeologist looking for the perfect place to begin my research. I made every effort to be polite and inoffensive, but then I would get carried away and start opening drawers without permission, asking excitedly about the contents.

The dressing table, in particular, had a number of drawers I was unable to resist. They were filled with cosmetics of all kinds, and each bottle or jar, from the makeup remover to the face powder, bore the image of two women, their heads pressed together, and the name of the brand: Twin Beauties Series. Their faces were perfect ovals, their hair adorned with large, pale pink flowers, their eyes fixed dramatically in the half-distance.

"Oh that, it works wonders," Grandmother Rosa would say, seating me in front of the dressing table. "It's beauty cream; the more you use, the softer your skin gets." She would spread a silk makeup cape over my shoulders and let me use her products, no matter how precious, including this, a sticky miracle cream in a round, milk-glass jar with a brown lid. The label read: RICH, NOURISHING FACIAL CREAM.

"You take a little on your finger and dab it on, dab, dab,

dab. You need just about an almond's worth. Too much, a
plum's worth, and it gets sticky; too little, a pearl's worth, and
it doesn't work."

She pinned back my bangs and applied the cream to my
forehead, my cheeks, my chin.

"You have beautiful skin," she told me. "It's very full."

"Full of what?" I asked.

"Full of health and moisture and elasticity, full of the
future, of everything."

She studied my reflection in the mirror as she spread the
cream with her trembling fingers, taking great care to avoid
missing any bumps or imperfections, applying it everywhere,
to the corners of my eyes, the ridges along my nose, the base
of my ears. I could feel her breath very close to me, and her
white hair, wispy as a down quilt. From time to time, her hair
brushed up against the makeup cape, making a rustling noise.
Her wrinkled fingers tickled me mercilessly.

"You mustn't say anything to Yoneda-san," she said, putting a finger to her lips.

"Why?" I asked.

"She doesn't like to have children using makeup. She thinks
that putting things on the skin can be bad for the body. I'd
like to put a bit of this on Mina as well, but I'm told I mustn't.
So, this will be our little secret," she said, winking at me in
the mirror.

It seemed that the two ladies were completely at odds on
the question of makeup. When Grandmother Rosa appeared
at the breakfast table each morning, she was already completely made up for the day, with lipstick and hairpins chosen
to match her outfit. If there were so much as a tiny chip to the
manicure on her pinky, she would redo all ten fingers.

With Yoneda-san, on the other hand, what you saw was what you got. Apart from a minuscule amount of loofah lotion, she used no makeup at all. Her pleasures came from stirring the pots in the kitchen rather than applying face cream, from sewing clothes for others rather than wearing fancy ones herself.

Once she'd applied the lotion to my entire face, Grandmother Rosa took a pink puff and patted my cheeks with a bit of powder—though not enough for Yoneda-san to notice—then applied lip cream and rubbed my fingernails with nail gloss. She picked up each of the perfume bottles lining the dressing table and let me take a sniff, and then put a drop of my favorite behind my earlobes. To be honest, they all smelled the same to me, so I chose by the shape of the bottle.

Her trembling hands moved uncertainly, rattling the bottles and jars, but the fingers that touched me were soft and warm. Her movements were relaxed, her back bent and padded almost as generously as Pochiko's. She wriggled her lips, rescuing the dentures that threatened to pop from her mouth.

I sat spellbound before the ranks of pretty bottles, all filled with colorful liquids and wonderful scents unlike any I'd ever smelled before. Though the sight of Grandmother Rosa's wedding ring, now that her hand was so close to my face, was a bit frightening. It seemed to have melted into the flesh of her finger, and the pattern engraved on the surface was an extension of the wrinkles on her skin. If it ever proved absolutely necessary to remove the ring, I had no doubt it would mean cutting off her finger, a scene that terrified me to imagine. The whole time I sat at her makeup table, some part of me was praying that nothing like this would ever come to pass.

"There now, all done." She pulled the cape from my shoulders and stood, nodding in satisfaction as she compared the real me with my reflection in the mirror. "Very pretty," she announced. "You look very pretty, Tomoko, but you mustn't say anything to Yoneda-san."

∿∿∿

In response to Grandmother Rosa's request, I wrote the Chinese characters for "Tomoko." She had been in Japan for fifty-six years, but she still struggled with kanji. She walked around with a little dictionary in her pocket, and when she encountered a character she didn't recognize, she would ask anyone she could find to help her. It seemed that she had been able to read more characters when she was young, but she had gradually forgotten them as she'd grown older.

"Tomoko." I took a fountain pen and wrote my name in large characters on a sheet of notepaper: 朋子

"I see," she murmured, as if it were somehow terribly interesting, while she retrieved the reading glasses that hung from a chain around her neck. "There are two identical characters lined up next to one another. They must be great friends."

"Yes, that's right. Two moons."

"Have they always had this kanji? I've never seen it."

"It means 'friend' or 'companion.'"

"How nice! What a lovely character. Especially since there's only one real moon, but here they are, two of them. What a wonderful thing, a great friendship. And they're just the same size, not one above the other but lined up together. That's the lovely part. Equal and not alone. Like these bottles here," she added, pointing at the makeup table.

The Twin Beauties were still surrounded by flowers, still

had their almond eyes fixed on the same point somewhere in the distance. Then Grandmother Rosa reached out and took a framed photograph from the wall.

"Just like us. Close to one another, lined up together."

The photograph was quite old. Two little girls in matching dresses with lace collars and puff sleeves, about the same age as Mina, standing side by side. Like the Twin Beauties, like the two moons in the character for my name.

"Do you have a twin, Grandmother?"

"I do . . ."

"Which one is you?"

"I'm here, the one with the deeper cleft above my lips, with the rounder earlobes." She pointed at the little girl on her left. But I couldn't tell the difference between them, no matter how much I looked. "And this is my big sister, Irma."

"Does she still live in Germany?"

Grandmother Rosa shook her head, but in an ambiguous way that made it difficult to decide at first whether it meant she was living somewhere other than in Germany or something else entirely. It was only as she took her handkerchief from her pocket to wipe the dust from the frame that I realized she'd meant the latter.

"The last time I saw her was in 1916, when we said goodbye at the station in Berlin."

I took the photograph from her and hung it back on the wall, checking to be sure it was straight. Grandmother Rosa drew the notepad closer and picked up her reading glasses to review what I had written, then she copied the characters again in her tiny, careful script, right beside mine.

9

The day of the opening ceremony for my middle school came at last. The morning was cloudy and cool. I had accepted the fact that I would probably have to attend by myself if my uncle didn't come home, though I hadn't mentioned it to anyone. But when the day arrived, the women of the house were all busy with their preparations.

"I would never let you go alone, Tomoko," my aunt declared in a tone that sounded quite unlike her.

Grandmother Rosa, Yoneda-san, and Mina had gathered at her closet, and they were all taking out their favorite dresses and holding them up in front of my aunt, one after another.

"The neckline on this one looks a bit tired," said Yoneda-san. "Have you lost more weight?"

"This one is just too sad." It was Mina's turn. "It's a celebration—you can't go looking sad. Don't you have anything brighter, with a bigger pattern? I'd lend you one of mine, but it would never fit."

"But not something too gaudy," added Grandmother Rosa. "That won't do for a roomful of children. Just find something that looks young and fresh."

With three very different views, it proved difficult to find the right outfit, and my aunt sat nodding, without expressing any opinion of her own.

Judging from the contents of her closet, it seemed that my aunt had little occasion to dress up or go out. The clothes on the hangers were all well made, but the designs were traditional and plain, as though their main purpose was to avoid drawing attention to themselves. And their number was equally unimpressive; you could see the back panels of the closet between the sparely arrayed hangers.

In the end, after a long debate, they decided on a dark blue silk chiffon dress and a mink stole that had the virtue of adding a bit of style while hiding the wrinkles on her throat. Her hair was done up and fastened with a sapphire clip, emphasizing her youth. Grandmother Rosa had gone to excavate both the stole and the clip from the layers of items in her room, and it was Grandmother as well who had redone my aunt's lipstick in a brighter shade and added rouge to her cheeks.

Compared to my aunt, things were much simpler for me, though I was to play the starring role. I put on the uniform that had just arrived from the shop in Nishinomiya and a pair of white socks. Thanks to the care my uncle had taken with ordering the uniform, it fit me perfectly. Since it was forbidden by the school rules, I couldn't add a ribbon like the ones that Mina and Pochiko wore, and, as I'd suspected, no matter how I tried to arrange the bra, it was ill-fitting, stiff, and uncomfortable.

"Are you ready, Miss Tomoko?" Yoneda-san asked. "The important thing is to be relaxed and confident," she added, patting my back. "First impressions matter. Don't be intimidated just because you're a transfer student. After all, everyone is in their first year at a new school. There's nothing to be afraid of." In reality, I wasn't particularly worried, but I nodded gratefully.

And with that, Mina left for her school as usual on Pochiko's back and my aunt and I walked in the opposite direction, toward the middle school.

〜〜〜

Y Middle School was farther up the hillside and away from the coast. To say that the road to the school was steep would have been an understatement. It was, for all intents and purposes, like climbing a mountain. The murmur of the Koza River could be heard through the trees. My aunt and I were out of breath and beginning to perspire, and her stole was slipping from her shoulders.

It was worse still for me, as my bra seemed to be pushing up with every step, moving in the opposite direction from her stole. By the time we arrived at the gate of school, it had slipped up above my breasts and was completely useless.

The school was in a far more rural setting than I had imagined, with nothing even vaguely urbane about it. The mountain came down right to the back of the building, and there was no sign of houses higher up the slope, just row upon row of trees. In that sense it didn't seem terribly different from the middle school in Okayama set among the rice paddies.

I'd been placed in the second class of the first year. As I looked around at the girls in our group, I realized I didn't stand out as particularly countrified. That had been my mother's main anxiety, but, as Yoneda-san had said, there appeared to be no reason to worry. The boys were even less impressive, and, sadly, at first glance I didn't see even one who interested me. The homeroom teacher, a short man who had just graduated from university, taught social studies.

~~~~

"Where do you live?" The girl seated next to me asked in a lilting Kansai accent, just as the ceremony was about to start. I told her my address. "Then you're near the hippo house?"

"Yes, that's the one."

"Oh?" she murmured, looking at me as though I were a hippo myself. "But you have a different name," she added, pointing at my badge. I wondered how to explain, but then the assistant principal solemnly announced the opening of the ceremony and the auditorium fell silent. I was relieved, but still I leaned in and whispered in her ear.

"It's not a hippopotamus. It's a pygmy hippopotamus, in the Artiodactyla order, Hippopotamidae family, common name pygmy hippopotamus."

~~~~

My aunt's conduct during the ceremony was exemplary. She had restored her mink stole to her shoulders, her left hand resting at her neck. The sapphire hair clip gave an elegant sparkle, with an unexpected accent from the cherry blossoms floating down from above. A smile on her lips and no trace of shadow in her eyes, she was the picture of refinement, even seated on a metal folding chair. The bright shade of lipstick suited her perfectly, and the soft material of her dress accentuated her slender figure.

The image she often projected as, a bit guiltily, she'd light a cigarette or bring a glass of whiskey to her lips had been cleverly concealed.

As the school year got underway, Mina and I fell into a daily rhythm. Returning home in the afternoon, we would have a snack and do our homework. In the evening, we would listen to Professor Marsha Krakower's radio course in "Basic English," and then help Yoneda-san or Kobayashi-san. Our chores were always simple ones, like peeling carrots or taking Pochiko her dinner. The job of lighting the gas heater for the bath with a match was always left to Mina. It had apparently been her duty since long before I arrived in Ashiya. We took our bath together after dinner and then went to sleep in our own beds.

My homesickness gradually began to ease. I was always in a good mood in the morning, being especially fond of the moment, on clear, springlike days, when the sun would slip through the curtains to wake me. I liked to lie in bed and watch as the features of my room appeared one after another in the morning light—the slippers I'd discarded the night before, the amber floorboards, the pattern of the wallpaper, the light in the shape of an oil lamp, the sturdy desk that promised to make me smarter just by sitting at it.

When I opened the curtains, the green of the garden sparkled with dew. The sea met the sky in the distance. No doubt Pochiko was still dreaming in her bed on the little hill, but the birds were already chirping merrily, gathered on the shore of the pond for a morning drink. I could tell that Yoneda-san was already busy preparing breakfast downstairs. She had baguettes delivered daily, and I could hear the bakery van pulling up to the kitchen door. The sound alone created the illusion that I was already smelling the delicious odor of freshly baked bread. The morning sun seemed to shed its blessings on everyone and everything.

But the night could be dangerous. The sun would go down and the lights would come on, in the entrance, in the kitchen, on the landing in the stairway, in the garden, and then here and there throughout the house, and as the shadows began to collect around me, the blessings of the daylight changed to curses. Whereas Mina, Grandmother Rosa, and the others were protected in principle by the places that had been reserved for them, I felt that I alone had been set aside in some irrelevant spot. Out of all the people in the world, the shadows had chosen me and seemed to be rushing in to claim me.

Pochiko presented particular problems at night too. Pygmy hippos are nocturnal, so her sphere of activity expanded as soon as it grew dark. She would wander around the flower beds, rest her head on the bench under the wisteria trellis to study the night garden, or simply roll about on the lawn at her leisure. Perhaps the meals that Kobayashi-san brought her were insufficient—she was constantly munching away, her head stuck in the grasses or underbrush. Sometimes she would slip into the pond and swim about on the surface with a serenity that was almost unimaginable given her stumpy form.

For some reason, as I watched Pochiko from my window, I felt a terrible sadness. Her behavior, which, by daylight, could only be seen as comic, took on a different meaning as soon as it grew dark. As she toddled about the garden, it seemed painfully clear that her frequent huffing and snorting were expelling a sadness that she was unable to express to us. Or perhaps she was hoping to dissolve it in the waters of the pond after Kobayashi-san had left for the day. Quietly, without anyone noticing, secreting it into the darkness.

I was the only person in the house who worried this way about Pochiko at night, and I came to feel that I alone understood her true feelings. Her deep green hindquarters, floating up in the darkness, seemed to tell of our shared sadness.

The letters that came from my mother were the best remedy for my homesickness. As soon as Yoneda-san would find one in the mailbox, she would drop whatever she was doing and call me in a loud voice.

"Tomoko! There's a letter from your mother!" And everyone else would gather around to celebrate the arrival of the letter with me.

"This one seems a little thicker than the last one," said Mina, always one for the sharp observation.

"Your mother has beautiful handwriting," said Grandmother Rosa, slipping on her reading glasses to study the address on the envelope. "Now I can read the kanji—two moons lined up together: Tomoko."

"Are you writing back to her? You need to make sure she isn't worrying. That would be the worst kind of ingratitude." As always, Yoneda-san couldn't avoid adding a little sermon.

"How can she read her letter with everyone hovering around?" said my aunt. "Leave Tomoko alone."

I came to understand why they showed so much interest in these letters the day that Yoneda-san announced that one had arrived from Ryūichi.

Letters from Mina's older brother, Ryūichi, who was studying abroad in Switzerland, were a source of unparalleled joy, gusts of fresh air blowing into the house atop the hill from the outside world. Grandmother Rosa would appear on the scene, tapping her cane more rapidly than usual, my aunt would immediately stub out her cigarette, and even Kobayashi-san, who should have been working in the garden, would come running. The letters were invariably addressed to Grandmother Rosa, so the honor of opening them fell to her.

"Go on, open it," Mina pressed, but Grandmother Rosa, intent on savoring the whole experience, would trace her finger over the address, study the postmark, plant a kiss on the sealed flap. Then, at last, she would rip open the envelope with her trembling fingers, without resorting to scissors or a letter opener. It bothered me that she was shredding the envelope of such an important letter, but no one else seemed to mind, their heads already occupied with what was written inside.

The envelope held not only a letter for Grandmother Rosa, but a separate one each for my aunt, Mina, Yoneda-san, and Kobayashi-san. Each of them would extract his or her letter from the stack in Grandmother Rosa's hand and begin reading it, right on the spot. Someone might give a stifled laugh, while someone else would nod knowingly. If someone started to recount what was written in their letter, it would set off a lively competition, with each one reading aloud, one after another. At last, they would settle into their preferred places on the sofa and listen to each other's news from Ryūichi.

I came to realize that they were people who took special pleasure in receiving letters—and people who knew how to share that pleasure. But I realized something else too: in Ryūichi's airmail envelopes, there were never any letters for my uncle.

IO

As I made my way home from school each day, I never tired of the moment when the view of the house gradually appeared between the trunks of the trees, at the bottom of the hill, at the last turn in the road. First the tops of the two towers, and then the graceful outline of the roof. The gently mellowed orange of the roof tiles and the cream-colored walls made an exquisite color scheme between the screen of leaves. Though the angle of my view changed as I rounded the curve in the road, this balance remained constant. You couldn't see the whole house, just glimpses coming and going of the bay windows, the railings on the veranda or the shutters, but still somehow even that gave the sense that something vast lay within. The elegance that made it hard to believe that the house was a place where people lived their lives—that was completely concealed.

The interior was, naturally enough, consistent with the exterior. I would often find myself standing in the entrance hall, school bag still in hand, looking up in wonder at the vaulted ceiling. The surprise I'd felt when my uncle had first led me through the door did not fade, nor could I ever grow used to the sight of the chandelier that hung in the hall, the curving staircase that disappeared into the upper floors, or the stained glass in the door of the parlor. No matter how often I stood there and gazed around me, I always found the sight unsettling.

As a middle school student, I didn't really understand at the time, but the art objects and decorations in the house were all of the highest quality. Most of the collection had been assembled by Mina's grandfather, and each object was arranged around the house in a place that seemed completely natural and appropriate, not in some showy, obvious way. The care for the seventeen rooms was consigned to professional cleaners, but Yoneda-san, a stickler for cleanliness, was also constantly polishing every last nook and cranny. The house literally sparkled. Whenever I left something lying about, she immediately noticed and gave me a scolding. My dirty gym uniform, photocopies from class, empty Fressy bottles—everything had to be put in its place immediately.

The one exception was books. Even if Mina left a book sitting open on the table in the sunroom, Yoneda-san would never presume to move it or put it away. Beyond the page lay an unknown world, and the open book was a portal to that world that should not be thoughtlessly disturbed lest Mina be unable to find her way back. Or so Yoneda-san believed.

In the house at Ashiya, books were considered more precious than any sculpture or piece of pottery. There were bookshelves in every room, so that a volume would be close at hand as soon as one thought of it, and the children were free to read the adults' books. Pharmaceutical texts in German, Mina's picture books, and the appendices to the issues of *The Ladies' Companion* that Yoneda-san collected were all viewed as equally important.

There had not been a single bookshelf in my home in

Okayama, the only printed materials being the fashion magazines or sewing pattern books my mother used in her work, so at first I was overwhelmed to see such an enormous number of books outside of a public library. I wondered whether one family really needed so many of them.

But soon I changed my mind about this. The books that lined the walls from floor to ceiling sat there quietly, never calling out for attention or advertising themselves with gaudy covers. But even if they appeared to be nothing more than unadorned paper boxes from the outside, they exuded a beauty equal to anything created by a sculptor or potter. Even though the meaning of the words printed on their pages was so profound it could never have been contained by those boxes, the books never let on to their depths. They waited patiently until someone picked them up and opened their covers. I came to have enormous respect for that patience.

One day, as I studied the shelves, Mina came in, lips drawn in a fine line, and ran her eyes over the spines. The box of matches in her skirt pocket made a dry, rustling sound as she paced back and forth in front of the shelves, until she finally found the book she wanted. Oblivious to the fact that her blouse was pulling free from her skirt, she reached up as far as she could and at last managed to extract the book, clasping it in her slender arms. Stretching out on the sofa, a pillow on her chest, she opened it and departed on a voyage to far-off places.

〰〰〰

A couple of weeks into the school year, on April 17, a Monday, Mina spotted an article in the newspaper that had been left on the breakfast table and let out a cry.

"Yasunari Kawabata has committed suicide!" She had simply read the headline word for word, but it sounded like a howl of despair. "He turned on the gas, in his study, perhaps from health concerns." She continued, reading the subheadings, her tone sounding like a protest to someone.

"But how could this be? Such an important man—he even won the Nobel Prize." Yoneda-san, who had been setting butter and jam out on the breakfast table, sounded truly despondent.

"Yes, how could he?" added my aunt, dropping a slice of lemon into her tea. Mina opened the newspaper and began reading the article.

"'On the evening of the sixteenth, Yasunari Kawabata, Nobel laureate in Literature, aged seventy-two, committed suicide by opening the gas line in his workplace on the fourth floor of the Marina Mansion in the city of Zushi. No suicide note was found, and those close to Kawabata have expressed puzzlement as to the reasons for the suicide, though it had been reported that his health had suffered after surgery for appendicitis last month . . .'"

Everyone had taken their places and was listening to Mina's recitation. Grandmother Rosa's hands were folded over her chest, Yoneda-san busied herself spreading strawberry jam on a piece of toast, and my aunt stirred her tea. The morning sunlight coming through the shutters on the windows to the east lit Mina's profile. She had read every character in the article correctly, even the most difficult ones.

"'The body was transported during the night to his home in Kamakura, where it was received by his family, the staff, and a contingent of neighbors.'" There were sighs from around the table as Mina finished reading.

"Was this Kawabata-san a friend of yours?" I asked to no
one in particular.

"No," said Grandmother Rosa, unfolding her hands.

"I just thought . . . since you're all so upset . . ."

"We didn't know him. We hadn't even met him. But Kawabata-san was a writer, a man who wrote books. We have some of them here in the house. He wasn't a friend, but we were connected to him. Everyone reads his books; that's why we're so sad."

Mina neatly refolded the newspaper and set it on the table. They sat with their heads down, as though observing a moment of silence, ignoring their rapidly cooling ham and eggs.

〰〰

"What does it feel like to die by putting a gas line in your mouth?" Mina asked, holding a bag of pellets in her arms. It was later that day; we'd come to help Kobayashi-san feed Pochiko after school.

"I wonder," I murmured. Mina often posed questions that were difficult to answer. Since I was older, I wanted to be able to say something that would satisfy her, but I never managed to do so. "The tubes are made of rubber, so they couldn't feel very good in the mouth. They weren't meant for mouths to begin with, and they must smell a bit."

I brought three bales of dried grass from the shed. Pochiko, who had been restless since we'd arrived, continued to root about between our legs.

"Hold on," Mina said, pushing her away from the grass while she measured exactly two and a half kilos of the pellets. "Why did he kill himself?"

There was no note of protest this time; she was simply trying to put to rest a lingering doubt. Pochiko drooled, looking back and forth between us, waiting for permission to begin eating.

"The stories he wrote became books, and those books found their way to the shelves of bookstores and libraries in Japan and all around the world. People he had never met, in towns he had never visited, read his work. Why would someone who had such amazing things happen in his life want to die? What does that mean?"

Mina gave a single clap, the signal for Pochiko to thrust her nose into the brick of dried grass and begin breaking it apart. Pochiko's tongue scooped the feed into her mouth. She ate with enormous concentration, though there was no one about who was likely to steal her food.

〰〰〰

It was late the next day that another painful piece of news arrived, a small article in the evening edition of the newspaper, so insignificant it might have been completely overlooked. "Elderly man commits Kawabata copycat suicide."

We held another moment of silence at the dinner table, this time for the lonely old man. Surely Kawabata's books must have lined his shelves too.

II

After Kawabata-san's suicide, I began spending time at the Ashiya Public Library.

"Can you do me a favor?" Mina said one Saturday afternoon. "Could you go to the library to get some books for me?"

The library was just to the north of Uchide Station on the Hanshin Line, a drive that would have taken no more than ten minutes. But for Mina, who suffered from terrible car sickness, it was impossibly far away. She was permitted to ride on Pochiko for the commute back and forth to school, but for nothing else. So, when necessary, she had been relying on Kobayashi-san to make the trip to the library for her.

"But he's got more than enough to do in the garden, so I feel terrible asking him. Besides, I'm pretty sure it's embarrassing for a man of his age to be borrowing *Anne of Green Gables* or *Pollyanna*. He'd never admit it, but I know he'd be relieved if you could go in his place."

"Of course," I said. "I'd be glad to. But with so many books in the house, do you still need to go borrow them from somewhere else?"

"Are you serious?" Mina's eyes widened with surprise. "When there are so many books in the world that you could never even read them all?"

"Fine," I said. "What do you want me to get?"

"Yasunari Kawabata."

"But didn't Grandmother Rosa say you have some of his books here?"

"Yes, *Izu Dancer* and *Snow Country* and *Kyoto*. I've already read those. So, the other ones."

"Such as?"

"Ones you've read and thought were interesting. That's probably easiest."

"Eh?"

I didn't know what to say. Not only had I never read anything by Kawabata, I wasn't sure that I'd ever even read a novel from start to finish. I had the feeling, though, that it was especially inexcusable that a middle school student had not read a single work by the first Japanese writer to be awarded the Nobel Prize for Literature. It left me a bit flustered.

"Fine," I said, trying to cover my embarrassment. "I'll see what I can find."

〰〰

The bus that I boarded at Kaimori Bridge passed along a line of cherry trees, their blossoms already fallen, crossed the train tracks, and then made a number of stops in a residential neighborhood. The pleasure I felt at being entrusted with the task of going to the library far outweighed my shame at not knowing Kawabata's novels. I had wanted to be of some use to the people in this house ever since I'd come to Ashiya. On the night of Mina's attack, each one of them had had an important role to play, but I'd been unable to help. So I had been waiting for the moment when it would occur to them that they were glad to have me here. Going to the library for Mina was the least I could do.

The library was a solid, stone building that sat facing the Uchide-ten Shrine. It was surrounded by impressive trees, the walls were covered with vines, and the old, double doors were carved with Chinese designs. The interior was chilly, as though the stones had been collecting the cold, and the regular rows of tall bookshelves receded into the shadows in the distance. The atmosphere was completely different from the libraries I'd known—those in Okayama, at the elementary school, or the children's corner in the public library. It was far more solemn, more grown-up.

"Excuse me," I said, addressing myself to the man at the counter. "I'd like to get a library card."

"Is this your first time here?" Unlike the other librarians, he was dressed quite casually in a white turtleneck sweater.

"Yes."

"Do you have your school identification card?"

"Yes, here it is." I produced the card, which I'd just received at school.

"Good. Then please fill out this form in pencil." He was tall and thin, and each time he leaned forward his long hair fell over his forehead. Though he seemed quite young, perhaps the age of a college student, he was clearly quite comfortable with his job and had the air of someone who had worked at the library for some time. He handled the books carefully but efficiently, and his calm voice seemed to match the peacefulness of the library.

"Do you have books by Yasunari Kawabata?" I asked.

"Of course," Mr. Turtleneck replied, looking up at me. "You

can find them in the memorial display we've set up next to Row Eight. It really is so sad what happened, don't you think?"

"I do," I said, as we both looked in the direction of Row Eight. "Which ones do you think are interesting?" I added.

"It's impressive for a middle school student to be reading Kawabata," he said with a kind smile.

I shook my head and was about to tell him it wasn't me, but then I realized the explanation would be a denial of his kind intentions, and I found myself unable to go on.

"What about *The Izu Dancer?*" he said.

"Oh, I've already read that."

"Is that so?" said Mr. Turtleneck, clearly impressed. Now I felt even more unwilling to disappoint him. "Well, there's *Snow Country*, and *Kyoto* . . ."

"Those, too," I said, telling myself that I wasn't lying exactly, just omitting the subject of my sentences.

"Amazing!" he said. I looked down, bewildered to be receiving such praise just for reading books—and fully aware that it was Mina who deserved the praise, not me.

"Well then, what about *The House of Sleeping Beauties?*" Mr. Turtleneck rested his hands on the counter and leaned toward me.

"Beauties . . ." The word echoed in my head. I was shaken, as though the handsome librarian standing in front of me had confessed that he found me beautiful. "No, I haven't read that one."

"Well then, that's what I'd recommend. I think it would be perfect for you."

He was right. "Sleeping Beauty" was the perfect title for Mina. Perhaps Mr. Turtleneck had understood everything. Perhaps he'd seen that I was no more than the messenger, that the real beauty who wanted a book by Kawabata was waiting in the big house at the top of the hill. If he hadn't, he would never have recommended the book about beauties to me. These thoughts came to me one after another, leaving me more and more confused.

"So, here's your library card. Take care of it," he said, handing it to me as though it were an important document. His fingertips were cold when they brushed against mine.

"I will," I said.

⌇⌇⌇⌇

I've kept that promise I made to Mr. Turtleneck. Today, more than thirty years later, I still have my card from the Ashiya Public Library. The paper has yellowed, and the corners are a bit tattered, but the titles of the books I borrowed in the course of that year—and which Mina read—are still legible. I have only to read them in order, beginning with *The House of Sleeping Beauties*, to bring back the memories of the time I spent with Mina. And along with them come the conversations across the circulation counter with the young man I secretly called Mr. Turtleneck. *King Arthur and His Knights of the Round Table*, *The Murder of Roger Ackroyd*, *The Garden Party*, *Franny and Zooey*, *First Love*, *The Metamorphosis*, *The True Story of Ah Q*, *Secrets of the Comets* . . . They are nothing more than titles, but to me they seem like engraved seals, offering proof of the immutability of our memories. Whenever I want to see Mina, I take out this library card.

⌇⌇⌇⌇

As soon as I was through the door, Mina, who had been waiting impatiently on the bench in the entrance hall, came running up, peppering me with questions.

"How did it go? Did you manage to find it all right? Did you figure out how to check out books?"

"It was fine. Here," I said, holding out *The House of Sleeping Beauties*. She clutched the book to her chest and thanked me, her gratitude all out of proportion to the small favor that I'd done for her. As I'd predicted, the *Sleeping Beauties* suited her perfectly.

For the time being, I decided to say nothing about Mr. Turtleneck.

12

When something was broken in the house at Ashiya, before calling for the repairman, the custom was to carry it to my uncle's study. Grandmother Rosa brought her pearl necklace with a loose clasp, Yoneda-san, a mixer with a damaged base, and Mina, a broken mechanical pencil. They attached no notes, put nothing in a bag, but simply placed their offerings on the absent owner's neatly arranged desk, and left the study. They clearly believed that simply by doing so, their broken objects would be restored to their original state.

As I could tell from seeing the saddle he'd created for Pochiko, my uncle had skills with his hands that surpassed those of the best jeweler or electrician or stationer. He easily repaired just about anything at all, and he did it with obvious pleasure. He would barely touch these things that no longer functioned, and, in an instant, they were returned to their proper form. Wires were reconnected, gears meshed, parts fit into place.

The only problem was that no one knew when he would return to work this magic. If he didn't come back, these things would remain on his desk in their broken state. Still, no one seemed impatient. Meals could be prepared without a mixer.

They all just waited, as the broken items waited on the desk themselves.

Since the study was on the second floor, just at the top of the stairs, I occasionally had a chance to see what was inside, when, for example, the door was left open by the house cleaners. If the opportunity arose, I couldn't help peeking in at that sturdy mahogany desk, situated next to a sunny window, and, over time, I watched the broken things pile up.

〰〰

My uncle finally returned in the evening, on the twenty-ninth of April, the first day of Golden Week. Apparently he'd given no advance warning, so when the doorbell rang somewhat ostentatiously and he appeared suddenly in the entrance hall, there were cries of surprise all around.

Ahh, I thought, now I could stop worrying about the desk overflowing with broken items.

As always, he was impeccably dressed, from his collar to his cuff links, with that wonderful, mesmerizing smile on his face. Though it was a holiday, we'd had nothing special planned and had been relaxing around the house, so when he appeared it felt as though a meteor had fallen among us.

"How have my princesses been getting along?" he said, kissing Grandmother Rosa, Yoneda-san, Mina, and even me. I'd never been greeted in this cheek-to-cheek, Western style before, so it felt awkward and embarrassing for me, though it clearly didn't for the others. Mina quickly found a spot next to her father and proceeded to tell him in detail about everything that had been happening at home and at school. At some point, my aunt, who had been upstairs, finally came down, but these two, who by rights should have been the ones exchanging a kiss, contented themselves with a glance and a nod, as though unwilling to interrupt Mina's elaborate story.

∿∿∿

My uncle had not returned alone. He'd brought with him two chefs and three waiters from the Mount Rokko Hotel. They greeted Grandmother Rosa with the utmost deference.

"It is a pleasure to see you again, madam, and a joy to see you looking so well," said one of the chefs.

"Today we would like to prepare for you the menu that you ordered on the occasion of the party given this day in 1956, when you celebrated your fortieth wedding anniversary with your husband, the former president of the company," said the other.

"But that was two years before Grand Papa died. Who could remember what we ate that long ago?" said Grandmother Rosa.

"Oh, but we do, madam. We remember perfectly." The chefs and the waiters all made another deep bow.

The family in the house in Ashiya had been clients of the Mount Rokko Hotel since it had opened. They had used it constantly, especially in the era when Grandfather had still been alive, for dance parties and business entertaining, family celebrations, or just to escape the summer heat. But after his death, and since Grandmother Rosa's legs had started troubling her, it seemed that they had visited much less frequently.

I had no idea what was about to happen, but I was sure it would be something extraordinary.

"Why are the people from the hotel here?" I asked Mina.

"Grandmother loves the food from the Mount Rokko, so they come to make her dinner from time to time."

"All the way from the hotel?"

"Yes." She nodded.

"Just for us?"

"Of course." Mina's answers were matter-of-fact, and, as often happened, there was a profound difference between the things that excited us. She barely glanced at the people from the hotel, having eyes only for her father.

"Come have a look at Pochiko," she told him. "She's been putting on a little weight, so we've changed to low-calorie kibble." With that, she took him by the arm and led him across the terrace and down into the garden.

〜〜〜

Taking care not to get in anyone's way, I shuttled back and forth between the kitchen and the dining room to observe the work of the hotel staff. It was all accomplished in complete silence and with a minimum of fuss, since they seemed to know everything about the house, down to the contents of each drawer. They covered the table in a snow-white cloth, decorated it with flowers, filled the candlesticks with fresh candles. In the kitchen, the chef pierced the roast with his knife, stirred spices into a pot, tasted a sauce with the tip of his little finger.

Yoneda-san alone seemed to share my sense of unease.

"You'll have nothing to do today," my uncle had said, foreseeing her dilemma, but from force of habit, without quite realizing it, she found herself folding napkins or laying out the dishes. Each time she did, however, the hotel waiters would come running.

"Please, madam, we'll take care of it," they would tell her, and Yoneda-san was forced to retreat. As soon as they touched

them, these familiar objects took on a different, more formal
air. The stainless-steel sink and the marble counter sparkled, and even Yoneda-san's old ladle seemed to play some new and secret role.

"Excuse me," I said to one of the waiters, unable to control my curiosity. "What's this?"

"It's a napkin ring," he said. "Each one has a name engraved on it."

"Were they made just for today?"

"No, we keep napkin rings at the hotel for regular clients."

The silver rings seemed heavy for their size, and there were the names, along with the hotel logo: "Rosa," "Toshi," "Ken Erich," "Hiromi," and "Mina." That was when I first learned that Yoneda-san's given name was Toshi. The rings labeled for Grandmother Rosa and Yoneda-san seemed well-worn and somehow subdued, but Mina's sparkled. The waiter folded each napkin in the shape of a butterfly, slipped a ring over it, and set it on the table. He had been working quietly, concentrating on the table, but suddenly he turned to me and winked. "Don't worry," he said. "We have one for you, too."

This ring was the newest of all, without a single scratch. I had the feeling that I'd find silver dust on my finger if I touched the place where *Tomoko* had been carved.

"The director sent instructions some time ago," he said, applying himself to folding my napkin even more carefully than the others.

〰〰〰

The preparations had been made. The sun had set, and it had grown dark outside. The white tablecloth was almost completely covered with an array of knives and forks, plates large and small that had yet to be filled, and glasses of all shapes and sizes. We had dressed ourselves up, combed our hair, and sat, backs straight, in our chairs. Even Yoneda-san wore a pale blue silk dress that I'd never seen before. And at the end of the table sat my uncle, in the seat that had been left empty for so long. The door leading to the kitchen was closed and we could not see the chefs, but the odors of warm food wafted into the room. The three waiters were lined up in the corner, ready to play their part when the moment came.

My uncle turned off the lights. As the waiters moved to light the candles, he interrupted them.

"No, no," he said. "We have someone who handles the matches here. Mina will take care of it. No one can light the matches as beautifully as she does."

13

If you wanted to describe Mina in a few words, you might say she was an asthmatic girl who loved books and rode a pygmy hippopotamus. But if you wanted to distinguish her from everyone else in the world, you'd say that she was a girl who could strike a match more beautifully than anyone.

I'm not sure how she came to love matchboxes the way she did or why the adults around her never put a stop to her obsession, despite the danger involved. But by the time I arrived at the house in Ashiya, it was clear that there was always a box of matches in Mina's pocket and that it was her responsibility to light the gas burner to heat the bath, to light the oil lamp in the light-bath room, and to light the candles when the electricity went out or for a special dinner.

Before I met her, matches were nothing more than matches, in my view. But from the first time she produced a matchbox in my presence, I realized that they could become a kind of silent ritual, a devout prayer.

Mina would slide open the box and select a single match with her delicate fingers. Then she would close the box and hold the rounded, reddish-brown tip at a slightly odd angle against the striking surface. Up to this point, everything would happen in a relaxed, tranquil manner. Nothing forced or hurried. Her lips pressed together, her eyes lowered. Only the tips of the three fingers that held the match seemed animated with the knowledge of the deed they were about to do.

Then, she would hold her breath for an instant and her fingertips would fly, followed by a sound so sharp that you wondered how such a frail girl could achieve this kind of velocity. And then the match was lit, and the darkness that had filled the room until that moment would recede like an out-going tide.

I was captivated, realizing for the first time how transparent the flame of a match could be. If not for the slight odor of phosphorus, I might have been tempted to believe that Mina had produced the flame magically, out of thin air, or that, given the clarity of the light, it was her finger itself that was burning.

〰〰

It was the same that evening. At the dinner celebrating my uncle's return, staffed by the men from the Mount Rokko Hotel. Everyone in the room watched in silence as Mina's hands moved to light six candles, one by one. Conscious that all eyes were on her, she performed her task with great elegance, and at the moment when the match in her hand was extinguished, the moment when the candles had been lit, the dining room became a magical place.

"Well then!" my uncle exclaimed, unfolding his napkin with a flourish. The flickering flames of the candles reflected in the sparkling dishes, wavered softly in the pupils of our eyes. The waiters came and went noiselessly between the kitchen and the dining room, passing behind us, setting delicious dishes before our eyes without a word from us, everything we could have wanted. Bottles of wine and Fressy were opened, and

then mushroom soup was ladled into our soup bowls from
a tureen shaped like a goldfish and sprinkled with croutons.

We all talked merrily of our memories, our little triumphs, our setbacks, of funny stories, stories of foreign lands, of Pochiko and our studies, and everything else besides. My uncle made us all laugh with his description of a strange old man who'd been seated next to him on his flight to New York for a business trip. The story was so amusing that none of us found the time to wonder whether the trip had been the reason for his long absence. Grandmother Rosa seemed to have a much healthier appetite that evening, and my aunt was so busy laughing that she drank less than usual. Yoneda-san joined her hands together gratefully as each dish was set in front of her, and Mina called out to her papa over and over again.

At first, I was nervous that I was using the various knives and forks incorrectly or in the wrong order, but before long I found myself mesmerized by the unfamiliar dishes, the ingredients of which I couldn't begin to imagine, and I stopped worrying about my manners. The thing that surprised me most was when the main dishes came out covered in big copper domes that were exactly the same shape as the shades covering the lamps in the light-bath room. The waiters glanced at one another, and then, with an exaggerated motion, lifted the covers high above the table. Were they meant to keep the food warm—or to preserve the surprise until the last possible moment? It wasn't clear, but the "lamb braised in red wine with truffles" certainly was delicious. So much so that it was hard to think of it merely as food.

⋀⋀⋀⋀

After we'd eaten the "bavarois of wild strawberries" (my uncle cut his in half and divided it between Mina and me), Grandmother Rosa and Yoneda-san started to sing. Mina accompanied them on the piano.

They stood next to one another, almost touching, and bowed in our direction. Then they lowered their eyes, as if gathering themselves, and waited for the introduction to begin. When and where had they managed to practice? From the first note, the voices of the two old women were in perfect harmony. I would never have imagined that they could be so talented. They sang some Japanese songs and some German ones—"Song of the Seashore" and "Children of the Sandcastle," "The Nomads," and "Moonlight on the Ruined Castle." There was no sign of the fretful muttering that usually came from Yoneda-san as she worked in the kitchen. Instead, she kept an easy rhythm, while Grandmother Rosa chimed in with a rich, resonant voice, seemingly unrelated to the body that relied on a cane to walk. Signals went back and forth through a glance or the touch of their shoulders. Though they were opposite in appearance, they sang with one voice.

They seemed like twin sisters to me, and I remembered when, in her room filled with products from the Twin Beauties Series, Grandmother Rosa had shown me the old photograph taken with her sister, Irma. These two women, one German and one Japanese, sang so beautifully together that they, too, must surely be twins.

When the last song ended, everyone applauded. Even the chefs who had appeared in the kitchen door at some point and the waiters who had been so completely focused on their work. The one who had winked at me clapped the loudest. Glancing out the window, I noticed Pochiko standing on the terrace.

Her nose was pressed against the glass, and she was looking in at us. The candles had continued to burn all this time.

~~~~

Later that night, when I got up to go to the bathroom, I noticed that the light was on in the study. The first floor of the house was sunk in darkness, the remnants of our lively party gone, and other than the faint glow coming from the study door, there was no sign of anyone.

"Ah, Tomoko. Trouble sleeping?" My uncle had noticed me outside the door.

"Just heading to the bathroom," I said. "I'm afraid I drank too much Fressy."

I took a few steps into the study. He was in his robe, sitting at the desk, working on something—repairing one of the broken objects, I realized right away.

"Thank you for the wonderful dinner," I said.

"You enjoyed it?"

"Of course! There were so many delicious things I barely knew what I was eating." On the desk I could see the mixer with the damaged base, a collection of spare parts, and a toolbox. Screwdriver in hand, he was staring at the bottom of the mixer. "Grandmother Rosa and Yoneda-san's songs were wonderful, too."

"Yes, they were. I'm a fan of their duets as well." He hadn't looked up from the mixer, but still I had the impression he didn't mind that I was there. "Ah, this wire is burned out."

"Can you fix it?"

"Probably." No matter where he was or what he was doing, my uncle's appearance was remarkably elegant, right down to the casual way he tied the belt on his robe.

"And the necklace, and Mina's mechanical pencil?"

"Those were simple. But the mixer's a bit of a nuisance." He seemed partial to the word "nuisance."

"And my aunt?" I asked.

"She's asleep." Her bedroom was the next room toward the east. From the balcony, you could see that it was dark.

"I was afraid the desk wouldn't hold all the broken things."

"Don't worry, there aren't so many, and it's a big desk." I noticed that the sofa in the study had been made up with sheets, a pillow, and a blanket. I realized my uncle would be sleeping here alone.

"Yoneda-san will be happy to have the mixer fixed," I said, trying not to look at the sofa, ready to leave.

"I'll have it running fine by tomorrow."

"Good night," I said, closing the door.

"Good night." I could hear his voice behind me.

14

When I think back to my time in Ashiya, the day Mina showed me her boxes of matchboxes stands out as the day she really took me into her confidence. Of course, we'd been on good terms before then, but the boxes of boxes opened the final door to our friendship.

I was the only one among her friends or family who knew her secret. In that enormous house in Ashiya, she and I were the only ones who knew what was hidden away in those little boxes.

We were knitting in her room one day when she suddenly stopped and turned to me.

"I'd like to show you something," she said. "If that's okay?" Her voice was oddly quiet, with none of its usual self-confidence. She put her hands against the bed and began pushing, and it seemed so heavy I stooped to help her. Before long, a whole array of boxes appeared.

There were various sizes and shapes and materials, but they were all small enough to hold in the palms of your hands—and they filled every available inch of the space under the bed. I had already spent a certain amount of time with her sitting or lying on this bed, but I had never suspected that something like this was hidden under it. It must have been pushed aside any number of times, since the floor was covered with scratches.

Soap, stationery, Band-Aids, perfume, chocolate, handkerchiefs, buttons—the boxes had once held a variety of things and their shapes varied according to their previous contents. Some looked as though they'd held imported luxury goods, while others were so crude they hardly seemed worth keeping around. But in any case, they were all just boxes.

Mina watched my reaction with an anxious look. I wondered what I was supposed to say. Should I praise their number, their variety, or the shape of the stacks? I couldn't tell. It was even more confusing than when I'd first been introduced to Pochiko.

"You can open any one you want," Mina told me. Her tone suggested that she was granting me special permission to this collection and I understood immediately that these were not simply empty boxes.

I took the closest one, which was decorated with red flowers. It must have held some kind of candy. There was a little seashell stuck to the top, and you simply had to pull on it to open the lid.

There was nothing inside that suggested it had once held candy. No waxed paper, no slips explaining where the bonbons had come from, no lingering smell of sugar. Just a single matchbox there at the bottom, like the ones that Mina always carried.

"Look closer," she said, bringing her head so near mine that I could feel her breath, hear the soft rasping at the back of her throat.

The little matchbox was glued to the bottom of the candy box, and there seemed to be a few matches left, since it rattled

when you shook it. But the air around it was still and peaceful.
A stillness like the deep sea, that could not be disturbed by
opening the lid or peeking inside or shaking.

I was reminded of a bug collection that a boy in my class
had once showed me. Rhinoceros beetles and cicadas and
long-horned beetles, all injected with formaldehyde. That box
had been peaceful too. When you shook it, loose wings and
antennae rattled a bit, but the insects themselves remained
silent, making it impossible to know whether they were living
or dead. The matchbox seemed to me just like those insects.

I soon realized that there was something written on the
inside of the box. At first, I'd thought that the floral design
on the outside was continued inside, but then I could see that
it wasn't flowers but words. The back of the lid, the sides, and
even the bottom were covered in the story of the matchbox,
all in Mina's handwriting.

"Are there matchboxes in all of them?" I asked, pointing at
the collection of boxes on the floor.

"Yes."

"Is this how you store them to make sure they don't get
damp?"

"No, no, I've never worried about that."

"Then are you hiding them from Yoneda-san?"

"Everyone knows I like matches, so I don't have to hide them.
But just look at them. Don't you think they're wonderful?"

My questions appeared to have missed the mark. Seemingly unable to wait any longer, Mina pointed impatiently at
the matchbox glued into the candy box.

It was obviously not new, with corners that had been worn
down and scuff marks on the striking surface, but the yellow
label was bright, and on it was the image of an elephant on

a seesaw. A magnificent elephant with tusks thrust up in the sky. The seesaw, resting on a green lawn, had been painted bright red, just the color to please children, and, in fact, there were several of them merrily swinging their legs as they balanced on the high end of the seesaw. That much was clear: the elephant was down, the children up. The elephant was using its trunk to hoist one of the children into the air, and the child had spread his arms with a look of supreme delight, like an opera singer accepting applause after an encore. A thin growth of hair could be seen on the elephant's trunk as it wrapped around the child's body. The gray skin was sagging at the base of the tusks and around the belly. Perhaps it was an old elephant. And above its head, the words SAFETY MATCH.

"You see? It's an elephant, on a seesaw," said Mina. "An elephant mesmerized by a seesaw."

Then she told me the story of the seesaw elephant that she'd written on the interior of the candy box.

◇◇◇◇

The elephant had always been envious of the children playing on the seesaw on the green lawn. It was captivated by the simple yet thrillingly suspenseful movement and the endless repetition of the curious sound. How wonderful it must be to go up and down like that. Just as you were about to touch the sky, you landed back on earth, only to mount again to the sky. His ears would no doubt flutter with joy.

One day, the elephant screwed up his courage and asked the children if he could join them in their game. The children on the lawn, who were all very kind, agreed immediately.

His heart swelling in anticipation, the elephant climbed

onto the seesaw, fitting his four legs on either side of the red
board. It was narrower than he'd imagined, but he managed.

And there he sat, waiting for the wonderful *click-clack*
sound, for the board to lift him into the sky. But nothing
happened.

The faces of children at the other end of the seesaw were
etched with inexpressible sorrow and chagrin. One of them
was trying with all his might to press down and lift the elephant even the least bit, but to no avail. No matter how long
they sat there, the elephant remained on the ground, the children in the air.

The elephant grew sad, gathering from the fact that the
seesaw had not moved since he'd climbed aboard that he was
the cause of the problem. And, of course, he was right. Looking down at his feet, he fixed his eyes on the red seesaw dug
into the ground and felt deep shame.

Soon, the children who had been playing on the swings,
in the sandbox, and on the jungle gym gathered around the
seesaw to see what was happening. The elephant used his
impressive trunk to pick them up and set them on the seesaw.
The children cried out with joy, posing and posturing like
clowns. After all, it wasn't every day that an elephant picked
you up in his trunk.

One by one, the number of children on the seesaw increased,
but the board gave no sign of moving. As the seesaw became
more crowded, the children squeezed themselves as close together as they could, clinging to each other's clothes to keep
from falling off, and all the while more and more children
were added to the board.

Gradually, they began to feel a bit uneasy, and soon there
were no more children to caper about or cry out with joy.

They were all on the board, where the sky was just over their heads and the ground seemed very far away. When the elephant reached out its trunk to search for more children hidden among the trees, his upthrust tusks flashed in the sun.

The children swung their legs as if begging to be let down. Those legs, dangling in the air, were now the only things they could move freely. As the number of children on the seesaw had increased, it became more and more difficult for them to breathe. But the elephant would not give up. He was determined to go on gathering children until he heard the *click-clack* sound of the seesaw.

If you should spy a red seesaw hereabouts, approach with caution. Especially if it seems it hasn't moved in years and years, and that one end is dug deep in the dirt. You'll find an elephant on that end, and on the other, a mass of children pressed into a block. They've floated up in the air there and they can't get down.

〰〰

"The end," said Mina, gripping the shell and closing the top of the candy box. The matchbox with the elephant on the seesaw receded into darkness once again.

15

Mina's obsession with matchboxes was not due to some sort of pyromania. The fact that she had an exquisite gift for striking a match was the result of having matchboxes always at hand, but that wasn't really the point. What fascinated Mina were the pictures printed on the boxes.

They were no more than tiny designs, could barely be called drawings, but that was exactly why they suited her. Neither heavy nor expensive, the boxes fit perfectly in the palms of a girl whose hands seemed as small as a seven-year-old's and could be studied wherever and whenever she wanted. And though they were simply matchboxes, as the elephant on the seesaw suggested, the subject matter varied widely. A frog playing the ukulele, a platypus swallowing a hammer, a baby chick smoking a pipe. You might have a mailman riding on a shell, making his rounds on the sea, or Okame and Fukusuke balancing on a ball, or Santa Claus bathing in a spring. The drawings had no context or perspective, nor any sort of logic. They were simply rough lines and bright colors printed on these small, rectangular spaces.

Mina took the box in her hand, held it for a moment to appreciate how small it was, and after running her finger over the rough striking surface and rattling the matches inside and touching the round tips of the matches, she extracted the story hidden in the picture on the little label. No one else, not the countless people who had struck the matches or even the one who had drawn the picture itself, knew what was hidden there, knew that the children captured by the elephant wept somewhere beyond the flickering flame.

In order to protect the secrets of the matchboxes, which would be doomed to be discarded once they were empty, or trampled underfoot or simply burned, Mina would build a box for each matchbox and write its story inside. For the frog playing the ukulele, with words suitable for a frog, for bathing Santa Claus, with words for Santa Claus, she would construct a space where they could live in peace.

Mina was kind enough to let me open any box I wanted, whenever I wanted. We would peer inside, and sometimes she would wait patiently while I finished reading in silence, while other times she would read the story aloud. The boxes were lined with white paper, and every inch, from the top to the sides to the bottom, would be completely covered in Mina's tiny characters. The story of the picture on the label would continue across the surface, even when the corners didn't fit properly, or the paper was swollen with a lump of glue.

The chain of words, which started as a simple collection, would form into a comforting cushion, woven together like a bird's nest, a bed to embrace and protect the matchbox.

I suppose the moments when she was constructing one of these matchbox boxes were Mina's only true chance to escape. She could wander freely, across a landscape or seascape, without having to worry about low pressure systems or exhaust fumes or steep slopes. Needless to say, she took Pochiko with

her, the two of them marching together through the tiny
worlds of the boxes.

∿∿∿

The return of my uncle was followed by an increase in the number of guests coming to visit, and the house became livelier. Most seemed to come on business, and he would receive them in his study. But there were guests of all sorts—some coming for dinner, some bearing presents, sometimes there were couples or even foreigners. Yoneda-san, whose work had increased abruptly, watched carefully over all the arrangements. The tailor from the dressmaker's in Motomachi came to take Grandmother Rosa's measurements, and an art dealer showed up hoping to buy the oil painting hung in the stairway landing on the second floor. Grandmother Rosa ordered three summer dresses, and the dealer left with a disappointed look on his face.

The visitor that day was a veterinarian from the Tennoji Zoological Garden who'd been summoned to examine Pochiko.

"Hey, Pochiko!" said the vet, holding the hippo's head in his arms. "How have you been? I'm sorry I always seem to leave you with unpleasant memories." His expression was warm, but it somehow suggested that Pochiko was in for some discomfort.

"You lucky girl, Pochiko!" my uncle teased. "Your boyfriend has come back for a visit."

"You're so happy your ears are twitching, aren't they, Pochi?" This was Kobayashi-san. The veterinarian had taken care of her for many years, since she'd first come from Liberia. Still, to Mina and me, as we sat atop the hill in the garden watching this show, it seemed that Pochiko's ears were twitching from annoyance more than anything else.

Short, with a rounded back, the vet wore a white coat covered with stains. A stethoscope hung around his neck. His completely bald head shone in the sunlight, as though complementing Pochiko's round bottom.

The examination started right away. Kobayashi-san rubbed Pochiko's muzzle to distract her, and the vet used his tape to measure the various parts of her body. My uncle wrote down the figures he read out on a sheet held in a clipboard. 62.5 centimeters, 18.3 centimeters, 1.72 meters, 4.8 centimeters. The vet bent down at Pochiko's feet, and then got up on his tiptoes to reach over her back, reading out figures the whole time, exactly the way the dressmaker had measured Grandmother Rosa's shoulders and bust. My uncle repeated them back, one by one, like a conductor making a safety check on a train, and then wrote them down on the clipboard. Some of the measurements were for parts that seemed to have nothing to do with Pochiko's health (the length of her tail, for example, or the distance between her nostrils), but nothing was overlooked.

Next, he took her temperature. Lifting her tail, he plunged the thermometer into her backside.

"Oh!" I gasped.

"That's the way to get the most accurate reading," said Mina, as if it were nothing.

"But doesn't it hurt?"

"Does she look like she's suffering?"

And, in fact, Pochiko seemed oblivious to what was occurring in her hindquarters. She just blinked her eyes gloom-

ily in an attempt to drive away any flies that might get too
close.

After they'd finished taking her temperature, they checked her heart. The vet got down on his hands and knees, ignoring Pochiko's drool dropping on his back, and pressed the stethoscope to her chest at a spot between her front legs. We held still so he could hear her heartbeat. But by this point the patient seemed to have lost patience and began to grow agitated.

"Excuse me, Kobayashi-san," said the vet, still on all fours, "but could you please hold on to her haunches?"

"By 'haunches,' where exactly do you mean?" asked Kobayashi-san.

"Somewhere around here," said my uncle, pointing to a likely spot on her round lump of a body. Kobayashi-san and my uncle took up positions on either side, and, working together, they did their best to keep her still.

"The haunches are fundamental for every living thing. If you can control them, you control the animal." The vet looked up at the sky, maneuvering the stethoscope and concentrating, as though trying to catch some important message coming from a distant place.

I wonder what kind of sound Pochiko's heart made? Seated on the top of the little hill, it occurred to me that perhaps it beat loud and strong, the better to come to the aid of Mina's heart, which could barely beat at all. The hill was really nothing more than a mound, but from up there we felt a pleasant breeze and could see the entire garden, including Grandmother Rosa, who seemed to be dozing on a lounge chair on the terrace.

"How old would Pochiko be in human years?" I asked the

veterinarian, who had finished with the stethoscope and was testing the hippo's leg joints and measuring the fat around her neck.

"Young lady, Pochiko is nothing like a human being," he said, continuing the examination. "So, the question itself doesn't really apply. Pochiko lives in her own time."

Mina and I nodded, but I suspect he sensed that we remained unconvinced.

〰〰〰

"Well then, I'll just go look in at the grave and be on my way." The vet had finished the exam and determined that Pochiko was generally healthy, other than a slight tendency toward corpulence.

"What grave?" I asked Mina.

"The grave for the Fressy Zoo, right over there."

I hadn't noticed it until that moment, but in the eastern corner of the garden, behind the toolshed, there was a little mound of earth surrounded with a ring of ill-assorted rocks. Sunlight filtered through the fluttering leaves of a myrtle tree. The only sign that it was a grave was a small wooden plaque carved with the words HERE LIE OUR FRIENDS FROM THE FRESSY ZOOLOGICAL GARDEN.

The vet took an apple from the pocket of his coat, set it in front of the mound, and put his palms together in prayer. My uncle, Kobayashi-san, and Mina joined him. I hurried to copy them. Then, before we realized it, Pochiko had made her way between us and swallowed the apple in one bite. Her lips smacked with enjoyment, while the vet continued to pray, the stethoscope around his neck swaying in the breeze.

16

"Saburō, the Taiwanese macaque, was the first to be buried here," said Mina, running her hand over the moss-covered mound.

The two of us lingered at the grave after my uncle had left to take the veterinarian home in his car and Kobayashi-san led Pochiko back to the pond. The shadows under the trees deepened and the ground seemed damp, despite the fact that it had not rained in some time. Through the gaps in the thick thatch of leaves, we could barely see the steep line of trees and the roof of the house next door.

"It was 1940, a little before the Fressy Zoo closed—so, long before I was born."

"Was he sick?" I asked.

"No, there was an accident," she answered, brushing away some pieces of skin from the apple that Pochiko had devoured a moment earlier. "Come over here," she added.

We walked hand in hand along the hedge behind the tool-shed on the eastern side of the grounds.

"Here it is," she said.

I looked down at my feet where she was pointing and could see a rail covered with rust and what looked like a rotting railroad tie half-buried in the grass.

"In the days when the Fressy Zoo was still open, there was a little train in the garden. The entrance was where the service gate is today, and from there the train ran down the slope, turned right around the back of the hill, and ended at Pochiko's pond—a nice little ride. And Saburō was the engineer. He sat up front, ringing the bell, wearing a cap with a brim and a patch with the Fressy star logo."

In fact, I could see that the rails still ran, though a bit sporadically, right up to the service gate. Next to the gate, there was a small square structure that until now I'd assumed was a storage shed, but as I looked closer, I could see the semicircular window of the ticket booth. Just above the window, where the paint had darkened, was a line of old nail holes. Had there once been a sign hanging there? WELCOME TO FRESSY ZOO or ENTRANCE FEE: ADULTS 5 YEN; CHILDREN FREE (TRAIN FARE INCLUDED)?

"After Pochiko, the train was the most popular attraction. Saburō just had to ring his bell and start down the line and the children would be completely delighted. It ran no faster than a quick walk, but they were so excited it might as well have been soaring through the sky. The children all wanted to touch Saburō, and the adults went on about his intelligence. As the train made its turn, the excitement grew, and when Pochiko came into view, there were cries of joy. All eyes were on Pochiko in her pond. But no matter how excited the children became, Saburō remained completely calm. He looked straight ahead, and once he was sure they'd reached the end of the line, he pulled the cord to ring his bell one more time. When the train stopped, they all ran off toward Pochiko, and no one paid any attention to Saburō."

"Well, I suppose a hippo is rarer than a monkey."

"But it never seemed to bother Saburō. He loved the little train, and he and Pochiko were great friends. He understood the role he played at the zoo, and he felt a certain
responsibility."

We pushed aside the grass, tracing the line to the ticket
booth at the entrance. The rails were much narrower and
more fragile than a normal train's, and now they were half-
buried in the ground, leaving almost no trace of the time
when the little railroad had brought such happiness to the
children.

"It was a day like today, a beautiful Sunday in early summer," Mina continued. "The little train was fully loaded, as
always. Crowded with children sucking on candies, clutching balloons, babies strapped to their mothers' backs, all
dizzy with excitement. The star patch on Saburō's cap shone
brighter than usual in the sunlight. The bell to signal the train
was departing rang out. But soon after the run got underway,
Saburō realized that something was wrong. The rails were
vibrating oddly, the air striking his face was different. That
was it!—the brakes had failed. The train was headed down
the slope, and without the brakes it would gradually pick up
speed. None of the passengers realized what was happening;
in fact, they found the speed thrilling. After all, there was a
conductor on board. Not the monkey, but a young man who
had been brought in as a temporary summer hire. He pulled
on the brake with all his might, but the train gave no sign
of slowing. If it continued like this, it would crash into the
myrtle tree at the bend in the tracks. The young man was
about to jump off to try to stop the train, but at that instant,
someone else intervened. It was Saburō, the engineer!"

"What happened?" I gasped, gripping Mina's hand tighter.

It was as soft as jelly and felt as though it would dissolve if I pressed the least bit harder.

"Saburō threw himself on the tracks, and his body stopped the train. Right here, under the myrtle tree that marks his grave."

〜〜〜

The sun was setting in the west, but the lawn on the south side of the garden had lost none of its brilliance, and there was a glow on the roses in the flower beds, on the bench beneath the wisteria arbor, and on the peaks of the two cupolas on the roof. Only the rails, extending out from where we stood, were lost in shadow.

Grandmother Rosa was still fast asleep in the chaise on the terrace. Pochiko, who had been led off by Kobayashi-san a few moments ago, had disappeared either into the pond or into her burrow.

"The only thing left undamaged was his cap. The engineer's hat he loved so much. It had rolled off when he threw himself on the tracks. Papa was twelve at the time, and they say he cried for three days, clutching it in his arms. They buried it with him in the grave here."

We had been holding hands all this time, and I had the feeling that it allowed us to more fully share our feelings of respect for Saburō, the brave Taiwanese macaque. A gentle breeze was blowing, and I caught a trace of a vaguely sweet odor each time it rustled Mina's hair. A mixture of Fressy, Bolos, and cough syrup.

"But Papa wasn't the only who was sad. They all showed it in their own way. The goat stopped giving milk, the peacock wouldn't open his tail, and the monitor lizard just froze, as

though he'd gone into hibernation out of season. And Pochiko,
who always loved her food, ate nothing for three whole days.
It was Grandfather who built the grave here. But I think you
could say that the Fressy Zoo never really recovered after the
death of Saburō. The little train never ran again, and the zoo
itself closed soon after, having been in existence less than two
years."

As Mina finished her story, the pond bubbled noisily and
Pochiko popped to the surface. Planting her front feet on the
edge, she pulled herself onto the grass and shook her head,
sending sprays of water everywhere.

"Mina! Mina!" we could hear someone calling in the distance. We turned to look and saw my aunt running across the
garden, a sweater clutched in her hands. "Here you are. I've
been looking for you everywhere." She was out of breath.

"What is it?" asked Mina.

"It's windy, put this on."

"I'm fine," said Mina. "You didn't have to come out here."

"You should go warm up in the light bath." Ignoring the
grave, my aunt wrapped the cardigan around Mina's shoulders as though she were hugging her.

Mina grunted but accepted the sweater in silence.

"You and Tomoko go back to the house, then."

I looked down again at the spot where I imagined Saburō's
body had fallen.

The next day Mina had a relatively minor asthma attack
that nonetheless kept her out of school for a week. The first
midterm exams for my new middle school were announced,
and I started studying in earnest. Rainy weather continued
for some time.

I'd sit at my desk, memorizing English vocabulary and

historical dates, and whenever I glanced out the window, I'd think for a moment that I could see the animals Mina had described, somewhere beyond the veil of raindrops. Vague images—an elephant on a seesaw, a peacock who couldn't unfold its tail, a Taiwanese macaque ringing the bell on a little train—floated up before my eyes before dissolving into mist. But, in reality, the only animal in sight was Pochiko. Occasionally, I could hear Mina coughing through the wall.

My uncle never came home the evening after my exams had ended, and after that he was gone from the house again for a time. The mixer was back in the kitchen, the pearl necklace hung around Grandmother Rosa's neck, and the mechanical pencil had returned safely to Mina's case, and, for the time being, the desk in the study had been cleared off.

17

"How did you like *The House of Sleeping Beauties?*" Mr. Turtleneck asked as soon as he caught sight of me. I'd gone to the Ashiya library nearly every Saturday since the day I'd received my library card and borrowed Kawabata's novel, but my timing must have been bad; I hadn't run into Mr. Turtleneck again. When I'd walked in that day, though, I saw him behind the counter and started pacing nonchalantly back and forth across the lobby, hoping he'd notice me.

"It was really interesting," I murmured, completely dismayed when the very thing I'd been hoping for had come to pass. It was June now, so he was no longer wearing a turtleneck, but the way he handled the books and the tone of his voice as it echoed from the high ceiling were exactly as I remembered them.

"I'm glad you enjoyed it. I was afraid I'd forced it on you when you didn't really want it."

"Not at all," I said, shaking my head.

"Really?"

"Of course. It did seem a little strange to write about that old man, when all the other characters were sleeping women who never said a word. But I think I understood. The old man was practicing his death. Spending the night with those young women who were drugged and slept like they were dead was his way of preparing for the end. He was trying to get used to it . . . so when the moment came, he wouldn't run away in fear."

I strung together words that I hoped would convince him he'd had nothing to worry about.

"I have to admit I'm amazed to meet a girl in middle school who can put herself in the place of an old man and understand his fear of death." Mr. Turtleneck leaned over the counter and smiled. His soft hair fell across his forehead. The smile seemed full of respect, with no hint that he was simply humoring a child. "I'm proud to have an intelligent young woman like you coming to the library," he added.

I could tell that he continued to watch me even after I'd looked down at my feet. Behind me, I sensed the people coming and going among the rows of books.

Please, please, I repeated to myself, please don't look at me anymore. I am not the person you should be praising like this. I had tossed the book aside before I'd even finished the first page, and everything I'd said about it was just what Mina had told me. I had repeated her impressions exactly as I'd heard them. The person who deserved your smile was a little girl who wasn't even in middle school yet, who lived in the big house on top of the hill. So, please stop looking at me.

"Have you decided what you're going to check out today?"

At this, I finally looked up, dug my hand into my bag, and pulled out the list Mina had given me.

"Uh, yes, *The Garden Party* by Katherine Mans . . . Mansfield."

"A wonderful story," he said. "Check in English and Ameri-

can Literature. There should be a volume of Mansfield's short
stories."

Mr. Turtleneck pointed toward the stacks. His arm was longer than I would have thought, and his fingers thicker than I'd have guessed from his thin frame.

"Thank you," I said, hurrying off in the direction he'd indicated.

Had he found it unusual that I needed a note to remember the title of the book I wanted to borrow—and that I'd stumbled over the author's name? Wasn't there something suspicious about a girl who could understand Kawabata's *The House of Sleeping Beauties* and yet seemed so shy and hesitant? I slipped into the English and American Literature aisle as if trying to hide, resenting Mina just a bit for wanting to read books with such complicated titles.

Please don't be wary of me, I pleaded silently with Mr. Turtleneck. You're not wrong, but I'm only the messenger, you can ignore me. The girl who read *The House of Sleeping Beauties* is just as intelligent as you imagined. You can be as proud of her as you want.

I found the book by Katherine Mansfield right away. When I got back to the desk and presented it to Mr. Turtleneck, I realized how strange it was to be constantly, silently pleading with him.

〰〰

I almost told Mina the secret of Mr. Turtleneck one day while we were playing Kokkuri-san in the light-bath room.

I hadn't really intended to keep my conversations with him from her, but somehow I'd neglected to mention him. I suppose I'd had a feeling that telling Mina about him might mean I'd end up telling even more lies, and, knowing her, I also suspected that she'd find it hard to take innocent pleasure in compliments from a librarian.

For the game, we traced a grid on a sheet of white paper and wrote one of the syllabary characters in each square. (This was called the "sheet of revelations.") Then we told fortunes by placing a ¥5 coin on the sheet, holding our index finger lightly on the coin, chanting "Kokkuri-san, Kokkuri-san," and letting the coin glide across the characters. The game was wildly popular in my elementary school in Okayama, but I'd been surprised to find that it was just as fashionable among students here in Ashiya. Furthermore, Mina was known as the mistress of Kokkuri-san at her school.

The light-bath room was an ideal place to play the game. In Okayama, we had chosen rooms with a certain atmosphere, such as the science lab or the storeroom for the school store, but none of them could hold a candle to the light-bath room. In this room, there was no chance we'd be interrupted by adults or hear any noise from the outside world, and, above all, our game was illuminated by the lamp Mina had lit.

As soon as we'd finished our light bath, we would begin preparations for Kokkuri-san. The room seemed dim for a few moments after the orange light had been extinguished, until our eyes had time to adjust. But soon the patterns on the tiles reappeared under the glow of the lamp. Still in our slips, we faced each other, kneeling on the daybed, and unfolded the sheet of revelations between us.

Our white slips added to the mood, making it seem as though we were great priestesses who had stripped ourselves

of all frivolous decoration in order to prostrate ourselves
before Kokkuri-san.

The creases in the paper and the characters that had been rubbed away by the ¥5 coin suggested how many revelations this sheet—Mina's own handiwork—had made in the past. She set the coin in the sacred, pentagonal space in the middle of the sheet.

"Okay then, let's begin," she said, sitting up straight, placing her palm on her belly, and bowing from the waist. She spoke like an adult, and her Kansai accent was suddenly gone, adding a greater solemnity to the occasion.

"First, I'd like Kokkuri-san to tell us the most important problem in your heart right now. Would that be permissible?"

"Yes, by all means," I said, matching my tone to hers.

She placed her finger on the coin, and I rested the tip of my finger on her fingernail.

"Not like that," she said, her accent coming back. "Your finger has to be at a right angle to mine."

"Really? We never did it that way in Okayama."

"Okayama Kokkuri-san and Ashiya Kokkuri-san aren't the same. If you don't put the fingers like that, the spirit vanishes. Okay?"

"Fine, I get it."

"Good, then I'll start again."

Though we'd just finished the light bath, Mina's fingernail was cold to the touch. The room was filled with tension, her tightly pursed lips and unblinking eyes revealing a strange suspicion in place of her usual sweetness. The flickering light of the lamp traced a rippling pattern on her hair as it cascaded down her back.

"Kokkuri-san, Kokkuri-san, Kokkuri-san, Kokkuri-san . . ."

Mina's murmured words slithered across the tiled floor before disappearing into the dark corners of the room. And then, suddenly, the sensation in my fingertip seemed to recede, and I had the feeling that my index finger, alone in my body, had suddenly become light. The next moment, the coin and our two fingers began sliding silently across the sheet of revelations.

To. It stopped first on the square containing the character *to*. Then *tsu* and *ku*. Then *ri*—spelling out the syllables for the word "turtleneck"! After that, the spirit seemed to pause for a moment, wandering a bit across the page, before returning to the sacred space in the center.

"'Totsukuri'? What's that supposed to mean? Do you suppose it was trying to say 'Kokkuri'?"

Mina slumped down and folded her arms with a skeptical look.

"That must be it," I said, anxious to placate her. "Look, the *to* and *ko* are right next to each other. After you told me our fingers had to be at right angles, that was all I could think about. My head was full of 'Kokkuri-san.' That must be it."

"What could be more boring? We go to the trouble to play Kokkuri-san, and the answer to the most pressing question in your heart comes out to be just that—Kokkuri-san." She seemed to still be upset.

"Okay, this time I'll do it for you. Quickly then, what's your biggest problem?" I said, pressing her.

The coin slid across the page again, stopping at *su* and *i*, *yo*, *u*, and *bi*.

"'Suiyoubi'? Wednesday?" I murmured, not quite understanding.

18

I still remember several of the predictions we received from Kokkuri-san. My future profession, the name of the man I would marry, the number of children I'd have, where I would live . . . Not one of them turned out to be correct.

I was never sure whether Mina actually believed in any of that. I suppose a silly game like Kokkuri-san was a way to use her imagination, which was so far beyond that of most sixth-grade girls, in compensation for her fragile body.

At the very least I think she believed in the existence of Kokkuri-san. There was something sincere about the way she looked in her plain, white slip, and a feeling approaching reverence as she manipulated the coin on the paper. So there must have been some invisible presence that found its way into the light-bath room to lend an ear to our childish whispers. We believed that presence was Kokkuri-san. Even if the predictions were all over the place.

But if it wasn't Kokkuri-san, how could it be that the predictions Mina and I played were actually correct? "Mr. Tokkuri"—"Mr. Turtleneck"—and "Wednesday." Though half the meaning was immediately clear to each of us, we never spoke about it to one another, pretending instead that the spirits from Okayama and Ashiya had gotten mixed up and confused the coin—even though those were the only correct predictions we'd ever made.

Though Kokkuri-san of the light-bath room responded to everything we asked of him, he never seemed to make a show of his powers. He answered somewhat indiscriminately for things we really didn't need to know—the name of the person we'd marry or how many children we'd have—while at the same time showing us much more important things we needed to remember for the future, gently, discreetly caressing our little index fingers all the while.

〰〰

The enigma of "Wednesday" became clear one day when Mina and I were helping Yoneda-san bake bread. We normally had the bread delivered from a shop run by a Frenchman out on the national highway. But when she could find good yeast, Yoneda-san would occasionally bake it herself.

I loved Yoneda-san's cooking. It was bold yet attentive to the smallest details, lovely and simple. She made dish after dish that seemed to reflect her own resolute character. Omelets stuffed with all sorts of things, grilled cypress buds, pirogis, mimosa salad, sand eels simmered in soy sauce, meatball stew, chestnut rice, deep-fried bites of whale meat, lamb pie . . . The dishes—and not just the flavors, but the presentation and even the design of the tableware—come back to me vividly, one after another.

Of course they weren't as spectacular as the plates sent out by the chefs from the Mount Rokko Hotel, but Yoneda-san's food had a certain warmth. You could feel her sincerity even in the finely spun noodles floating atop the bowls of shaved ice she would make for us during summer vacation.

But what I liked even better than her cooking was the chance to work with Yoneda-san in the kitchen. In Okayama, I had occasionally taken over the dinner duties from my mother, but that was simply another household chore. In Yoneda-san's hands, however, the same activity became an act of beauty, a manifestation of wisdom.

The kitchen was spacious and elaborately equipped, like some sort of precision machine, and sunlight poured into it through an east-facing bay window. An L-shaped sink was made of glittering stainless steel, and the stove, oven, and refrigerator were all imported from Germany. In the middle was a large, marble-topped table, with a surface so smooth you might be tempted to press your cheek against it.

Everything in the kitchen—be it the tiniest drawer or light switch or spice bottle—was infused with Yoneda-san's will. And it wasn't just that she kept everything so neat and tidy; the kitchen itself was defined by an order determined through her long years of use. The evidence was in the stack of half-completed contest entry cards on one corner of the table (contests being perhaps Yoneda-san's one and only hobby) or in the cans of condensed milk always stacked next to the refrigerator (suggesting that, despite her strict principles, she often gave in to the temptation of a sip or two of this beloved treat).

All these trivial things made the kitchen an even more pleasant place, and it was here that Mina and I, using our hands and our ingenuity, applied ourselves to simple tasks and learned the pleasure of making food that acknowledged the bounty of the earth.

"Be sure to measure accurately. When it says 'lukewarm,' it should be forty degrees. Two-and-a-third teaspoons of yeast.

One teaspoon of sugar." Yoneda-san was in her element giving orders.

Mina took the thermometer and I grabbed the spoons, and we nervously made our measurements. The first step in making bread is sprinkling the yeast on lukewarm water and waiting for it to begin bubbling. It's mysterious to see these sand-like grains start to wriggle and squirm, with no more than a bit of sugar to get them going. Our faces bent over the bowl, Mina and I inhaled the slightly sour smell as we watched, transfixed.

Gifted chefs often cook by instinct, but not Yoneda-san. She had the exact measurements in her head for each dish, and she stuck to them.

"The world is founded on the golden ratio," she was fond of telling us. "They used it building the pyramids, which is why they're so solid. So, if you carefully follow all the proportions, your food will be delicious."

Yoneda-san stood back and left everything to us as we scattered the flour and mixed together the ingredients. Hands thrust in her apron pockets, she limited her involvement to the occasional comment—"No, no, more slowly" or "That's right, just like that."

When we reached the next step, kneading the dough, Mina suddenly came to life. For a girl who usually seemed so fragile, she showed unbelievable energy.

"Okay! Here we go! He! Ha! Ho!"

Urging herself on, she leaned over the table and slapped the dough down on the marble. Ignoring the cloud of flour that turned her hair white, she punched the dough, stretched it into the air in an arc, then let it fall back on the table. At this point her breathing started to get a bit ragged, so Yoneda-san, no doubt fearing an attack, ordered her to let me take over. But, try as I might, I couldn't match Mina's energy, and soon enough Yoneda-san broke in again.

"Miss Tomoko, you can't be quite so delicate," she told me, ordering us to change back. Mina seemed unable to conceal her joy at being able to behave so brutally.

We let the dough rise in the light-bath room. It seemed that the orange light rays were effective not just for delicate children but for activating yeast as well. In no time, the dough had expanded, overflowing the bowl. To see if it had risen sufficiently, we poked our fingers into the center of the ball. It trembled slightly in response, as if to tell us that tiny living things were concealed inside. Dimples from the three finger-holes, Mina's, Yoneda-san's, and mine, remained in the dough. That was the sign it was ready.

Our six hands divided the dough into eighteen equal parts and fashioned them into balls. We cut a cross into the top of each with a knife, heated the oven, and then all that was left was to wait for the wonderful smell to fill the room. We passed the time while the bread baked washing the bowl, spatula, and board, and mopping the floor.

〰〰〰

Mina and I were peering through the oven window, anxious to make sure that the bread wasn't burning, when we heard a car pulling up out back and then someone ringing the bell at the service entrance. Soon the young man who made the weekly delivery of Fressy from the factory appeared in the kitchen.

"Hello!" he called as he entered. Tanned and solidly built, he wore a uniform with the Fressy insignia and a baseball cap.

"Thanks for coming," Yoneda-san called back. He opened a

trapdoor in the kitchen floor to reveal a storage space, pulled out a case of empty bottles, and replaced it with a new case of Fressy. Despite his large frame, he moved carefully to avoid getting in our way, maneuvering the full bottles as easily as the empty ones.

"You've timed it perfectly," said Yoneda-san. "The bread is just coming out of the oven, so you can take some with you." And, indeed, the wonderful odor of bread had filled the kitchen—a smell so splendid that we had trouble believing it was the result of our efforts. "Mina, put a few rolls in a sack for him."

At Yoneda-san's suggestion, Mina took the rolls, hot out of the oven, dropped them into a paper bag, and handed them to the young man, who was waiting by the kitchen door. As she passed the bag, steam rose from the opening, floating around her face like a veil.

"Thank you," said the young man with a bow, lowering his face into the cloud of steam as well.

"Not at all," Mina answered in a ladylike tone that seemed unimaginable coming from the girl who had been kneading the dough so violently just a short while ago, and, as she spoke, she discreetly brushed away a bit of flour still clinging to her hair.

I couldn't help noticing that the young man took something out of his uniform pocket and passed it to Mina as he was on his way out the door. In the blink of an eye, a signal had passed between the two of them—a matchbox.

At that moment I realized: It was Wednesday.

19

I should have realized sooner how strange it was that Mina had managed to accumulate such an enormous collection of matchboxes. Other than her trips back and forth on Pochiko to school, she hardly left the house. Neither of us were permitted to have money, and if Mina wasn't allowed to spend a few yen buying candy or pencils in the Yamate shopping district near Ashiya Station, how much less likely was it she'd be visiting the kinds of markets where matches were sold?

So how had she managed it? She'd had them brought to her by the young man who delivered Fressy every Wednesday. He was in charge of deliveries for Ashiya and Nishinomiya, and every day he would load his truck with Fressy and make the rounds of the supermarkets and liquor stores, the restaurants, hotels, and cafés. And whenever he found an unusual matchbox abandoned by the service entrance of one of the stops on his rounds, he would ask if he could have it and then bring it back to Mina.

More than likely, it was the young man from Wednesday who had offered her the first matchbox that led to her collection. Perhaps Mina had picked up a matchbox that had fallen out of his pocket and, fascinated by the label, had formed a secret exchange with him from that time on.

"The next time you find an interesting one, could you bring it to me?" she must have asked him.

Every Wednesday evening after that, she would find some excuse to come down to the kitchen. After the delivery had been made, as he was climbing back into his truck, he would hand over his new acquisition—an interaction that invariably took place at the back door.

"He doesn't find a new box every week," Mina told me. She wasn't in the habit of talking about the young man from Wednesday, but she did like to keep me up to date on the state of her collection. "The mass-produced ones are boring, so I got interested in the ones with unusual labels, old ones from the Meiji and Taisho periods or the ones they make for export."

"It must be hard for him to find them," I said.

"Sometimes he won't bring any for several weeks, and then he'll show up with three at once. It varies a lot. I think some of the places where he makes deliveries have started to save the good ones for the 'Young Man from Wednesday,' as you call him."

"Hmm," I murmured.

This young man was quite different from Mr. Turtleneck. He was polite enough but a bit shy, and there was something brusque about the way he silently went about his job. No doubt his slightly dirty uniform and muddy tennis shoes suited him better than a white turtleneck sweater would have. But I liked the image I had of him in my head, his cheeks stuffed with our fresh-baked bread, the steaming bag in his hand.

Even after the Young Man from Wednesday had handed off his matchbox, climbed back in his truck, and driven out the gate without a backward glance, Mina would linger outside the kitchen door in the gathering gloom. Yoneda-san, busy preparing dinner, paid no attention to us. Once she'd finished studying the illustration on the new matchbox, Mina would slip it into her skirt pocket.

∿∿∿

Later that summer, Mina was hospitalized. It seemed she'd been unable to cope with the successive waves of low pressure that had started at the beginning of July, and the long string of rainy days that came with them. Once again, the crisis had come in the middle of the night, and she'd been driven to the hospital in Kobayashi-san's car, but this time she did not return home the next morning and remained in the hospital for some time.

And yet for everyone else in the Ashiya house, the situation did not seem particularly alarming. Her toiletries, clothing, and everything else she might need for a stay in the hospital had been packed in advance, and other than my aunt going each morning to look after Mina in the hospital, there was no noticeable change to the rhythm of life in house.

One day, after final exams for the first term had finished and I'd came home from school before noon, I was allowed to go to the hospital with Kobayashi-san when he drove them all their lunches. Yoneda-san packed lunches every day for my aunt and for Mina, who had lost her appetite and found it impossible to eat hospital food, and Kobayashi-san made the round trip to the hospital any number of times during the day.

Konan Hospital, in the Higashinada Ward of Kobe, was about twenty minutes by car from the house. After coming down the mountain and continuing west for a time on the national highway, you turned north around Mikage and then climbed into the mountains again. The road was as steep as the ones in Ashiya. Halfway along, you skirted a lake before continuing up.

Needless to say, the little truck was much less comfortable than my uncle's Mercedes, but Kobayashi-san's way of driving was relaxed and reassuring. Perhaps because he'd so often driven Mina when she was sick, he held the steering wheel gingerly, as though it were a little kitten.

He said almost nothing as we drove, though I was sure it wasn't because he was in a bad mood. Rather, I suspect he had no idea what to say to a girl my age. He asked just one question.

"How were the exams?"

"Not bad," I answered.

Finally we passed through a stone gate and came to a building made of light brown bricks—an elegant, stately hospital surrounded by tall trees. The ceiling of the entrance hall was decorated with stained-glass windows, and the waiting area looked out onto an interior courtyard. But the trees were so lush and green, very little light reached the hall regardless.

Mina's room was on a dim corridor that stretched to the left as we got off the elevator. Wrapped in a blanket, she did not look at all well, and it seemed almost more than she could manage to turn to look at us. Her head was resting on an ice pack. The worst of the attack had passed, but the fever that followed it was proving stubborn. My aunt was sitting on a chaise lounge next to the bed.

"Thanks, as always," she said to Kobayashi-san and then turned to me. "Tomoko, how did it go?" They had all been worried about my final exams.

"Not bad," was all I could find to say.

Yoneda-san's bento boxes were magnificent. Sandwiches,
apple salad, and pineapple Jell-O. The sandwiches were filled
with all sorts of things—ham, cheese, tuna, egg, strawberry
jam—cut into bite-sized morsels and wrapped in multicolored
cellophane. The apple salad was spooned into lovely paper
cups with floral patterns, and the Jell-O was molded in the
shape of stars. No effort had been spared in trying to spark
Mina's appetite.

"I'm going to warm some milk," said my aunt. She took a
small pan from the shelf and the milk bottle from the refrigerator by the bed and headed toward the kitchenette at the
end of the hall.

"I'm afraid I left my bag in the van," I said to Kobayashi-
san. "Could I have the keys?"

"No, don't bother. I'll go and get it." And as I'd hoped he
might, Kobayashi-san left for the parking lot, leaving me
alone with Mina. I held out the matchbox that the Young
Man from Wednesday had given me with this week's delivery.

"Here," I said, setting it next to her pillow. I could feel the
fever coming from her body and wondered whether the picture on the box was appropriate to have brought to a sick
room: a naked angel, sewing basket at her feet, in the act of
reattaching her broken wings. Mina thanked me, staring at
the image with her moist, swollen eyes. Her voice was so weak
it seemed about to disappear altogether, drowned out by the
constant wheezing at the back of her throat.

Kobe spread out below the window, and tankers could be
seen floating on the sea beyond. But the light was far away,
and Mina's face was in shadow.

"The Young Man from Wednesday was worried, too," I
told her. "He said he was praying for you to get well soon."

In fact, he had simply murmured that he wasn't surprised she'd had another attack, but I'd thought I'd sensed something more in his softly spoken words, so it wasn't exactly a lie. Mina brushed her finger over the box, over the angel repairing her wings, just as she had at the kitchen door, before slipping the matchbox into the pocket of her pajamas.

~~~~

On our way out, Kobayashi-san treated me to a fruit-flavored milk from the kiosk in the hospital. Mina's room had been overheated, and we were so thirsty we opened the bottles right in the hallway in front of the shop. Kobayashi-san had chosen coffee-flavored milk.

"Isn't it nice to have something besides Fressy every once in a while?" I said.

"Hm? I suppose so," he muttered, the bottle still to his lips, and then gulped down the rest of the coffee-milk.

Looking out on the courtyard, I realized it had begun to rain. The fire escape, the exhaust fan, the basement ramp, the palm trees—large drops were pelting all of it. I sipped my drink and we stared as the rain poured down.

20

Nights when Mina wasn't in the house seemed longer than usual. After my bath, I would go to her room, fish out one of the boxes under her bed, and read the story written inside. Leaning against the windowsill, I would light just one small lamp to illuminate the hidden world. This was my way of saying a prayer for her quick return.

The boxes that held the matchboxes all fit easily in my palm. When I shook them, the matches rattled like moonlight shimmering on the surface of a swamp.

The one I opened that evening, a soap box that she must have received from Grandmother Rosa, contained a matchbox with two seahorses perched on a crescent moon on the label.

∧∧∧∧

"It's getting worse," said the first seahorse.

"Not to worry," said the second, trying to be helpful. But the sliver of a moon had grown as thin as a closed eyelid, and they pressed closer together.

"If it gets any thinner, we're going to fall," said the first.

"Listen," said the other, "when the time comes, we'll jump to that blue star over there."

"That star? The tiny one so far away?"

"It must be a wonderful place."

"How can you tell?"

"It's perfectly round without a single piece missing."

"And what will we do if we get separated on the way?"

"Why would we? If we attach ourselves tail to tail, like this!"

So they wound their tails together so tightly it was impossible to tell one from the other, like a knotted piece of yarn.

"You see, nothing to worry about."

"No, nothing at all."

They tried to look each other in the eye, but their tails were so tangled they lost their balance and were about to fall. The horns of one ended up propping up the head of the other. Meanwhile, the crescent moon had grown so thin it was about to vanish.

"I would have liked to stay here a bit longer."

"Me, too."

"It was only three billion light-years."

"There must be time on that blue star, too."

"I hope so," sighed the one.

The moment seemed to have arrived at last. The moon became a single strand and then no more than a point of light.

"Shall we go?"

"Let's."

Taking a deep breath and concentrating all their force in their tails, they jumped through the darkness toward the spot of blue in the distance.

But despite their best efforts, they fell, fluttering through the air like dry leaves, and their tails, which had been wound together so tightly, came apart without a sound as they traced an arc in the darkness.

The seahorses floated away, unsure who they were or where

they had come from—or what to do with their too-long tails, the purpose of which they could no longer recall. From time to time, they'd try to escape from an eel that had darted out at them or a shell that threatened to snap them, but they could do nothing more than float like dry leaves.

If they were always looking overhead, it was because they were hoping for a better view of the moon. They loved to stare at its light glinting on the surface of the sea. It seemed to recall for them a scene from a distant past, perhaps even before they were born. They had the feeling someone or something might be revealed to them, like invisible ink held up to the light. Especially on the night of a crescent moon.

But in the end, they remembered nothing. They continued to float, forever alone in the depth of the sea.

∧∧∧∧

I closed the soap box. The garden was pitch dark. Pochiko's pond, the remains of the train tracks, the old ticket booth— everything was invisible. A crescent moon floated in the sky.

I felt then that Mina, who must have been asleep in her bed at the hospital, weighed as much as a matchbox in the palm of my hand. And at the same time, I was somehow sure she was there in that pale moon, so very far away. Perhaps her trips to school on Pochiko and our feasts of Milk Bolos and the tale she'd told me of the seesaw elephant—perhaps all these things had taken place on a star three billion light-years away.

I put away the story of the seahorses, slipping it quietly back where I'd found it, careful not to disturb the other boxes, all so neatly stacked under the bed.

∧∧∧∧

The members of the household all seemed to have their own way of passing the long nights. Grandmother Rosa would become completely absorbed with her facials and manicures, while Yoneda-san, once the kitchen had been tidied up for the night, would sit at the counter and write postcard after postcard, entering every contest she could find.

My aunt would shut herself away in the smoking room—or as Mina called it, "the place Mama goes to drink so that Grandmother doesn't find out." It was on the first floor, to the north of the main salon, and apparently it had originally been reserved for guests, who went there to smoke their cigars. The open fretwork on the ceiling and the decorations on the built-in shelves seemed extremely elaborate for a room that had been intended for just that one purpose. It was impossible to miss the smell of nicotine—it permeated every corner—and despite its fancy design, the room itself seemed dark and cold.

"Have the results of your exams come back?" asked my aunt one night as I went in to see her.

"Some of them," I said, sitting down across from her. In addition to her whiskey and cigarettes, the round table between us was filled with books, magazines, dictionaries, and pens and pencils. The ashtray was full of butts, and a cloud of smoke enveloped her. She was forced to limit her smoking when she was at the hospital with Mina, so she made up for lost time in the evening.

No matter how much she drank, my aunt never seemed drunk. She didn't act outrageously or lose control of herself—her face didn't even get red. Still, she could invariably be found sitting in a corner of the terrace or on the sofa in the smoking room, drinking discreetly, making sure not to disturb anyone.

"Are you working?" I asked her.

"No . . ." she said, shaking her head. "I was just looking for
typos."

"Typos?"

"Printer's mistakes. In books or pamphlets, anywhere I find them. I'm always looking for mistakes hidden in the printing."

"And what do you do when you find them?"

"Nothing in particular. It doesn't amount to much," she said, shaking her head again and then draining the rest of the whiskey in her glass. "Look at this, for example."

The spine of the book read *Folklore Beliefs: Agony and Chaos.*

"My," I groaned, "that doesn't seem very interesting."

"It's not a matter of interesting or not, the problem is the typos. Look, here, on page 319. Instead of 'nun' they've written 'gun.'"

"Oh, you're right . . . 'in this instance, the only person speaking the truth is the gun.'"

"It makes you wonder what sort of truth they think would come out of a 'gun.'" She chuckled as she poured herself a fresh drink. "And here, on page 116 in this romance novel set in Venice: 'I never wanted to meet you under these circumferences. It's too late, it's all too late.'"

"I see, they've put 'circumferences' where it should have been 'circumstances.'"

"I suppose the heroine must be partial to geometry," my aunt laughed. She had drawn circles around "gun" and "circumferences" and inserted bookmarks at those pages.

"How do you find them?" I asked.

"There's no special method. I just read each character very carefully."

"And do you ever spend days going through a long book and not find a single typo?"

"Of course. They're actually quite rare. It's a bit like mining for gems."

"Ahh," I sighed. She shook her glass, rattling the ice.

"Most of the time they're not gems at all, though. Sometimes they're quite vulgar." And with that she held out a copy of a publicity brochure from my uncle's company. On the first page was a picture of him seated in the president's office. "Right here in your uncle's greeting, they have 'Fleshy' instead of 'Fressy.' Now who would want to drink something called that?"

She coughed quietly, took another sip of her whiskey, and brought her half-smoked cigarette to her lips. The ash fell on my uncle's photograph, along with a drop from the bottom of her glass.

∿∿∿

On the way to my room, I peeked into my uncle's office. Several more broken things had been left on his desk.

21

Dear Sir,

I apologize for the sudden intrusion, and I hope this letter finds you in good health. I am an avid reader who takes great pleasure in your publications.

As such, I have read with interest the fascinating *Folklore Beliefs: Agony and Chaos,* Volume Thirteen in your series on the History of Contemporary Thought. I have, however, discovered the following typographical error, and, rude as it may seem, I feel it is my duty to call it to your attention:

On page 319, fourteenth line, thirty-eighth character from the top of the page:

"gun"—"nun"

I am sure I will continue to enjoy the highly informative works that you publish, and I continue to wish your enterprise every success.

Respectfully yours,

When my aunt discovered a typo, she invariably sent this sort of letter to the publisher. She rarely received a reply, and most of her letters were apparently ignored, but occasionally a particularly polite publisher would answer, apologizing for the mistake and thanking her for pointing it out. On rare occasions they included bookmarks or a book cover or a pen with the letter.

"Did you get an answer from Uncle's company?" I asked, remembering the typo in the brochure.

"No," she said, her voice flat. "Even though I signed the letter from Yoneda-san, to avoid being recognized—please don't tell her that."

It seemed to me that it would have been better to mention the typo directly to my uncle, but I decided against saying so.

"They misspell the name of the product, and they don't even send a bottle to apologize. Rude, if you ask me," she said, giving a shrug.

Needless to say, for her the goal of searching for typos was not to receive gifts of thanks. Nor did I really believe that my aunt was so meticulous she found it impossible to overlook the tiniest mistake. No, she was content simply to journey through the desert of characters, searching for every single typo buried at her feet. They were jewels glittering in a sea of sand, she said, and if no one dug them up, they would always remain hidden. If no one noticed them, they would be trampled underfoot and left behind—something my aunt couldn't bear.

The smoking room, as its name suggested, was for smoking and drinking, but at the same time it was a place devoted to these voyages through the desert. It was there that my aunt spent the better part of her days, and no one but her had any business there. Mina, of course, was forbidden to enter for fear that the smoke would bring on an attack, and Grandmother Rosa hated the smell of whiskey. The drawers of the display cabinet, which presumably had once held imported cigars, now contained boxes of the domestic brand of cigarettes that my aunt preferred, and my uncle had long ago stopped inviting guests into the room.

I was the one exception. I'm not sure why, but whenever my aunt shut herself away in the smoking room, I felt restless. I'd go and press my ear against the door. My parents in Okayama never touched a drop of alcohol, which may be why I feared the stuff more than I needed to. No matter how hard I listened at the door, though, I could never hear anything, and so eventually I'd always end up knocking.

My aunt would be sitting there, pencil stub in hand, puffing incessantly on her cigarette and tracing her finger across pages of characters, sifting one by one through her grains of sand. She never seemed annoyed when I interrupted her; she just murmured my name and then went right back to her task. At times she'd be reading a leather-bound book, others nothing more than a crude leaflet, but the distinction seemed not to matter to her at all. The important thing was not the quality of the territory she was traversing but the endless characters themselves. She'd sift and sift, but only perfect, proper characters would flow through her fingers. Yet she never gave up, bending over again and again, plunging her hands into the sand. Back bent, breathing low, even forgetting to blink, she'd stare intently at her fingertips.

I pretended to have free time, said I had nothing better to do, and hovered about, peeking between the curtains or flipping through the dictionary. But in reality I was worried about her. The desert was boundless, the oasis a mirage, and my aunt a lone traveler.

"Ah!" she said, her hand stopping for the first time as she looked up. "Look, here . . ."

I hurried over to read the words she was pointing to.

"'His clergy exhausted, he collapsed on the spot.'"

"It should read 'energy' instead of 'clergy,'" she said, circling the character for spirit. A circle to honor this single grain left in her palm, to comfort this wandering spirit for which no one had a care.

Though she could have had all the real jewels she might have wished for, the only ones my aunt wanted were the typos. She found comfort not in glittering rings or necklaces that so insistently called attention to themselves, but rather from typos abandoned in inconspicuous places. On nights when my uncle wasn't at home, or when Mina was in the hospital, she pored over her typos with the same care someone else might have reserved for real jewels, and the next morning she'd slip the errant words into an envelope and, praying that they'd find their way back to their places of origin, take them off to the mailbox.

〰〰

Mina came home from the hospital in the afternoon on the first day of summer vacation. Her face was even paler than usual, and one of her arms, visible below her short-sleeved blouse, bore painful traces of the injections that she'd received, but her voice was full of energy as she stood in the entrance hall and announced her return. Grandmother Rosa took her face in her hands and covered it with kisses, and Yoneda-san turned her around, inspecting her from all angles to be sure nothing was amiss. Mina, who was terribly ticklish, squirmed under all the attention.

No sooner had we settled onto the couch in the living room than the adults sent us off to the light-bath room.

"They don't have this at the hospital. Even though that's where she needs it most. That's why I hate having to send her there. It makes me nervous," Grandmother Rosa said to Yoneda-san as soon as the door was shut. Everyone in the house believed that Mina's therapy could not be complete until she'd been bathed in the light.

As usual, Mina lit the lamp with a match. The movement of her hand, decisive yet somehow sweet, was unchanged after her trip to the hospital, and it was only when I saw the flame at the end of her fingers that I felt she'd truly come home. She was using the matchbox with the angel mending her wings, the one I'd delivered to her for the Young Man from Wednesday.

"Have you written that story yet?" I asked her, looking at the angel's wings.

"No, but I'm thinking about it. I asked the nurses and they gave me lots of boxes to hold the matchboxes. It turns out that the kind that the ampoules of anti-inflammatory medicine come in is just the right size."

She turned on the lightbulbs and set the timer.

"When you're finished, you can tell it to me," I said.

"Of course."

"I can't wait for this Wednesday."

"Wednesday?"

"You might get another matchbox, and I know he'll be happy to see that you're all better."

"I wonder . . ." Mina scrambled up onto the lounge chair.

"He will," I said, emphasizing the words, but Mina had nothing more to say on the topic. She tossed a Bolo in her mouth and took a sip of Fressy.

"It's true, it always tastes better at home," she murmured.

22

I'm not sure what happened while she was at the hospital, but when she got back, Mina had become a fanatical volleyball fan. The same Mina who generally spent the better half of gym class watching from the sidelines and who'd previously had no real interest in sports was suddenly explaining to me the strengths of the Japanese volleyball team in great detail. Apparently, her sudden interest in them was due to a TV program she'd watched in her hospital room.

The show was called *The Road to Munich*, and it followed the Japanese men's volleyball team as they prepared for the upcoming Olympics and pursued their dream of winning the gold medal. No one in the Ashiya house was in the habit of watching television, except for the news, children included. But after Mina got back from the hospital, we began gathering by the TV every Sunday evening at seven-thirty to watch *The Road to Munich*. We started the summer of 1972 under the spell of volleyball.

〰〰

I caught Mina's volleyball fever almost immediately. The team was coached by Yasutaka Matsudaira, and Jungo Morita was my favorite player. He was Number 8 and, along with

Okō and Yokota, was part of a group of attackers known as
the Big Three.

"Everyone thinks Morita is the most handsome," I said.

"So, you think looks are the most important thing?" Mina
shot back.

"No, but he looks so good when he's playing. His jump
serve is fantastic. Or the way his arm strains when he's diving for a ball, or the way his eyes fix on a set, or the arch of
his back when he strikes . . ."

I imitated Morita's jump serve. Mina took the opportunity
to correct my form, suggesting I'd lose power if I cocked my
elbow, that I should bend my knees a little more . . .

Mina and I took great pride in our encyclopedic knowledge
of everything to do with the Japanese men's volleyball team—
the player profiles, of course, but also the stories behind their
secret weapons and even the timing of their attack patterns.
That year, in 1972, the men's team had its heart set on winning the gold medal at the Munich Olympics. They'd won the
bronze medal at the 1964 Tokyo Olympics and the silver at
the 1968 Olympics in Mexico, so the only thing left for them
was the gold. Coach Matsudaira had assembled a group of
idiosyncratic players and had built an offense around hitherto
unimaginable decoy sets and quick kills. He planned to overcome the superior size of the foreign teams with quickness
and precision.

Morita had the most stylish game of the Big Three in every
conceivable way, far more than Okō, with his crewcut and his
power game, or Yokota, who always seemed ready to burst
into tears when he spiked the ball. No matter how sweaty
Morita got, his neatly parted hair never seemed mussed. His
profile as he looked up at the ball was intensely masculine,

and his play was powerful, yet full of intelligence. It seemed to me that he would have looked just as natural behind the counter of a library as he did on the volleyball court. In fact, something about him reminded me of Mr. Turtleneck.

Mina's favorite player, on the other hand, was Number 2, Katsutoshi Nekoda, a setter. He was said to possess a once-in-a-century talent; Coach Matsudaira had entrusted him with carrying the gold medal campaign. But while I pursued Morita like a fan following a pop star, Mina's interest was solely in the volleyball—meaning that her attraction to Nekoda was purely due to the vital role he played in the team's success.

"To become the best team in the world, you have to have the world's best setter," Mina told me. "That's why Nekoda does what he does. He keeps track of the ball with his left eye while he watches the blockers across the net with his right. And even after the point is finished and everyone else is running around the court celebrating, he never stops watching the opposing players. He notes everything they do and immediately figures out the next attack—even though it's the strikers who carry it out. It would be amazing if he were the one to actually strike the ball. But setters just set. And don't say a word."

Mina, who, needless to say, had never played the game, nor even so much as touched a volleyball, spoke with such animation about Nekoda that it almost seemed as if she were taking the court in his place.

"When Nekoda has set the ball and the striker has scored the point, doesn't it seem like they're having some sort of silent conversation? Like their feelings join together in the ball as it pierces the enemy defenses and smashes to the

ground? Nekoda sets the ball with tremendous feeling, holding out his hands to the striker as if to convey how much he's
relying on him."

Mina pretended to be setting the ball. Though she'd just
spoken so vividly about that very motion, her actual imita-
tion of Nekoda was so feeble that she seemed to be doing an
O-Bon dance for the dead rather than playing volleyball. Still,
I nodded.

"I know," I said. "It's so beautiful when Morita makes a
quick attack. Nothing gets in his way, as though the ball has
become a shooting star. Like when you strike a match and
the spark brings out the story in the box, that's how it feels
when Nekoda offers up the ball and it meets the explosion of
Morita's arm."

I pretended the wall was the net and demonstrated a quick
spike. The point of the quick spike, a move Morita invented
by chance when his shoelace had come undone at the exact
moment of his jump, was to get the blocker to commit to a
direction based on an almost instantaneous arm fake, and
then execute the spike beyond him without losing any force.

As perhaps was inevitable, Mina was dissatisfied with my
performance and offered critiques of my swing, of the depth
of my crouch.

〰〰〰

The television sat on a sideboard in the living room. Every
Sunday evening, right at seven-thirty, Mina and I installed
ourselves on the rug and waited for *The Road to Munich* to
start. We could just as easily have viewed the show from the
comfort of the couch, but as we grew more and more eager,
we naturally found ourselves kneeling right in front of the

screen. Perhaps we thought that in enduring the pain in our legs we were, in some small way, partaking of the sacrifices of Morita and Nekoda.

For some reason, Yoneda-san was in the habit of joining us, kneeling beside us on the rug. Perhaps she just wanted to know what sort of program it was that had captured our attention. Grandmother Rosa watched too, from the couch, but her interest in the show had less to do with volleyball than it did with the fact that Munich, a city from her homeland, was mentioned in the title.

In each episode of the *The Road to Munich* there was an animated film focusing on one of the players on the national team and highlighting his role in the fight for the gold medal. There were photographs inserted here and there amidst the animation as well, a technique that, at the time, seemed incredibly novel and impressive and made us watch all the more eagerly.

"It's just soccer with the hands," observed Grandmother Rosa, seemingly a bit disappointed that, despite the title, there were no scenes of Germany.

"Not at all," said Mina.

"Oh," Yoneda-san blurted out, "that one's really short." She had a habit of saying whatever it was that came to her mind.

"That's Matsudaira, the coach. He's the most important of all. And he's not actually that short, it's just that everyone else is so tall." It was my turn to answer; no matter how many questions they asked, Mina and I took turns responding without taking our eyes off the screen even once.

"They certainly make a big fuss about it . . ."

"There's no goal, like in soccer, so how do you score a point?"

"You score a point when the ball hits the floor on your opponent's side."

"When you've got the serve."

"Got the serve?"

"We'll explain the rules later, Grandmother, but could you keep quiet for now? It's too much to go into while we're watching."

Mina and I would have preferred to concentrate on the program without their company, but there was only one television in the house, so we didn't have a choice.

The first strains of the theme music and the sight of the red-and-white uniforms on the screen were enough to throw us into paroxysms. We'd be moved to tears by shots of a player, ignoring his bloodied body, flying across the court to dig out a spike, or another practicing alone in a dimly lit gymnasium until all hours, trying to perfect some new technique.

"Which one is your favorite, Mina?" Grandmother Rosa asked.

"Number two," Mina replied. Nekoda was on the screen now, tossing up A-quick sets, one after another.

"Number two? The one who's always bent over? As though he's groveling?" For once, Grandmother Rosa's observation seemed right on target.

"That's the one," said Mina. "Even if you don't know the rules, you can get a sense of what's so amazing about volleyball just by watching him."

Nekoda was making delicate adjustments to the angle of his sets according to the height and quickness of the attacker, guiding the ball to its ideal point, a point that existed for only an instant. Mina held her breath and fixed her eyes on his hands; each finger seemed to possess a soul of its own.

〰〰

"Twenty-seven days until the Opening Ceremony."

As the program ended and this line came on the screen, Mina and I looked at each other and let out a long sigh. The Japanese team just *had* to win the gold medal, they had practiced so long and hard they just *had* to, somehow or other the gods just *had* to look out for the team, please, *please* hang those gold medals around their necks, *please* . . . Our heads were filled with thoughts like these. With no idea what else to do, we could only sigh.

23

As soon as the rainy season ended, summer came to Ashiya as though rising from the waves. The sea, which had been absorbed by the gloom of the overcast sky, rediscovered its brilliance, and the eye could once again follow the horizon from end to end. The wind and the light passed over the waves and drifted up the hillsides, bringing with them the scent of the tides. You found yourself thinking the sea was closer than it had been the day before—and that was the signal summer had come.

"Look," said Mina. "The court is eighteen meters by nine meters. So, from where I'm standing, the length would be about to that hawthorn, and the width to the lantern. Can you picture it?"

Grandmother Rosa and Yoneda-san, seated on a bench under the wisteria arbor, nodded in unison.

"The net divides it down the middle, and six players face off on either side." After indicating the approximate size of the court, Mina raised her arms as high as they could go to emphasize the height of the net.

The bright sun reflected from each blade of grass. The color of the shadows under the trees seemed to deepen in response to the sparkling light, casting shapes across the lawn. Pochiko, apparently exhausted from the heat, had submerged herself in the pond with only her head protruding above the surface, floating along with a distracted air. The birds and cicadas, so noisy during the cool of the morning, seemed to have vanished, and the garden was silent, except for our voices echoing across the lawn.

"Let's say Tomoko is the Soviet Union, and I'm Japan. It starts with the service. Everything starts with the serve. I stand here behind the back line, toss the ball in the air like this, and hit it so it lands on the Soviet side. The Soviet team has to return the ball back across the net in three tries or less, and if they do, then Japan has three hits to get it back to the Soviets. Nekoda receives the ball, sets it, and Okō spikes it. Okō's spikes are amazing, so the Soviets can't reach it and it rolls across the floor. Since Japan had the service, that's one point for us. Fifteen points is a set, and three sets are a match."

Mina had moved around from position to position, pretending to be Nekoda and then Okō. I had performed the role of the hapless Soviet player who missed the ball and went tumbling to the ground. It was difficult to explain the rules without a ball or net and with only two players, but Mina managed quite well. She used vocabulary that two old women with no prior knowledge of the sport could grasp and balanced a general account of the game with a smattering of useful specific details.

The two ladies listened intently. By then Yoneda-san seemed to have realized that *The Road to Munich* wasn't some tasteless TV program, and Grandmother Rosa's disappointment that the city of Munich never made an appearance had long been forgotten.

"Who decides who gets to serve?"

"What happens if you hit the ball back on the first try?"

Their questions were naïve but not ridiculous. Grand-mother Rosa was dressed in slacks made of a silky material and a blouse printed with yellow flowers, while Yoneda-san's thin frame was even more obvious under her plain linen dress. They wore matching straw hats. On the table was a silver bowl full of ice that held four bottles of Fressy.

"In volleyball, the thing to remember is that the serve keeps passing back and forth between teams when no one scores. In any given set, you'll always have a stretch like that, where you're going back and forth without scoring. You have to be patient and wait for your opportunity. Even if the serve changes hands hundreds of times, you have to take each ball as it comes, without getting anxious. Volleyball is a waiting game."

"That's why the setter has to do more than just set up the spike," I added. "He has to be the psychological support for the whole team."

"I couldn't have said it better myself, Tomoko," said Mina. "And do you remember the name of the setter for the Japanese team?"

"Number two, Nekoda," the two old ladies said together, as if reprising their duet.

"Exactly," said Mina, her forehead glistening with perspiration.

〜〜〜

Mina and I demonstrated the A-quick, the B-quick, and the quick spike, emphasizing the originality of each attack. The sun was directly overhead, and the shadows under the trees had deepened. Two bees seemed to have discovered the sweet odor and were buzzing around the Fressy.

"Tomoko, come over here. These are the Soviet blockers. The ball comes back over to Japan. Nekoda makes a quick horizontal set along the net. Yokota jumps and seems about to complete the spike but then simply swings at thin air. Like idiots, the Soviet blockers fall for the fake and jump, and at the exact moment their long arms retract back harmlessly, Nekoda's pass reaches its zenith, and the real attacker, Okō, spikes the ball."

Mina played Nekoda and then Yokota and then Okō. I was the Soviet blockers, then the decoy, and then Morita for the quick fake. Mostly we switched parts freely, but when it came to Nekoda, it was always Mina.

"Do you see?" she said, glancing repeatedly back toward the arbor. Each time the ladies would dip the brims of their straw hats. Pochiko was the lone holdout. Seemingly uninterested in the quick set, or anything else, she had extracted herself from the pond and, after giving a thorough shake that scattered drops of water everywhere, settled into her nest on the hillock.

For the benefit of the ladies, whose vision was less than perfect, we exaggerated our demonstrations, running after the ball or jumping or swinging our arms with abandon. The whole performance was especially tricky for me, since I had to switch back and forth across the net as I alternated between roles, first the Soviet players and then the Japanese. Soon enough, we were both dripping with sweat. Mina's shirt was plastered to her back and her hair was knotted at her neck.

"Now the D-quick." From the tone of Mina's voice, we

might have been tied two sets all in the Olympic gold medal match, the score 13–14, with the Soviet Union to serve.

"Okay," I answered.

The Soviet ball came over the net—a float serve. It seemed to have some spin on it, but the Japanese team managed to dig it out. Seeing that Nekoda was looking left, the Soviet front line shifted in that direction. Nekoda crouched under the ball, and four Soviet arms stuck up over the net, preparing to block the spike. But, at that moment, Nekoda set the ball behind him, in the exact opposite direction from where he'd been looking. His knees became supple springs, his back arched, his ten fingers offered a silent prayer to the attacker. The invisible ball slid to the right above the invisible net. None of the Soviet players could lay a finger on it.

Mina, Grandmother Rosa, Yoneda-san, and I watched as the ball slammed into the Soviet side of the court and rolled away. The sound of the referee's whistle echoed through the garden.

〰〰

That week, when I wrote to my mother, I knew just what I wanted to ask her.

Dear Mother,

How have you been? I'm fine. Everyone here is fine. Mina was in the hospital for a couple of weeks at the beginning of July, but she's better now. There's no need to worry.

My aunt says she's going to send you my grades from the first semester, so you can see them for yourself. I've been taking your advice and listening to the English lessons on the radio every day, so I'm satisfied with my English grade at least.

You once wrote that if I needed anything, clothes or pens or whatever, to match Mina's, you could send it to me. Well, I've thought of something: could you send me a volleyball? A white one, like they use in the real game. I don't need a Snoopy pencil case or a frilly blouse, but I'd like a volleyball. So Mina and I can play together. It doesn't have to be an expensive one . . . I hope this doesn't sound selfish.

When you've saved up enough ¥10 coins, please call again. Take care!

Tomoko

∿∿

Just as I was getting back to the house after dropping this letter in the nearest post box, the mailman arrived.

"What wonderful news! I could almost cry!"

Grandmother Rosa had put aside her cane and was waving a blue airmail envelope above her head. I knew right away that it must be a letter from Ryūichi, since they were all gathering in the entrance hall, even Kobayashi-san.

"Ryūichi's coming home from Switzerland! He'll be here August first!" Grandmother Rosa kissed the envelope again and again; it was covered with red lipstick in no time at all.

24

On August first, Ryūichi returned to Ashiya. It was his first trip home since he'd left over a year ago. We'd all waited impatiently since early that morning, checking the clock again and again until he finally arrived—the hope of the family, Grandmother Rosa's prince—at the hour before dusk, when the wind had died down and the slopes of Mount Rokko were just beginning to light up with the rays of the setting sun.

I don't know why, but he arrived with my uncle. We hadn't seen my uncle at the house in some time, but he was just the same. Perhaps he had timed his return to coincide with his son's. Or perhaps he had gone all the way to Haneda Airport in Tokyo to meet him. Since he was so rarely at home, who would have communicated these details? And how had they managed to do so? I had so many questions about this homecoming, but they all vanished the moment Ryūichi stood in front of me.

First, Grandmother Rosa wrapped her arms around him and covered his face with kisses, leaving his cheeks as red as the envelope had been. He bent over and gently hugged her, taking care not to disturb her cane. Her body disappeared completely into his arms.

They all celebrated his return, in their own ways. My aunt

and Kobayashi-san, in true Japanese style, were reserved in expressing their emotion, while Yoneda-san was nearly in tears, and Mina, in a display of innocence unlike anything I'd seen before, kept repeating over and over how happy she was to have him safely home. My uncle stood nearby and watched them all with an air of satisfaction.

"So, you're Tomoko?" Those were the first words Ryūichi spoke to me.

"Yes, Tomoko. I'm Tomoko." I couldn't take him in my arms the way Grandmother Rosa had done, nor could I grab his hand and jump for joy like Mina, so I contented myself with repeating my name. What else could I say . . . to a boy like Ryūichi?

〰〰

Ryūichi's beauty was different from my uncle's or Mina's, which had the transparent clarity of a cold, clear lake. His was more passionate, more powerful, like the earth itself. His hair and his eyes were the purest black, not chestnut like theirs. Black that brought to mind obsidian extracted from deep in the earth.

He was not as tall as my uncle, but his shoulders were broad and he was muscular. His navy blue school blazer and tie suited him perfectly, and even though he'd just arrived home after a long journey from a place that was, to me, unimaginably far away, there wasn't a single wrinkle on that blazer nor any sign of fatigue on his face.

At first glance, my uncle and Ryūichi didn't look much alike, but when you lined them up, their appeal seemed to resonate one with the other, forming a bright light that illuminated everything around them. Each one alone was remarkable

enough, but together there was something about the differences in the color of their hair and eyes, their physiques, their
ways of talking that seemed to merge to create a new kind
of charm—which was, in turn, proof beyond doubt that they
were father and son, despite their apparent differences.

"Thank you for being Mina's friend," Ryūichi said, turning
to me and extending his hand. "I'm glad you're here." I knew
that it was nothing more than a standard greeting, no matter
how warmly he'd said it, but I couldn't help feeling ecstatic.
Shaking hands with someone that wonderful! How was I supposed to stay cool, calm, and collected? Of course, I'd been
excited the first time I'd met my uncle at Shin-Kobe Station,
but an uncle was, after all, an uncle. Ryūichi, on the other
hand, was an unbelievably handsome, accomplished young
man, even if he was also my cousin's older brother.

I reached out to take his strong, tanned hand and realized
then that I'd done something unforgivable: I had forgotten to
wear a brassiere.

I have no idea why this occurred to me at such an important moment, even though I'd given absolutely no thought to
bras since the middle school opening ceremony. In any case, I
was wearing nothing but a white slip under my blouse and felt
deeply embarrassed by my meager, childlike chest. My head
was suddenly so full of bras that I was unable to smile charm-
ingly or make a witty remark . . . or even breathe properly.

By the time I came to my senses, that precious moment
when I could have shaken Ryūichi's hand had fled, leaving
behind only the vaguest sensation, like a passing breeze.

I hurried back to my room, opened a drawer in my dresser,
and pulled out the bra that had been wadded in a corner, worn
only once for the school ceremony. Perhaps I was imagining

things, but I had the feeling that I filled it out more fully now than I had in the spring. I carefully adjusted the straps and raised my arms over my head several times to be sure it wasn't riding up.

〰〰〰

Ryūichi possessed many qualities that Mina did not. He was healthy, for one thing, and he had lots of friends. He preferred to act rather than simply imagine things, and he was perfectly capable of going off on adventures wherever he wanted to, without riding on Pochiko.

A silver Jaguar served as his legs, a quick, stylish car that had nothing in common with a pygmy hippo. It seemed a high school friend had lent it to him just for the summer, but the little hood ornament that cut through the wind seemed to suit him perfectly.

Mina questioned Ryūichi about life in Switzerland, pestered him to look at her summer homework, invited him to the light-bath room—anything she could think of to extend her time with her brother—but it did not go well. He was constantly on the move, determined to take full advantage of his short summer vacation. He'd promise Mina that he would help her with her homework in the evening and then drive off in the Jaguar early in the morning and still be out when it was time for us to go to bed. He seemed to have an endless list of places he had to go: a part-time job as a swimming instructor at the pool, the tennis club in Ashiya Park, Mount Rokko, the movie theater in Sannomiya.

With no other options, Mina and I passed the time spoiling Pochiko, telling her how much cleverer she was than any

Jaguar, and making scrapbooks about the Japanese National Volleyball Team with articles and photographs we found.

〰〰

On the rare occasions when Ryūichi was home during the daytime, he invariably had several friends with him. They seemed to be college students, polite, neatly dressed, and all carrying musical instruments, records, books, or cameras. There were girls among them, too, and they generally came bearing cakes or pastries.

"Here, these are for you and your sister." They all had pleasant smiles and musical voices.

Mina never looked particularly pleased, even when they brought her absolute favorite: madeleines from the finest patisserie in all Ashiya.

"Thanks," was her curt reply, in a voice that was anything but musical.

"She's my cousin, not my sister," I would never forget to add.

Ryūichi and his friends would listen to records in the living room, go out on the terrace to play cards, or do nothing at all, relaxing in the shade in the garden. There was endless conversation and laughter, and Ryūichi was always at the center. They were nice enough to Mina and me, but in the way you were nice to children, and it was clear we were not part of their group. Still, to be as close to Ryūichi as possible, we would pick a nearby spot that was unlikely to disturb them and apply ourselves to our scrapbooks.

"Do you think Pochiko is napping?" one of them came to ask us. She was wearing a snow-white dress with lace at the neck and sleeves.

"You haven't had a chance to meet Pochiko?" Mina asked, scissors still in hand.

"I've been here lots of times, since I was a child," said the girl. "But she's never come out of hiding."

"Are you a classmate of Ryūichi's?" I asked in turn.

"Yes, I was in the girls' school. But in high school we were in the same fencing club."

She smelled good, not like Bolos or Fressy, but perfume.

"During the day, she's usually in her burrow. Look, you can see just her butt sticking out." Mina pointed at the hillock in the garden. "We can take you down there if you'd like."

"Really? That would be wonderful! Please."

We left the terrace and walked down to Pochiko's hill. The girl in the lace dress followed, as though trying to hide behind us, but eventually she came forward. Pochiko's rear end was as impressive as ever.

"There's nothing to be afraid of," Mina said. "She particularly likes to be rubbed right here by her tail."

"Like this," I added, demonstrating.

"Go around and around, like you're drawing a circle."

Following our instructions, she rubbed the area around Pochiko's tail. Pochiko, for her part, erupted in the usual way just below the girl's hand, and her tail sent the offering flying in every direction.

The girl's scream was more or less simultaneous with the soiling of her white dress. We comforted the girl as best we could and scolded Pochiko, but inside I was praising her for letting fly with a mess even more magnificent than the one she'd bestowed on me.

25

I hadn't slept well since Ryūichi's homecoming. I had washed out the one bra I owned in the bathroom, dried it on the curtain rod in a sunny window, and slipped it under my mattress; the mere thought that Ryūichi used to sleep in this same bed made my whole body tense and kept my brain wide awake.

"I'm sorry I've taken your room," I said to him.

"Don't worry about it," he said, as though it meant nothing at all. "There are plenty of other rooms, and this one isn't really mine. I don't need a nursery here anymore."

It made me a little sad to think that even if you were born in a wonderful house like this, you couldn't just stay there, warm and cozy, for the rest of your life. But in any case, the fact that I shared this bed in common with Ryūichi gave me a chill and made it impossible to sleep.

〰〰

"We're all going swimming at the beach at Suma," my uncle declared one Sunday morning. "The weather is good, and Mina's healthy. What do you think, Yoneda-san?" In this house, if you could enlist Yoneda-san's support, you could pretty much have your way. "You have the day off, don't you, Ryūichi?"

My uncle's tone was somewhat different when he addressed his son. Instead of his usual cheerful, stylish self, there was a hint of the severe paternal figure.

I thought it was a shame that I hadn't had a chance to swim even once during summer vacation, so I was the first to agree. Mina seemed delighted as well at the opportunity to monopolize her big brother's time. Ryūichi, who must have had other things in mind for his day off, seemed less than enthusiastic, but in the end he agreed.

We quickly set about getting ready. Yoneda-san made rice balls, and my aunt gave Mina some medicine for motion sickness. Grandmother Rosa opened a drawer in her dressing table and produced an assortment of makeup for the beach. My aunt, Grandmother Rosa, and Yoneda-san took their places in my uncle's Mercedes, while Mina and I climbed in Ryūichi's Jaguar. The two groups formed naturally, without anyone saying anything. Unfortunately, Pochiko was left home to watch the house.

The weather was clear and magnificent, perfect for the beach—the sky cloudless, the sun shining down on everything around. The glittering Ashiya River appeared and disappeared between the thicket of reeds, and Mount Rokko traced a sharp outline across the sky. We had only to follow the national highway due east to arrive at the beach at Suma.

The Mercedes and the Jaguar rolled gently along, never losing sight of each other. Grandmother Rosa, Yoneda-san, and my aunt turned one after another to be sure we were still following, and each time I would wave at them. I was unbearably happy to be going out with all of them, not to mention the chance to ride with Ryūichi.

Soon after we'd passed Motomachi, just as the smell of salt air began filtering in through the window, the sea made its appearance between the pines.

"Mina! Look! The sea!" I said, pointing to the expanse of blue beyond the windshield. But Mina was wearing a mask to avoid inhaling the exhaust fumes, and she had covered her head with a towel, apparently to help with car sickness. The scenery was the last thing on her mind. I could barely catch what she said through the layers of material.

"The exhaust is outside the car," Ryūichi said, sounding a bit exasperated. "The mask won't do any good."

"But Mama says you can never be too careful," replied Mina. She looked like an Arabian princess with her eyes peeking out from the towel.

"Such a worrywart! Are you still riding Pochiko to school? Wouldn't it be healthier to walk? What do you think, Tomoko?"

This sudden need to choose between them confused me; just as I started to mutter something noncommittal about health and the places where only a hippo's legs could take you, the cars arrived at the Suma beach.

〰〰

My uncle and Ryūichi unloaded the trunks of the two cars, planted two beach umbrellas in the sand, and unfolded the deck chairs. The beach was crowded with families and couples who had come for the day. Mina and I had worn our bathing suits under our clothes, so we didn't need to make a trip to the bathhouse. Instead, we simply slipped off our dresses. We were about to run down to the water when Yoneda-san stopped us in our tracks, ordering us to do proper warm-up exercises. For no other reason than to please her, we imitated some of the calisthenics we'd learned from the radio.

The water was much colder than I'd imagined. I found myself shivering from the tiniest waves lapping at my ankles. The sea was calm, but the sound of the surf was surprisingly loud. Broken seashells pricked the soles of my feet.

Mina, who could not swim at all, contented herself with clinging to a life preserver and floating near the shore, while I did a gentle breaststroke that allowed me to look up and check on her. Don't go out too far . . . come in before you get tired . . . watch out for jellyfish . . . We could see the anxious adults under the beach umbrellas waving their warnings, but their voices came to us only intermittently on the wind.

Grandmother Rosa and my aunt rubbed coconut oil on each other's backs. Yoneda-san opened her basket and began preparing for lunch. And my uncle and Ryūichi stared at the sea in silence, never exchanging a word. Perhaps it was the brilliance of the sunlight, but they all seemed to me much farther away than they were in reality. Only the shadows on the sand appeared solid, the rest seeming to dissolve into vague outlines in the brilliant glare. An island appeared to float in the offing, small fishing boats passed back and forth, a flock of seagulls rested on the sand.

"Tomoko!" Mina called. "Stay with me. I don't like it when you leave me."

"Of course, I know."

I spun her life preserver in circles to keep her amused, tickled her belly with a strand of seaweed. She laughed out loud, but her hands gripped tightly to the ring.

Mina looked even more fragile soaking wet than she did

in the light-bath room, or even than when she was having an attack. In the sea, there were no matches, no matchbox boxes, no Pochiko. Her clavicle and ribs and backbone—all her bones, suddenly more visible under the dazzling sun— seemed awkwardly assembled. Her legs, drooping from her swimsuit, and her brown hair, spreading out behind her, swayed forlornly in the sea.

"Are we being carried away?"

"Don't worry, I've got you."

"Are you sure we can get back?"

"Of course, they're all just right over there."

"I can't really see them with the waves shining like that."

"Do you want to go back?"

"Hmm. I guess we could stay out a little longer."

We floated like lost seahorses. The commotion from the beach receded. We were surrounded by the drone of the waves.

〰〰

Back on the beach, we ate our rice balls, taking care not to get them sandy from our damp hands. Wrapped in every bath towel we could gather to prevent her from catching cold, Mina was once more the proper Arabian princess. And I tried to position myself so that Ryūichi wouldn't notice my flat chest.

"Tomoko, you're a good swimmer," said Grandmother Rosa, reaching for a third rice ball. Her breath was scented with the coconut oil she had too liberally applied.

"She's good at volleyball, too," said Yoneda-san. The two of them were again wearing their matching straw hats.

"Are you in the volleyball club?" Ryūichi asked. He had not gone in the water yet, and his back glistened with sweat.

"No, no," I said. "I only play it in my imagination."

"She's a whiz at the jump serve and quick spike," Mina offered from her knot of towels.

"It must take a lot of effort to learn all that in your imagination. Not everyone could manage it." As always, my uncle was a master at paying a compliment.

Lunch was nothing more than the rice balls and cold barley tea, but everyone seemed to enjoy it as much as the feast we'd had from the staff from the Mount Rokko Hotel. The presence of Ryūichi made the atmosphere even more jolly. The rice balls in the basket, stuffed with salmon and umeboshi and tiny dried sardines, disappeared in no time.

But all the while, my uncle and Ryūichi avoided looking at each other. Though everyone pretended not to notice, we could see that Ryūichi was staring out to sea for just this reason. The tide crept gradually up the beach.

"Okay," said Ryūichi, getting to his feet. He brushed the sand off his body and pointed far out to sea. "Papa, I'll race you to that buoy."

26

Before Yoneda-san could say anything about warm-up exercises, my uncle and Ryūichi had run off toward the water. They swam freestyle, straight toward the buoy that marked the limit of the area where swimming was permitted. I could tell from the height of the spray they were kicking aloft that the competition was more serious than I would have imagined. The casual bathers floating beyond the breakers hurried to get out of their way.

It was difficult to tell who had won. The sunlight reflected off the spray, turning them into glittering masses, and no matter how much we squinted, it was impossible to tell them apart. As the rust-colored buoy bobbed in and out of view, it began to seem strange that they hadn't reached it, despite swimming so frantically. Their glittering masses grew smaller and smaller, and yet the buoy seemed just as far away.

"No!" cried Mina, jumping up from under the umbrella and throwing off her towels. "They shouldn't go out that far!" The people on the beach turned to look at us. Mina ignored them. "They'll drown!" she shrieked, staring out at the waves. "Please come back!"

But her voice could not reach them, no matter how much she cried.

"Papa and Ryūichi are both great swimmers," said my aunt, patting Mina on the back. "Don't worry."

"Men like to race like that. They'll come in as soon as they finish."

"That's right, no need to worry."

"Yes, come back in the shade."

We did our best to calm Mina, but to little effect. She stood there, feet planted on a towel, lips trembling. Seen from behind, she seemed painfully vulnerable, as though the circuit that proved Mina was Mina had somehow blown a fuse.

"They can't stand up way out there, and the current's too strong. What are they going to do if a shark shows up? They won't come back! They're just tiny points of light, about to disappear . . ."

It was true, they'd been reduced in the distance to a single point of light, bobbing on the crests of the waves.

Mina was weeping. Each time she blinked, tears fell from her eyelashes, wetting her cheeks, which were turning red in the sun. She wept as though she didn't really know why she was crying.

That was the first and last time I ever saw Mina cry. We had lived through any number of situations in which it would have been natural enough to shed tears, but she never had. The one time she cried in my presence was on that hot Sunday in August, watching from the beach as her father and brother raced to the buoy.

〰〰〰

In the end, they came back safe and sound. By that point, Mina had regained her usual composure. She was able to greet them calmly from her spot under the umbrella, her tears for the most part dried.

My uncle and Ryūichi were still gasping for air, and their bodies were wet and chilled. In the end, we never learned which of them had won. My uncle lowered himself into one of the beach chairs, and Ryūichi lay down on his back, oblivious to how sandy he would get.

"How fast you swim!" said Grandmother Rosa. "Just like flying fish."

"Yes, it was a wonder to watch," added Yoneda-san. But they could only huff in reply, still completely out of breath. The buoy continued to bob in the distance.

～～～

On the way back to the car, we stopped at a stand on the beach and ate shaved ice. An affable lady cheerfully ground up seven cups of ice for us, working so efficiently it occurred to me that if Yoneda-san had been a shaved-ice lady, she would have gone about it in much the same way. Grandmother Rosa chose strawberry-flavored syrup, melon for my uncle and Ryūichi, honey for my aunt, pineapple for Mina, grape for me, and for Yoneda-san, of course condensed milk.

Sitting on a bench in front of the shop, shaded by a reed screen, we ate our ices, each with his own flavor. There was no Fressy in the cooler on the porch, just drinks from rival companies, but no one seemed to notice. A pleasant sea breeze blew up, rustling the ribbons on the straw hats and causing the paper lanterns hanging from the eaves to sway. From time to time, one of us would howl "Cold!" and press our hands to our temples, letting our spoon rattle in the glass.

Everyone is here, I thought, looking at each of them in turn, lined up shoulder to shoulder on the short bench. Everything is all right, no one is missing.

My aunt was neither smoking nor drinking. She was gazing at the menu board on the side of the stand, but she didn't seem to be searching for typos. Mina had forgotten how hard she'd been crying and was eagerly devouring her ice, Grandmother Rosa and Yoneda-san were happily sharing the strawberry and the condensed milk. Ryūichi had returned from distant Switzerland, and he'd made it back safely from the buoy too. Even my uncle was here now, here where he belonged, not off on his own, repairing broken things.

Pochiko at that hour was no doubt napping in the underbrush, avoiding the intense heat. Kobayashi-san would be enjoying a leisurely day off, freed from his usual duties taking care of Pochiko or chauffeuring Mina back and forth to the hospital.

And me? I, too, had nothing to worry about. I knew the address and telephone number of the place where my mother was living. I knew where my father was too; my mother had shown me his resting place on the day of his funeral. It's a bit far away, she told me, but we'll both be joining him there someday, so we're not likely to lose track of the spot. Your father is kind, she added, so he's gone on ahead to see where we'll be.

But now here I was with Mina's family. When we laughed, our tongues peeked out, red and yellow and violet. My uncle and Ryūichi had the same pale green from the melon. Everyone is here. No one is missing. Once more I repeated those words to myself, deeply comforted, as I stirred the ice melting in the bottom of my glass.

Ryūichi's summer vacation was over in the blink of an eye, and soon the day came when he had to return to Switzerland. On the morning of his departure, a photographer was summoned, and pictures were taken in the garden. Chairs were set out on the lawn for Grandmother Rosa and Yoneda-san, and the rest of us gathered around them.

The only problem was Pochiko. Kobayashi-san had carefully bathed her and tied a ribbon around her neck to match the one that Mina was wearing. Ryūichi had brought the ribbon, with a lovely Tyrolean design, from Switzerland, but unfortunately Pochiko's was half hidden in the thick furrows of fat on her neck.

Kobayashi-san was determined to get Pochiko to look at the camera, and we all joined him in the effort.

"Hey, Pochi, be a good girl. Look at the black box over there."

"When we're done, you can have an apple or some watermelon, anything you want!"

"It won't take long, just be patient for one second, Pochi!"

Ryūichi murmured encouragement and rubbed her hindquarters, as though he were comforting a baby, while Kobayashi-san held her head in his hands, tugging on the ribbon. The photographer held the shutter release and watched, his expression making it clear that he was happy to wait as long as need be until Pochiko assumed the proper pose. Clearly it was challenging to include a pygmy hippo in a group photograph, but we were all determined that Pochiko be in the shot.

All this while, Grandmother Rosa and Yoneda-san had been sitting, backs straight, hands folded on knees, eyes focused on the camera, ready for the moment when the shutter would be released. Holding their most elegant expressions.

"Here we go then, three, two, one . . . Cheese!"

Brandishing the shutter cord above his head, the photographer gave it a firm click.

~~~~

I keep the photograph taken that day close at hand, like a precious treasure that holds the memories of my days in Ashiya. A great deal of time has passed since then, but my uncle and Ryūichi remain as extraordinarily handsome as ever. My aunt has the same reserved smile, while Kobayashi-san is still holding fast to Pochiko, whose ribbon has come undone in the long struggle. Grandmother Rosa and Yoneda-san still sit next to one another, like twin sisters. And Mina's brown eyes are focused somewhere in the distance, far beyond the camera lens. Behind all of us, in the background, is that wonderful house that I loved so much.

Every time I look at the photograph, I murmur to myself. Everyone is there. Everything is okay. No one is missing.

27

Ryūichi returned to Switzerland, but not before whispering to me that he was counting on me to look after Mina. His manner suggested that he was asking this specifically of me, not of his parents nor of Yoneda-san.

I nodded, my heart full of joy that he had singled me out for this duty but also with the sadness that I would not be seeing him anymore.

Of course, I understand. Leave it to me. I'll be here for Mina. Though no one had told me, I had more or less gathered that the reason my uncle could not be with us all the time was because he had another home he had to return to. The letters Ryūichi wrote to everyone except his father and their little battle out in the waves—these were no doubt related as well. He knew that his father was unlikely to be there when Mina needed him most. That my aunt might very well be drinking. But I would always be there, would always be willing to help. I promise. Don't worry, Ryūichi, go back and focus on your studies.

I bowed, knowing that all those feelings were implied by my lowered head.

And as though confirming my conjecture, my uncle took

advantage of the commotion surrounding Ryūichi's departure and vanished from the house.

〜〜〜

While I seemed to lose my head over every man I met—
Mr. Turtleneck from the library, Morita from the national
volleyball team, my cousin Ryūichi—Mina only had eyes for
the Young Man from Wednesday. To be honest, as someone
who placed a lot of value on physical appearance, I found it
hard to understand why she would have chosen him. The
Young Man from Wednesday was a typical, if rather tight-
lipped, workman of the sort you might see anywhere.

Perhaps she was a bit numb to normal standards of beauty,
having been surrounded from birth by such handsome men.
Perhaps she had no further need for mere appearance, having enjoyed, by her last year in elementary school, more male
beauty than most women encounter in a lifetime.

Still, there was no doubt that her feelings had something to
do with the matchboxes, that things might have been very different if he had merely been the boy who delivered our Fressy.

When he snapped open his thick fingers, Mina stared at
the box resting in his palm as though he had just performed a
magic trick. In reality, he was a deliveryman. A role much like
the one I played when I took her books back and forth to the
library. But in her eyes, he was a traveler arriving on a magic
carpet. A traveler who moved freely from the meadow where
the elephant played on his seesaw to a starry sky filled with
floating seahorses, who carried with him a single matchbox
for a young girl every time he rang the bell at the service
entrance.

To afford them as much privacy as possible, I avoided using

the kitchen door on Wednesday evenings. But, conscious of my promise to Ryūichi, I would hide myself in the shed that had once been the ticket booth for the zoo, ready to appear in an instant if the need arose. If you were willing to ignore the spiderwebs, the little semicircular window made an ideal place for discreet observation.

But I realized before long that my vigilance was unnecessary, and that the situation was not progressing. In his presence, Mina became a gloomy, bashful girl, while he seemed even more distant and unsociable. Perhaps chitchat while on duty was against Fressy company policy. It almost seemed he was worried that she would tell her father he'd committed an infraction.

 Their interaction was limited to the single instant when the matchbox passed from his hand to hers. A moment later, he was back in the truck and Mina was watching him drive away. Hiding in my shed, I heaved a sigh.

 Say something to him, Mina, say anything. It's up to you to keep him there longer, so make an effort! From my hiding place, I sent one encouraging message after another.

〰〰

That day I made a plan. The next time he came, I clutched the brand-new volleyball my mother had sent from Tokyo against my chest, working up my nerve. Just as their brief moment of contact was ending, I rolled the ball down the hill toward them and ran out of the ticket booth.

 "Sorry!" I called. "It slipped out of my hands."

 I'd imagined that the young man would pick the ball up and ask me if I liked volleyball, and that then I'd invite him to play with us. But, in the end, both he and Mina simply stood there dumbfounded as I realized how contrived my entrance must have seemed—though it was too late to do anything about it now.

"Tomoko," said Mina, pointing at me, "you have spiderwebs in your hair."

"What?!" I shouted, running my hands over my head. Mina, however, had already moved on to volleyball—but why was the young man so unresponsive?

"It's been hot, hasn't it," I observed, still brushing my hair. He stood there, saying nothing, as the setting sun reflected off the empty Fressy cases on the back of the truck.

"Do you want to play volleyball with us?"

It was the line I had been planning all along, but now that it was out of my mouth it sounded even more artificial than I'd imagined.

"How about it, Mina? I'm sure he could show us a thing or two." I held the ball up in front of him. It had rolled down the hill just once, but it was already covered with dust.

"Okay, sure, here goes," he said, barely trying to hide his reluctance as he sent a sudden pass in my direction. Though it had been my suggestion, I was unprepared for the ball. I managed to get in position to receive it, but I struck the ball with a strange thud, and it went flying off in the wrong direction.

"Now you," he said. The pass to Mina was somewhat less abrupt, but too quick nonetheless. An image of Nekoda making an overhead pass went through my mind as the real ball sailed above Mina's outstretched fingers. The box of matches she had just received made a dry, rustling sound in her pocket.

In the end, despite repeated tries, Mina never managed to make contact with the ball, and I spent most of my time running after it as it rolled away across the garden. Though in her imagination she had been making brilliant flying saves or back sets, with the Young Man from Wednesday nothing worked out as planned.

"So, I have to get back to the factory," he said at last, and, without a word of advice or encouragement, he got in his truck and left.

〰〰

That evening in the light-bath room, Mina told me the story she'd written based on the matchbox with the picture of the angel repairing her wings. She set this one down in a box that had held ampoules of an anti-inflammatory medicine.

She didn't appear to be angry about my meddling. Rather, she seemed almost sorry for me that nothing tangible had come of my efforts. But what was more surprising still, her affection for the Young Man from Wednesday seemed even stronger than ever.

〰〰

Most human beings don't likely know the most important gift that angels have. It is, in fact, a talent for needlework. The hemming work of a gifted angel leaves a trace that is nearly as invisible as the silver trail of a snail. Every angel carries its sewing box on its back. Mine is made of wood and was inherited from my grandfather. It has many small compartments and is very easy to use.

As the Chinese characters in our name suggest, we are envoys from heaven sent to earth to deliver messages. It annoys us that we are often mistaken for fairies or sprites, which generally manifest themselves as ice or flowers or wind. They can't stand to remain hidden and always end up taking material form. About all we have to say about them is that they lack consistency.

By contrast, we angels are much more reticent. The important thing is the message, not the form it takes. Humans tend to create images of angels that are the products of their own imagination, but they are all somewhat inaccurate. Which is natural enough, since no human being has ever seen a real angel.

But one point is accurate: we do have wings. Yes, we have wings, and we deliver our messages by beating them.

Messages that make the heart beat faster, heartbreaking messages, messages of solace. We deliver all sorts. An angel swoops down, coming to rest next to the recipient, hovering in place. It's not easy work. Sometimes the human lacks sensitivity; other times the wind is too strong. We continue our deliveries even when our wings get damaged. Eventually, the human will signal that he has received the message, by means of a smile or a sigh or a tear.

There may be people who say that they have never received a message from an angel, but they shouldn't worry. They may have simply failed to realize what happened. Everyone receives our messages. At times we use the voices of others to communicate; at times we use our own, our voices echoing in a human's heart. No matter how they're sent, our messages from heaven protect anyone who receives them.

If you hear a strange rustling noise in your ears, don't rub them too hard. An angel may well be mending its wings there, perched on your earlobes.

28

The Munich Olympic Games finally began on Saturday, August 26.

We had wanted to watch the live broadcast of the opening ceremony on NHK at eleven o'clock at night, but no matter how we pleaded, Yoneda-san refused to give her permission.

"Only juvenile delinquents are still awake at eleven at night." That was the pretext she offered, but in reality I suppose she was worried that staying up late would be bad for Mina's health. In the end, we had to settle for watching the rebroadcast the next morning.

We assumed our usual positions, which had been fixed since we'd started watching *The Road to Munich*. That is, Grandmother Rosa sat on the edge of the sofa, and Yoneda-san, Mina, and I knelt in a line on the rug directly in front of the TV. Whenever men's volleyball came on, Mina and I sat up even straighter, our backs almost rigid.

I urged my aunt, who was in the smoking room, to join us, thinking it would be a shame to miss a ceremony that took place only once every four years.

She came to sit next to Grandmother Rosa, bringing a German dictionary with her.

"There might be typos on the scoreboards or the signs, the placards or the flags," she murmured. We told her we doubted they would make mistakes like that for such an important occasion, but she would have none of it.

"It's actually even more likely when the stakes are so high," she said. "Grandmother, you watch, too. If we see a single typo, I'm going to write to Avery Brundage, the president of the International Olympic Committee." She propped open the dictionary, ready to check a spelling at any moment.

The teams filed into the stadium—Greece, Argentina, Australia, Vietnam, Ethiopia, Jamaica. Mina and I struggled to read aloud the names printed on the placards. When we were unsure how to pronounce a country, Grandmother Rosa spoke up to correct us. Kuwait, Mongolia, Poland, Somalia, the Soviet Union . . . New countries appeared one after another, as though sprouting up from the horizon, so many we started to worry they would never stop. My aunt flipped through the dictionary each time she saw a particularly complicated name.

The team from Liberia, Pochiko's homeland, marched in as well. When the Swiss team appeared, we all leaned forward, as though hoping to find Ryūichi there among them. Grandmother Rosa applauded with equal enthusiasm for both East and West Germany.

"Which one were you born in?" I asked, but she shook her head.

"Neither," she said. "I was born in Germany, in Berlin. They divided it after I came to live in Japan."

Their order of entry, their uniforms, and their flags were all different, but for Grandmother Rosa they were both Ger-

many, and not to be distinguished one from the other. Half
rising from her seat, her swollen hands raised nearly to her
forehead, she continued to applaud even after the athletes had
disappeared from the screen.

While we showed our respect for Grandmother Rosa's
Germany, needless to say, Mina and I were most enthusiastic about our homeland. The moment we caught sight of
the blue signboard with JAPAN written on it, we yelled out
the name even louder than the announcer in the stadium and
bent farther toward the TV. The red of the athletes' blazers
sparkled against the blue sky. When the camera moved in for
a close-up, we could hardly keep ourselves from caressing the
television.

"The volleyball team is tall. That must be them in front."

"Look! There's Minami!"

"And that must be Okō!"

"I don't see Morita."

"And Nekoda, where's Nekoda?"

As we called out, the Japanese delegation disappeared from
view—without a sighting of either Morita or Nekoda. Though
the screen was covered with fingerprints.

Gustav Heinemann, the president of West Germany, pro-
nounced the games open, five thousand doves were released,
and a blond young man lit the Olympic cauldron. The flame
flared up even more suddenly than when Mina lit a match.
Finally, the Olympic Oath was recited.

"Every four years, as we return to this joyous competition,
rejecting combat, give proof of dear friendship . . ."

The TV broadcaster read the Japanese translation, but we
focused on the German that Grandmother Rosa was repeat-

ing from the stadium announcement. It was the first time that we'd heard Grandmother Rosa speaking in her native language.

She seemed to be a completely different person from the woman who needed a cane to walk, who spoke Japanese with so little assurance. She seemed filled with self-confidence, full of impressive energy. Even though we understood none of the words she was saying, it was clear that she had lost none of her German, and the brilliance of her language came through as though the past fifty-six years had never happened. When the door of her memory was opened, she was able to bring back every syllable with perfection, despite having no one around her to speak them to. She faced the Germany she saw on the television now and spoke to it in her native tongue as if singing a song aloud in full voice.

When the ceremony was over, Yoneda-san turned to the television, joined her hands in prayer, and thanked it for showing us something so rare and extraordinary; while my aunt snapped shut her dictionary, apparently disappointed not to have discovered a single typographical error. Mina and I could barely contain our excitement at the thought that the difficult road to the gold medal would begin tomorrow.

〰〰〰

As for our own playing, we realized that we would need at least some basic level of skill if we were going to have the Young Man from Wednesday coach us, so we began practicing in secret. On evenings when the sky was cloudy and the heat less oppressive, we brought the volleyball out of the storage shed.

My mother had said in the letter that she'd included with

the ball that it was assembled from eighteen pieces of high-quality leather and made by the same manufacturer that had been chosen to make the balls for the Munich Olympics.

"They say that every volleyball player who comes to Japan from overseas goes home with this ball." My mother's letter had been filled with pride, but we knew that having a first-rate ball didn't mean that we possessed the ability to go along with it.

Our first objective was to be able to make a basic pass five times without missing.

"It's not the hands that receive the ball, the important thing is the legs. A properly controlled pass starts with the legs. You have to slide quickly under the ball, bending your knees, keeping your head down, and flexing your elbows. Then you relax completely, and once you've absorbed the energy from the ball, you send it back using your legs and hips like a spring. It's as though your ten fingers are the earth receiving the force of the ball. For that one instant, it's completely at rest, so still you could see every stitch in the leather, and you hear a pure sound more perfect than any musical instrument."

Mina's explanation was impeccable—logical yet poetic at the same time—and all gleaned from her study of Nekoda. When I listened to her, I felt I could follow the graceful track of the ball as it went back and forth across the lawn and hear the satisfying *plock* echo in the air. Why then did these images crumble the moment we took the real ball in our hands? It struck me as endlessly strange.

Five successful passes proved to be an unreachable goal. Mina seemed to send the ball off in impossible directions intentionally, and the sounds issuing from the tips of her fingers were less like music and more like cracking cartilage in her joints.

Our official Olympic ball spent much more time rolling across the garden than flying through the air. After falling repeatedly into the pond or bouncing through Pochiko's droppings, it had started to take on a slightly disreputable look.

But Mina and I were in no way discouraged. In fact, the more we understood how difficult it was to play volleyball, the more our admiration for Nekoda and Morita grew. As we were using the garden hose to wash off the ball at the end of our practice each day, we would imagine once more that Morita was gracefully receiving one of Mina's terrible passes, that Nekoda was gently setting the ball for me.

〰〰

The preliminary rounds of the Olympics began on August twenty-eighth, and the Japanese men's team performed well. They beat Romania and Cuba without any trouble at all, and then swept past East Germany, thought to be their toughest competition at this level. Meanwhile, summer vacation had come to an end and exams were approaching, but I said nothing about them, and Mina and I continued to take up our positions in front of the television every evening at seven twenty. Matches with Brazil and West Germany presented no problems, and the Japanese team, which still had not lost a set, moved on to the finals.

On the eleventh day of the games, the evening of September fifth, as we were waiting for the start of the final round, the broadcast shifted from scenes of the competition to a shot of a dormitory in the Olympic Village. An announcer in a black tie began to speak.

"This morning, at five o'clock local time, members of a Pal‐ estinian militant group forced their way into the residence of the Israeli team in the Olympic Village. After killing one athlete and a trainer, they have barricaded themselves in the building with nine hostages."

29

At the time, I understood nothing about the significance of this event. I didn't know what a Palestinian militant group was, why it would target the Israeli dormitory, or why any of this would be happening during the Munich Games. I knew nothing.

There were eight terrorists in all. They called themselves the Black September Organization, and they were using the nine hostages to demand the release of two hundred Palestinians who were imprisoned in Israel as well as a plane to leave the country.

I can still remember the pictures on the television of these men, of them appearing on the balcony with their rifles. They were nothing more than knots of black shadow, only their eyes visible above the scarves that hid their noses and mouths, but the sight on the screen was somehow so vivid that you had the sense you could see the tattered edges of the cloth and the sweat soaking their masks. Or perhaps it wasn't sweat but the blood of the Israelis they had killed.

Grandmother Rosa was more shocked than any of us by these events. I think it was the sight of her grief that made me able to pray for the Israeli victims. If it weren't for her, I'm afraid I would have seen the terrorists as nothing more than

annoying men who were preventing the Japanese men's volleyball team from winning the gold medal.

She grew even more worried as night fell, and the Japanese
announcer reported that the guerillas had left the Olympic
Village with the hostages.

"At ten o'clock this evening, Minister of the Interior Hans-
Dietrich Genscher announced that he had accepted the de-
mands of the terrorists. They are moving to the heliport near
the Olympic Village along with the nine Israeli athletes, to
make the transfer to Munich International Airport where they
will board a flight out of the country. The hostages left their
dormitory tied together like beads in a rosary, eyes covered
and arms bound behind their backs, and were loaded into a
military van."

"Beads in a . . . rosary?" murmured Grandmother Rosa to
no one in particular. The word was beyond the scope of her
Japanese vocabulary.

"It means the hostages were tied up like the little beads
in a bracelet you wear for prayers," I told her. At this, she
looked up at the ceiling, shook her head, and let out a long
sigh. I worried that I had said something I shouldn't have,
but her sorrow seemed so profound that I had no idea how to
comfort her.

〰〰

Looking back now, I think the moment she heard the words
"beads in a rosary," she somehow knew how things would
end—that the gun battle between the guerillas and the German authorities would result in the deaths of all nine hostages.

The newspapers printed a picture of the gutted helicop-
ter. Its top was blown off, the frame laid bare, and the seats

burned. A lone soldier stood guard over it, as though protecting the corpses awaiting burial.

Grandmother Rosa gathered all the photographs of her twin sister, Irma, from the walls of her room and dusted the frames with a white handkerchief. She polished the glass with great care, working the cloth into the corners far longer than seemed necessary. All the while, Yoneda-san stood behind, never taking her hand from Grandmother Rosa's back.

Mina gave me a look that seemed to convey that only Yoneda-san could comfort Grandmother Rosa in a moment like this. I nodded in silence.

The attack had clearly reminded Grandmother Rosa of her sister. I realized that the photo of her and Irma together— the one in which their resemblance was so startlingly clear— must have been one that she'd brought with her when she'd moved to Japan. The more recent ones of Irma must have been sent later from Germany. When you lined them up by date, you could trace Irma's marriage, the birth of her three children, and their successive growth and development.

The last photograph showed a happy family of five, enjoying lunch at a table that had been brought out into a garden. It must have been early summer. The dogwoods are in bloom. It doesn't seem to be a formal occasion, just an early afternoon meal on an ordinary day. Mugs of beer are lined up on the table. The three children, two girls and a boy, appear to be college-age or perhaps in high school, and Irma and her husband perhaps fifty. The oldest child, the boy, bears some resemblance to Mina. They are all smiling, their eyes squinting against the bright sunlight.

That was the last. The date on the back of the frame was 1938. Though no one would have guessed it, Irma, so very

young in the image, was the twin of my old grandmother sitting there before me, holding the frame on her lap and caressing it, as though lamenting the fact that these two who had
once been so similar were now so different.

For a brief moment, there was talk of canceling the rest of
the Games, but in the end they continued, with only a day's
delay. A commemorative ceremony was held on September 6
during which IOC president Brundage declared that the
Olympic Games would never surrender to political pressure
or to violence.

Eliezer Halfin, wrestler; Ze'ev Friedman, weightlifter;
Amitzur Shapira, track and field coach; Andre Spitzer, fencing
coach . . . The names of the victims were read aloud.

Just as Grandmother Rosa learned the meaning of the
Japanese word for rosary beads, in watching that ceremony, I
understood for the first time the significance of a flag flown
at half-staff. The five rings of the Olympic banner fluttered
forlornly, halfway up the pole.

It was my aunt who told me that Irma's whole family
had died in a Nazi concentration camp during the war, that
Grandmother Rosa was the only one who had escaped, since
she was already living in Japan.

"One day they rang the doorbell of their apartment in Berlin, and the whole family was led away. They were sent to the
gas chambers. Israel was founded by the Jews who survived
the persecution," she told me. "So, when Grandmother Rosa
saw their team being attacked, it must have reminded her of
that time."

I went to the library and asked Mr. Turtleneck to help me
find a book of photographs from Auschwitz. It was the first
book I borrowed for myself rather than for Mina.

There were pictures of exhausted and battered Jews being forced out of freight cars and into long lines leading to the gas chambers. I searched the faces among them for the grandmother of the wrestler, the brothers of the fencing coach, the boy who looked like Mina, for Irma. They were making their way toward death, each following the other, like beads in a rosary.

30

After a day's delay, the semifinals of the volleyball tournament got underway.

We went off to our morning classes at school that day having avoided turning on the TV or opening the newspaper. But we were nearly beside ourselves with excitement. I had no idea how I was going to explain my terrible grades on the exams, but that didn't keep me from running straight home once school had ended. Mina asked Kobayashi-san to pull harder than usual on Pochiko's reins, and they hurried home as well.

Yoneda-san had made her special rice with brown sauce for lunch. We worked our spoons without a word.

"You're awfully quiet today," she said as she poured us cold barley tea. "Have you had a fight?"

"No," Mina told her. "This evening is the rebroadcast of the semifinals. We're just waiting."

"The matches are already over, so we're plugging our ears to make sure we don't find out what happened until tonight. We want to enjoy the excitement as if it were live," I added.

"So, if you know anything at all, you mustn't tell us," Mina emphasized.

"No, no, I don't know a thing," Yoneda-san said, ladling a large helping of vegetables into our bowls.

We thought we already knew the results. Since their real rival was the Soviet team they would meet in the finals, we were sure the Japanese team had beaten the Bulgarians in the semis. But we still wanted to watch the victory on TV.

In fact, we had it all wrong. We didn't know that the Soviets had lost their semifinal against East Germany or anything about the match against Bulgaria. Like Yoneda-san, we were completely in the dark.

Mina and I passed the time while we waited for the broadcast to begin at seven twenty by playing Kokkuri-san in the light-bath room (Japan had a 97 percent chance of winning the gold medal), read stories from the matchboxes, and, come evening, had our usual practice session passing the volleyball.

〰〰〰

We knew, of course, that the campaign might end in defeat despite our hopes. It would have been unexpected if they had lost to the Bulgarians instead of the Soviets or East Germans, but we realized that there was no guarantee of a gold medal. But we knew how hard they had tried. We had seen it all on *The Road to Munich*. So, even if they lost, we wanted them to keep smiling, to keep their heads up . . . or so we thought as we watched the match, as we stopped looking ahead to the gold medal.

Japan lost the first two sets to Bulgaria in the semifinal match. The usual players were on the court, but there was a subtle sense that something was wrong. It wasn't just that the Bulgarians seemed to read all the quick sets and staggered attacks, but their ace, Zlatanov, was hitting blistering spikes.

Grandmother Rosa, Yoneda-san, and my aunt had joined us in front of the television, but as the game went on, we said less and less. Each time Zlatanov scored with a spike, Mina and I glanced at each other, trying to keep from breaking down in tears.

It was such a critical moment in the third set and neither Nekoda nor Morita was on the court. Except for Okō and Yokota, all of the regulars had been benched, replaced by Minami, Nakamura, Shimaoka, and Nishimoto. Mina was beside herself that Nekoda was absent; everything we'd heard in the lead-up to this day had said that there could be no gold medal for Japan without him. The quiet, ever-present rasp at the back of her throat became louder and louder.

"This is Minami's third Olympics, after Tokyo and Mexico, and he plays on Asahi Kasei in Okayama . . . my hometown," I said, hoping to cheer them up even a little, but it had no effect. The air seemed chilly, as though Minami's origins were of no importance at all.

But the change in lineup proved effective. The moment Nakamura, the team captain, and Minami, who was a reserve in Munich but for years had been the ace of the Japanese national team, made their appearance, the gray cloud that had seemed to hang over the court dissipated and the white tape on the top of the net glittered. The two veterans brought fresh life to the game and Nekoda and Morita got a moment to catch their breath.

Quick passes, blocks, receptions—the veterans seemed to be everywhere, and somehow Japan took the third and fourth sets.

"Japan's looking good now."

"Sometimes it's better to have to play catch-up."

The two old ladies had brightened and began to offer more optimistic assessments. But Mina and I were still terrified

Japan would lose. At some point we'd begun holding hands as we stared at the screen.

In the fifth set, Nekoda and Morita returned to the court.

"It all comes down to this set," said Mina.

I knew it as well as she did, but I also understood why she couldn't help saying it aloud.

"Yep, this is it," I confirmed.

The Bulgarians led 8–3 at the changeover. Our first-string players seemed to have returned to form, their combinations clicking again, but Bulgaria retained its large lead, and soon the score was 11–7; they needed just four more points. If they got them, there'd be no gold medal for Japan. Every time Bulgaria scored, I did the subtraction anew in my head. I was afraid of miscounting; I folded and refolded the fingers of the hand that wasn't clutching Mina's. The ladies had fallen silent.

We couldn't let them get any farther ahead. It was as though we were balanced precariously on our tiptoes, the court shrouded in unbearable tension. Our legs, folded under us in proper fashion, had gone numb and cold, beyond painful. But that wasn't enough. If we were going to help the players on the court, we needed to suffer even more. Mina and I squeezed our hands even harder, not caring if we broke bones.

∧∧∧

That's when it happened. My aunt, who had been quiet until now, suddenly spoke up.

"Look, there!" she said, half rising from the sofa.

"They've written *Mastudaira* instead of *Matsudaira*!" She was pointing at the team lists below the scoreboard.

"Here," she said, but by the time her finger touched the place on the screen, the shot had changed.

"Mama, could you be quiet, please," Mina said, clicking her tongue.

"But the name of the coach is wrong . . ."

"It doesn't matter right now. You must know that. You can write all the letters you want to Mr. Brundage or anyone else, but later. For now, please be quiet." Mina was so insistent that my aunt returned reluctantly to the sofa.

〰〰

Looking back on it now, the moment when my aunt discovered the typo perfectly coincided with the most crucial point in the fifth set of the match. At the very moment her fingerprint smudged the screen as she tried to point out the error in *Mastudaira*, it was as though a switch was thrown somewhere and tiny gears began to turn. Everything seemed to stop for a moment. The shadows of the players on the court, the cheers of the spectators coming from the stands, the referee's whistle—the flow of time altered. The change occurred so quickly and subtly that mostly no one noticed, but Mina and I did.

In the next instant, Nekoda served an ace. Calmly struck, his ball seemed to be drawn to the one tiny, unprotected spot on the court, where it landed almost without a sound. The Bulgarian players stared at the floor as if unable to comprehend how the ball could have landed there.

The alteration in the flow, once begun, seemed unstoppable. Okō and Shimaoka managed five more points between them, and after some expert blocks and feints from Minami, we arrived at 14–12, match point for Japan.

When Shimaoka's spike scored the final point, Mina and I shouted for joy and hobbled on our numb legs to throw ourselves into the arms of Grandmother Rosa. Yoneda-san joined us, and we hugged each other in our delight. Nekoda and Morita had wrapped their arms around Okō, who was sobbing, his face buried in his hands. I apologized to them silently for having lost faith during the match. We continued to hug one another, as though Nekoda and Morita and Okō and Minami and all the other members of the team were there in our arms.

The final score was 13–15, 9–15, 15–9, 15–9, 15–12. Time of the match, three hours and fifteen minutes.

"Look, there it is. The *T* and the *S* are reversed."

My aunt continued to point at the team list. For the Japanese men's volleyball team, it was a precious error indeed.

〰〰〰

To be honest, I have very little memory of the final match. Perhaps it was because Mina and I had given everything we had to the semifinal with Bulgaria. By the time we got to the final, we had little energy and no tension; we felt almost refreshed. The joy the players felt at getting to the finals after their long road to Munich was far more important than winning or losing.

Our state of mind was probably also due to the fact that the opponent in the final was East Germany rather than the Soviet Union. Grandmother Rosa applauded with equal enthusiasm whether it was a quick spike from Morita or a block by Schulz. She sighed with admiration at the controlled play of Nekoda and the thrilling smashes of Schumann, and her reactions all seemed perfectly natural and unforced.

"I'm happy no matter which team scores," she said, winking at Mina and me. "What luck!"

She had only a vague grasp of the rules, but every time

a point was scored, she would lean forward on the couch, and as I watched her applaud with enough energy to propel herself all the way to Germany, I was reminded again of the long journey she had made to get here. It seemed that Grandmother Rosa had grown old not so much because of the passage of time but because of the distance between Germany and Japan. The thought somehow made me sad.

When Japan arrived at 14–10, match point, Nekoda raised his finger in the air to let everyone know—"One more, just one more." In the end, when the East German ball fell out of bounds, Japan had won the gold medal.

The closing ceremony took place on September 11. The Israeli team was represented by a placard, but no players entered the stadium. The Olympic Flame was extinguished at eight o'clock that evening.

Unnoticed, summer, too, had ended.

〰〰〰

Over ten years later, on September 4, 1983, Katsutoshi Nekoda, former setter for the Japanese National Men's Volleyball Team and gold medalist at the Munich Olympic Games, died of stomach cancer. He was thirty-nine years old.

The news, when I heard it, left me paralyzed. I felt the events of that summer in Ashiya return with almost suffocating power. The texture of the carpet we sat on in front of the television, the shape of the scarves worn by the Black September group, the smell of Pochiko's droppings on the volleyball . . . everything came back to me in an instant, and with it came sadness; much like Nekoda, that summer had disappeared to some faraway place where I'd never be able to find it again.

"Retiring at the end of the qualifying rounds for the Moscow Olympics, he ended a seventeen-year career with the Japanese national team. He had taken a position as coach for Hiroshima, but a malignant tumor was found in his stomach, and, after a brief battle with the cancer, he died on September 4. His final words, 'One more, just one more,' speak to just how much he wanted to return to the game."

Images of the Munich Olympics played nonstop on the television, with Mina's beloved Nekoda in all of them, the man whose ten fingers had set each ball in absolute silence, as if offering a prayer to the striker.

〰〰〰

As soon as the Olympics ended, my aunt, Mina, and I all wrote letters. My aunt wrote Avery Brundage of the International Olympic Committee to point out the misspelling of Coach Matsudaira's name, and Mina and I wrote fan letters, I to Morita and she to Nekoda.

In the evening, when we went out for our walk, we headed down the hill to the post box near the Kaimori Bridge, where the three of us mailed our respective letters.

I remember asking my aunt whether hers would, in fact, reach Mr. Brundage, since she had addressed it in Japanese.

"I'm sure it will," she said, unconcerned. "There's a branch of the Olympic Committee in Japan as well." Her letter was quite formal and proper, beginning and ending with the customary pleasantries.

Mine was just a fan letter, one more in the mountain of letters that young girls must have been sending to Morita then.

But Mina's letter to Nekoda was something else again, and there was no danger it would have been overlooked, no matter how many letters he received. Though her volleyball passes inevitably always went astray, with her letter, she sent Nekoda a pass like a ray of light.

∧∧∧

Dear Mr. Nekoda,

Congratulations on the gold medal! I was practically in tears, clapping in front of the TV. I wanted to call out to you: "Thank you for bringing the gold to Japan!"

I looked for you after you jumped into Coach Matsudaira's arms, but I couldn't see No. 2 anywhere in that crowd of taller players. I knew you were there anyway, though, in the middle of the circle as ever, right where nobody notices you, playing the most important part. Just as you've always done.

When the ball is spiked, all eyes turn to the striker; everyone is captivated by the power with which it hits the floor.

But even at those moments, my eyes are on you. After you've made your set, you stay low and look up at the ball you've lofted above. Sometimes you're all the way on the floor, on your hands and knees. And though the spike can only be as spectacular as the pass that gave birth to it, you never conduct yourself in a way that would suggest that. You just continue to work your way under the ball.

The grace with which you set the ball is remarkable. There's far more mystery to your talent than the brute power of the strikers, which almost tears the ball to pieces.

The moment the ball touches your hands, it seems to grow calm. No matter where it's come from, once it reaches you, it suddenly becomes obedient, moving peacefully in the direction of the striker. It's in that peacefulness that the final preparations happen for the ball's explosion across the net.

It's extraordinary that the human body can express itself in so many ways through a single ball. I'm only 130 centimeters tall, weigh twenty-five kilos, and have asthma that causes endless problems for my family, but somehow I feel that even I could hit a smash with enough force to send the Soviet players scattering, if you were the one to set the ball.

Thank you for reading my boring letter to the end. I look forward to the next chance to root for you on TV. I'll always be there for you. Really, really congratulations on the gold medal!

Good-bye.
From a sixth-grader,
Ashiya City, Hyogo Prefecture

31

One day in autumn, we had a bit of an incident. It started with a postcard Yoneda-san had sent to a contest—that happened to win first prize.

To enter, she had clipped three coupons from boxes of laundry soap and attached them to a mail-in card. First prize was a trip: three nights and four days in Hokkaido. Everyone in the family was terribly excited and said how jealous they were of her good fortune.

It was the biggest prize she had won in decades of entering contests. In the past, the best she'd done was a magnetized "health" mattress, a dozen mosquito coils, or ten coupons good for an ice cream cone in shops all over Japan.

And yet despite the fact Yoneda-san's extraordinary perseverance had finally paid off, she didn't seem pleased at all. If anything, she looked a little put out.

"Hokkaido is so far, I don't really feel like going."

"How can you say that? When will you get a chance like this again? It must be a wonderful place, Hokkaido!" My aunt was the first to react—perhaps because a trip to Hokkaido was so vastly superior to the meager rewards she had received for pointing out all those typos.

"The cold is no good for an old woman . . ." Yoneda-san

muttered, slipping the envelope with the prize tickets into the pocket of her apron before pulling it back out and slipping it in again, as though she didn't quite know what to do with it.

"Then wait and go next year," said Mina, trying to peek into her pocket. "How long are the tickets good for?"

"Do they have spring in Hokkaido? Do they have summer?" Grandmother Rosa weighed in.

"Spring? Summer? What difference does it make, if you're afraid of flying?"

"Haven't you ever flown in a plane?" I asked. Yoneda-san shook her head despondently.

"Then you don't know if it's scary or not. Who knows, it might be fun. And we all know how much you need a vacation." I said aloud something I had been thinking for a long time. Since I'd arrived in Ashiya, I had not seen her take a single day off. Not a day without performing all her household duties, nor a day off to run errands for herself or just have fun. She had spent all day every day caring for us.

"I'd have been much happier with fourth prize, a set of clothespins . . ." It was clear that my proposal wasn't enough to overcome her hesitation. "Besides," she added, "the trip is for a 'couple.' Two people."

We passed the envelope around the circle, one after another, extracting the tickets to confirm this new information. She was, of course, quite right: the tickets were for two people, and there was even a disclaimer in small print that they could not be used for travel for one person.

"Then there's no need to hesitate. Just take me with you," said my aunt.

"But that's impossible," said Yoneda-san. "What would happen if Mina had an attack while you were gone?"

"We could ask Kobayashi-san to come sleep at the house."

"I don't want to go off to Hokkaido if it's going to cause everyone problems," countered Yoneda-san.

"If my legs were in better shape, we could have gone together," put in Grandmother Rosa, rubbing her knees and heaving a sigh. "What a shame."

"Is there someone at Papa's company who comes from Hokkaido and might want to make a trip home?" Mina offered.

"Or what about going with Kobayashi-san?"

Our suggestions just made Yoneda-san all the more uncomfortable—and made it even clearer that she had no friends or family to travel with.

"There's no need to decide immediately," said my aunt at last. "I'm sure we'll think of something. You should just take some time to enjoy your good luck."

But the very next day, Yoneda-san would no longer be enjoying her luck or suffering embarrassment. A burglar stole her tickets to Hokkaido.

〰〰〰

He was, in fact, a very particular sort of burglar. He paid no attention to the valuable works of art in the house, but instead drank a bottle of Fressy, took a sip of condensed milk, and made off with some of my aunt's whiskey and cigarettes—and the tickets to Hokkaido. None of us noticed a thing, and we slept peacefully right through the night.

At six o'clock in the morning, as usual, Yoneda-san came into the kitchen and took her apron from its hook. She noticed an empty Fressy bottle on the counter, but she must have thought one of us children had left it, so she washed it (along with any possible fingerprints) as she muttered under her breath.

Eventually, Grandmother Rosa woke up and came down to the kitchen, and the two of them chatted while they drank their coffee. At some point, Yoneda-san, deciding it was time to fry some sausages, peeked into the refrigerator and noticed an unfamiliar drip running down the side of a can of condensed milk.

Discontent with limiting her intake of condensed milk to just a slather on a slice of bread or a pour over strawberries, Yoneda-san was in the habit of taking a sip of it as a snack. But she would never have wasted those drops, and invariably would have wiped them with her finger when she was done. Still, when she noticed the drip on the can that morning, it didn't occur to her that there may have been an intruder.

Just at that moment, however, the bakery truck appeared.

"Your doorknob's broken," the apprentice to the French baker announced, and it was only then that Yoneda-san and Grandmother Rosa finally realized that something unusual had taken place.

That, in outline, is what Yoneda-san reported to the policeman who came to investigate.

〰〰

The baker's apprentice was young, but he seemed to be a sensible man. He managed to calm the two old ladies, who were in a state of shock, and immediately called the police. He even gave them some useful advice: "Better check if anything's missing besides the Fressy and the milk. If they took your passbook, you should notify the bank right away."

Soon, police officers began arriving, one after another. The house filled with noise and activity, and the chance for breakfast was lost. Grandmother Rosa trembled violently; Yoneda-

san, pale as a ghost, stood rooted to the spot; and my aunt
paced around frantically, as though the effects of her hang-
over had suddenly evaporated.

But Mina and I were not at all frightened. We followed
after the officers as they took plaster casts of footprints and
collected fingerprints. We peppered them with questions
about the white powder and other paraphernalia they were
using. We were completely caught up in the sudden excitement and secretly hoped we might be allowed to skip school.

As usual, Pochiko alone seemed totally unaffected. She
sneezed, thrust her head into some bushes, and then went to
slurp water from the pond. When the police officers began
searching the garden, she shook her tail in annoyance.

In the end, the investigation confirmed that the safe in the
house had been undisturbed and the only things missing were
the Fressy, the condensed milk, a carton of cigarettes, and
two bottles of imported whiskey my aunt kept in the smoking
room. The police decided that either the burglar had ignored
the works of art because they would have been too easy to
identify, or that it was not a real burglar at all but simply a
hungry drifter.

"So, there was nothing else missing?" the police repeated,
encouraging us to keep looking. "Are you sure?"

Mina's theory was that the burglar, energized by drinking
Fressy, was just beginning to search for the safe when he was
startled at the sight of Pochiko at the other end of the terrace
and went running off into the night.

"If he didn't know about Pochiko, he couldn't have been
from around here," she whispered in my ear.

Yoneda-san was more upset by the incident then the rest
of us. No one had said as much, but clearly she was convinced

that it had been her responsibility to check whether the door was locked. And yet, no matter how badly she felt about what had happened, she still didn't give us permission to skip school.

"Why should you take the day off? That would be just what the burglar would want," she said, patting Pochiko on her behind. Then, as she was hurrying us out the door, she thrust both her hands in her apron pockets and, after a moment's hesitation, let out a cry.

"The tickets are gone!"

〜〜〜

The day after the burglary, my uncle appeared with a team of locksmiths in tow and proceeded to have all the locks in the house traded out for elaborate new models. He also had alarm bells installed in each bedroom and in the hallway. He seemed to me as dashing and handsome as ever, giving orders in his crisp voice, making snap decisions, and in general going around to check every detail. He wielded his fountain pen like a pointer, indicating spots on his diagram and sending the workers scurrying off to perform his every desired task. He struck me as extremely dignified without being in the least bit self-important.

I had secretly thought that the person who should feel responsible for the burglar affair was not Yoneda-san but my uncle, who had been absent from the house, but as soon as I saw him, so magnificent, I felt inclined to forgive him everything.

When the work was completed, they tested the alarm. Grandmother Rosa pushed the new red button, which set off an ear-splitting screech. Even Pochiko, who never let any-

thing upset her, slipped backward at the edge of the pond and
fell on her behind.

"That will do," my uncle said, folding his arms. "That
should wake up everyone in the neighborhood."

We were impressed with the volume of the alarm and told
each other we would be safe now.

Still . . . I thought to myself . . . the alarm might be powerful, able to alert us to danger, but was it loud enough for my
uncle to hear it wherever it was that he went?

But of course, I said nothing. If everyone was happy with
the new locks and alarms, that was good enough for me.

Despite the unexpected nature of his trip home, my uncle
stayed until he had repaired all the broken things that had
accumulated in his absence. In this case, though, it was
nothing more than a jammed stapler and an umbrella with a
bent rib.

ᗯᗯᗯ

The next day as we took our light bath, Mina and I discussed
the burglar. The box of matches she'd just used lay on the
floor next to the lamp. She was wearing a housecoat with a
little brown bear in a funny pose on it, completely covered
in little felt balls, like *marimo*, the famous moss orbs of Lake
Akan. The bear seemed to be twisting about, trying to make
the balls bristle.

"He was clumsy," Mina said, "but there was a logic to the
things he took."

"What do you mean?"

"He chose things that were valuable to him but not to us."

Mina was still as slender as Bambi, but since she hadn't

had an attack all summer, the marks on her arms from the intravenous needles were fading.

"Grandmother was probably happy that he stole Mama's whiskey and cigarettes, and I'm sure Yoneda-san was actually relieved that the tickets disappeared."

"You think so?"

"I do. She doesn't have to worry anymore about who to invite to go with her."

"I see what you mean."

"She's probably thinking how much easier it is to have some unknown burglar go to Hokkaido in her place."

"I wonder who a burglar would invite to go along?" I said.

"I wonder," echoed Mina. Then, after thinking a moment, she went on. "Someone he met in prison, no doubt."

"No doubt."

Having finished bathing our front sides in the rays, we turned on our stomachs and rested our chins on our hands to expose our backs. As we listened to the grinding of the rotating bulbs, we imagined the burglars' trip to Hokkaido. We pictured them drinking whiskey on the plane, smoking cigarettes on the shore of Lake Akan, buying moss orbs in a bottle or wooden carvings of bears at the souvenir shops. If anything, we wished them a wonderful trip.

〰〰

A few days later, the police came to tell us they had arrested the culprit—thanks to a footprint left in Pochiko's droppings.

"What did I tell you? The credit goes to Pochiko," Mina said, quite pleased with herself.

We forgot to ask whether the burglar had found time to get to Hokkaido.

32

Looking back on that time now, I feel comfortable saying that Yoneda-san had sunk her roots in the Ashiya house more deeply than anyone else.

Grandmother Rosa still clung to her memories of distant Germany, and my aunt was originally from Okayama. Mina went off to school each morning, enjoying her fifteen-minute ride on Pochiko, and Ryūichi had abandoned his childhood room at an early age. And my uncle was . . . my uncle.

But Yoneda-san had nowhere else to go home to, nowhere else to go at all. She had only her contests to send mail to, with almost no hope of ever getting an answer. She passed her time caring for others, and lived like a member of a family to which she was in no way related.

Perhaps Yoneda-san had appeared at the Ashiya house long before Grandmother Rosa or my aunt or Pochiko or anyone else; perhaps she had been doing what she had always done for all that time. I had the impression that she had already been an old woman at birth, had always been baking bread and washing windows and darning socks.

Yoneda-san was like the glittering white bits inside a snow globe. The scene of the Ashiya house was reflected in the glass of the globe. The rooms were all perfectly clean and tidy, the aroma of a delicious meal wafted here and there, laughter echoed through the house. You had only to invert the globe to send the snow falling, collecting on the floor, protecting the inhabitants.

But no matter how hard you shook it, the snow could never leave the globe. Breaking the glass would be a foolish mistake. Everything that had looked like snow before would become something much more uncertain, something dirty and viscous and unable ever to return to its original form. That's why Yoneda-san could never be taken too far away from the house.

〰〰〰

One Sunday not long after, Grandmother Rosa and Yoneda-san separated for once, a rare event precipitated by the lingering agitation of the burglary. Grandmother Rosa was supposed to go to the Shin-Osaka Hotel with my aunt to attend the wedding of the daughter of an old acquaintance. Normally, Yoneda-san would have gone with them, but since it was so soon after the burglary and there was some concern about leaving us children alone to watch the house, it was decided that Yoneda-san would stay with us.

After Grandmother Rosa and my aunt left in a hired car, Kobayashi-san, who should have been off that day, arrived at the house. He was carrying a baby in his arms.

His daughter and her husband had business elsewhere and had left the baby with the grandparents for the day, but his wife had fallen in the bathroom and strained her back. Could we perhaps look after the child while he took

his wife to the emergency room? The baby slept peacefully
in his arms as Kobayashi-san explained the situation with
an embarrassed grimace. Knowing how often he had accompanied Mina back and forth to the hospital on his days off,
we agreed immediately and told him to go look after his
wife.

"I'm terribly sorry," he said. "I can't tell you how grateful I
am. If it won't stop crying, try tickling the feet. That usually
works. Everything you should need is in here."

The bag that he passed us was several times heavier than
the baby.

First, we settled the baby on the couch in the living room.
Mina, Yoneda-san, and I were reluctant to leave it for a
moment, so we sat there staring at its sleeping face, forgetting
about the homework and cleaning that awaited us.

The baby was wrapped in a yellow velvet onesie with locomotive appliqués. It slept with its little fists balled up next
to its ears, completely oblivious to the world around it. Its
hair grew in unruly clumps, there was a trace of milk at the
corners of its mouth, and its eyes were buried in its fat little
cheeks.

"Is it breathing?" Yoneda-san said, drawing her ear close
to the baby's mouth.

"Please! Don't say things like that!" I told her.

"I can't hear it," she said, frowning and listening more
closely. Finally, she reached out to touch its cheek, carefully,
almost fearfully.

"It's warm."

"Of course it is."

Just then, the baby's little fists twitched, and Yoneda-san, taken by surprise, leapt up from the sofa, knocking her elbow on the corner of the table.

"Look, I think it's waking up," Mina said. It had started turning its neck back and forth, as though it were uncomfortable, and as its little bottom began to squirm, its eyes opened just a crack. They met Yoneda-san's as she was rubbing her sore elbow, and with that the baby began crying lustily.

∿∿∿

Far from being on its last breath, this child proved to be almost too healthy. Its cries sounded through the house like an alarm bell.

"It might fall if we leave it on the sofa. Better put it on the floor," said Mina.

"Yes, you're right," said Yoneda-san, spreading a towel on the rug. Mina picked up the baby and carried it to its new bed. Little by little, the crying grew louder.

"First thing to check would be the diaper," Mina observed, which sent me rooting around in the bag Kobayashi-san had brought. As he'd said, it contained everything a baby could possibly need. A bottle, powdered milk, cotton balls, antiseptic ointment, a rattle, an apron, a woolen vest and hat, talcum powder, camellia oil, a vaccination booklet. And, of course, a change of diapers.

I gazed at the material, folded into a triangle, half amazed that this constituted a diaper. We had assumed, naturally enough, that Yoneda-san, the oldest among us and the one who had disturbed the baby, would change the diaper, but she seemed bewildered and a little pitiful.

"I'm sorry, but I'm not good with babies. It's not that I don't like them, but they frighten me."

"But you took care of Mina and Ryūichi when they were small . . . ?"

"We had a live-in nurse in those days. I had my hands full with the house," Yoneda-san said apologetically. It was the first time I'd seen her so hesitant.

"Okay," Mina said suddenly. "I'll do it. Yoneda-san, bring me some damp cotton, please." Mina knelt next to the baby and pulled off its diaper cover—at which point we learned for the first time that it was a boy.

"Of course, right away," Yoneda-san said, running off to the kitchen.

It could not be said that Mina's technique was practiced, but she was clearly gentle and careful as she went about her work. She seemed to use just the right amount of force as she lifted the baby's legs or wiped his bottom with the cotton, working quickly but calmly. Her movements were precise and controlled, even when handling the soiled diaper.

"Right then, next we need to feed him." Mina continued to give instructions as she tested to see that the diaper fit properly. I extracted the bottle and a can of powdered milk from the bag, and Yoneda-san scurried back with them to the kitchen. All this time, the baby went on crying, and I went on tickling the soles of his feet. They were soft and warm, nice to touch, but despite what Kobayashi-san had said, tickling them did nothing at all to calm him.

Still kneeling on the floor, Mina picked him up in her arms. She tested the bottle on her wrist to make sure it wasn't too hot and then offered it to the baby, who began to drink eagerly. At last, the crying stopped, and the only sound was the quiet sucking on the rubber nipple.

I wondered why Mina was so good at changing and feed-

ing the baby. She seemed off balance as she sat there holding him, her body too frail for the weight. Even when she
grasped him with both arms, his little legs had stuck out on
either side. But the baby had rested his head in the crook of
her jagged elbow and was drinking contentedly, his freshly
diapered bottom nestled comfortably on her lap. He'd look up
at us every once in a while, with one hand on his bottle and a
tear in the corner of each eye. Unblinking, Mina studied the
milk as it gradually disappeared and adjusted the angle of the
bottle accordingly. Yoneda-san, apparently worried she might
disturb this peaceful scene, stood a few steps away, lips pursed
in a nervous smile.

〰〰〰

In the afternoon, we put the well-fed baby in the carriage and
went out for a walk in the garden. We had spent a good deal
of time and effort extracting the fancy German carriage from
the storage shed and dusting it off. Even though the wheels
squeaked a bit from lack of oil, it was still extremely elegant,
and the baby seemed to enjoy the ride, pulling on the cord of
the music box and kicking his legs on the cushion.

When we got to the edge of the pond, Pochiko came to
peek in the carriage. Her tongue darted out and gave the baby
a lick on the cheek, at which he burst out laughing.

〰〰〰

That evening, he was returned safely to Kobayashi-san, and
my aunt and Grandmother Rosa came home from the wedding. Yoneda-san and Grandmother Rosa went to sit under
the arbor to watch the sunset. They seemed relieved and
happy to be back together after a long day of separation. They

had traded their matching straw hats from summer for brown felt berets, perched lightly on their heads at exactly the same angle. The berets bent close, touching as they exchanged accounts of the day's events, the last of the sunlight illuminating the scene.

33

"I haven't heard what you thought of Katherine Mansfield's *The Garden Party* or the collection of photographs of Auschwitz."

Mr. Turtleneck had stopped what he was doing and faced me across the circulation desk.

"Ah . . . yes." I looked down at my feet as though I'd been scolded. As usual, I was incapable of behaving naturally when it mattered.

But in fact, I was overjoyed he'd remembered the books I'd borrowed. All sorts of people must borrow all sorts of books from him every day, so it seemed wonderful that he could recall the titles he'd lent to an unremarkable middle school girl.

"Ah," I stammered. "I'm not quite sure."

"What? I'd have thought someone like you would have a lot to say about them," he said, straightening a stack of library cards by tapping them on the counter. He could perfectly arrange everything on the circulation desk with just the slightest movement of his hands.

"Well, no . . ."

Naturally, Mr. Turtleneck never fully understood. He didn't realize that I was nothing more than a proxy for Mina. The more he complimented me, the more flustered I became.

"It's just that . . ."

"Just that what?" he said, not a hint of doubt in his voice as he looked at me, waiting for me to continue.

"The ending of *The Garden Party* surprised me. At first, I thought it was just a boring story about a rich girl who feels sorry for a poor boy. But I was wrong."

"Ah, I see."

"What I mean is, it didn't have anything to do with being rich or poor. It all comes down to the moment when Laura discovers beauty on the face of the man who died falling from the horse," I said, failing to add that this was Mina's assessment, word for word. "Laura is struck by the nobility of someone who can accept death almost willingly, without rebelling," I added, trying to recall whether this was everything Mina had told me about the story.

"Maybe you're something like Laura," Mr. Turtleneck said.

"What?" This remark was so unexpected that I had no idea how to respond. And there was nothing left in the stock of words Mina had provided.

"I'd imagine a girl like you, who could empathize with the old man in Kawabata's *The House of Sleeping Beauties*, would have been able to see the nobility—just as Laura did."

The light from the high ceiling of the reading room fell softly on his face. For a Saturday afternoon, the library seemed quiet and empty, the only sound the occasional rustling of pages from somewhere deep in the stacks.

"That's why it's so sad," I said, barely loud enough for him to hear me. "The people in the photographs of Auschwitz had nothing left at all. Not their nobility, not even their names or their hair or anyone to mourn them."

Mr. Turtleneck nodded. As always, his shaggy hair hung down on his forehead.

"Of all the middle schoolers who use this library, you make me most proud," he said, handing me the books I was borrowing for the week and my library card, as though they were proof of this fact.

"Thank you," I said. Stuffing the books quickly in my bag, I bowed and hurried out of the building. In fact, I ran all the way to the bus stop at Yamauchide, without quite knowing why.

~~~~

That day, I had broken my record for the longest conversation I'd had with Mr. Turtleneck. It surprised and troubled me that we could talk so much with nothing more between us than some books, without my even knowing his name or age. But the real reason I'd run away from the library had nothing to do with that. It was, I'd realized, because of the title of one of the books I'd borrowed: Turgenev's *First Love*. Why, of all things, had Mina wanted to read a book with such an embarrassing title? Had Mr. Turtleneck found it suspicious? That's what I'd been afraid of when I'd run away from the counter, what I'd been thinking about the whole time I ran, past the Uchide-ten Shrine, along the national highway, all the way to the bus stop.

But I'd understood something that day too. What I'd said about the book of photographs did not come from Mina or from someone else. Those were my own thoughts. I'd spoken to Mr. Turtleneck for the first time using my own words. Was I running now too out of sheer joy?

~~~~

There had been some progress with Mina's first love as well. Things had been at a standstill since the volleyball strategy had ended so poorly, but then, on the last Wednesday in Sep-

tember, the young deliveryman took the highly unusual step
of speaking to Mina before she'd spoken to him.

"Did you know that you'll be able see the Giacobini meteor shower on the night of October eighth?" he asked.

Mina shook her head.

So that's it, I said to myself as I stood in the ticket booth, he prefers stars to volleyball. And from my hiding place, I sent brain waves to Mina, encouraging her to pretend to be interested even if it was an act.

"When the Giacobini comet passes close to the Earth, it's going to create the biggest meteor shower of the century."

"Is that so?" said Mina, her tone as cold as always.

"I guess I thought you might be interested because Fressy's logo is a star . . ." he said, pointing at the bottles he'd just brought from the house. They stood silently for a moment, looking at the truck.

You'll get nowhere staring at empty bottles! Say something! Talk about stars, anything! You've read so many books, Mina, surely one of them was about stars. I was practically squirming in the shadows of the ticket booth.

"Is there an observatory where you can see them?" she asked at last.

"You don't have to go to an observatory, all you have to do is look up at the sky. I'm thinking of going up Mount Rokko, all the way to Okuike. The viewing is better the farther you get from the city lights."

"Is that so?" Mina said, looking once more at the empty bottles.

Ask him to take you with him! It's your golden opportunity!

"Hmm," Mina muttered, watching as he got into his truck, my silent encouragement having come to nothing.

I came out of the ticket booth and she held out her hand as she saw me; she seemed delighted. "Hey, look at this," she said. She had a box of matches in her palm with a picture of a young girl holding a bottle up to the night sky, trying to capture within it a blaze of shooting stars.

∧∧∧∧

The next evening, Yoneda-san sent me on an errand.

"Would you please get some boiled beef at the butcher's just across from the confectioner's on the left as you enter the Yamate arcade? They come in small, medium, and large packets—I need two medium. And don't forget to ask them to gift wrap them. Two, medium, gift wrapped."

She repeated the instructions again and again, as though speaking to a small child.

When I'd finished making her purchase, I cut through the crowd of people emerging from the Ashiyagawa Station on the Hankyu Line, and, as I reached the pedestrian crossing, I noticed a truck stopped in front of the kindergarten on the other side of the river. I realized immediately that it belonged to the Young Man from Wednesday.

He was there, sitting on the bank of the river, dressed in his usual work uniform and baseball cap. Apparently, he had completed his deliveries for the day and had only to return the truck to the factory. He seemed relaxed, legs stretched out on the grass, and there was a smile on his face unlike anything Mina and I had ever seen. Sitting next to him was a young woman.

So, I thought to myself, clutching the boiled beef to my chest, the Young Man from Wednesday does know how to smile. The noise of the water falling over the stone dam in the river and the sound of the train on the Hankyu Line made it impossible to hear what they were saying. Their faces were half in shadow as the sun set, so I couldn't tell whether the woman was as beautiful as Mina.

But I could tell one thing for certain—there was a special bond between them. I could see it clearly. They were holding hands.

34

I never supposed that Yoneda-san, who had considered us delinquents for wanting to stay up until eleven o'clock at night for the opening ceremony of the Olympics, would easily grant permission for us to go up to Okuike to see the Giacobini meteor shower. Mina knew this, too, so she used all her skills of persuasion, insisting, in effect, that observing the meteor shower was not just an amusement but a full-fledged scientific experiment.

"What is this 'Jacko' thing?" Yoneda-san asked. She was too wary to be easily taken in.

"It's a comet. When it passes, it's going to bring meteors falling like rain. More than anytime this century. It's a wonderful opportunity and a chance for scientific study."

Yoneda-san crossed her arms, dubious.

"Even if we stay up late on Sunday, Tuesday is a holiday, so I'll have a chance to rest." Mina was anticipating the anxiety that the outing might bring on an attack. "I'll be sure not to overdo it, and if I start to feel bad, I'll come home right away. You can only see the stars at night. You have to stay up late if you want to study them. You see that, don't you?"

She grew more and more insistent. I wanted to join her

in petitioning Yoneda-san, but having seen the Young Man from Wednesday with his girlfriend, I hesitated.

I was sure he would ask the young woman on the riverbank to go with him to Okuike to see the meteor shower. It was the perfect place for a romantic date. The girl hadn't been dressed for going out on the town. She might have been a salesgirl from one of the shops near the station. Her casual dress seemed to speak to the depth of their connection, though.

Mina's desire to see the meteor shower was no doubt sincere, but was it also based in part on the suggestion from the Young Man from Wednesday? . . . And if she ended up seeing him with the girl . . . At that, I started to hope that Yoneda-san might not grant us permission after all.

In the end, she said: "I'll ask your father. I can't decide this myself." Though we children did not know what it was, it did seem there was a way for the Ashiya house to contact my uncle when necessary.

〰〰〰

My uncle had just one condition when he granted us permission to go: that we write a report about our observations.

"Your father will want to check what you write after you get back," Yoneda-san told us.

"That'll be simple," said Mina, skipping around the room. "We can do that, can't we, Tomoko?"

I pretended to be as excited as she was, careful to avoid letting her see how I really felt.

Okuike was a reservoir halfway up the slope of Mount Rokko. You took the toll road toward Arima that started next to Y Elementary School, where Mina attended, and climbed a bit farther up the mountain. There was a sanitorium in the area and some youth hostels, but it was far removed from the neon lights of the city, and there was a playground with restrooms on the shores of the reservoir. As the Young Man from Wednesday had said, it was the perfect place for stargazing.

Though my uncle had set the conditions, there was no sign that he would be returning home for the event, so, as so often happened in situations like this, we were left to rely on Kobayashi-san. It had been decided that we would set out after dinner on the evening of Sunday, October eighth, in Kobayashi-san's van.

Mina had bought a new notebook and had written the title on the cover in big characters: "Record of Observations of the Giacobini Meteor Shower, October 8, 1972 (Sunday)." I'd run off to the library and, at Mr. Turtleneck's suggestion, had borrowed three books: *Wonders of the Night Sky*, *Secrets of the Comets*, and *In Search of Shooting Stars*. Mina had read all three and used the information she'd gleaned to write an introduction for our study.

1 GOALS OF OBSERVATION
To see shooting stars falling like a rain shower is a rare and beautiful phenomenon. Stars move on a timeline that is much longer than the one for human beings, so there's no telling when this chance will come again if we miss it this time. Observing the Giacobini Meteor Shower is a wonderful opportunity to understand the nature of the universe. Furthermore, a star is an important symbol for our house. We should be able to observe this phenomenon with the same sense of familiarity we have when we open a bottle of Fressy.

When the dust scattered by a comet burns upon entry
into the Earth's atmosphere, it forms shooting stars.
When the Earth passes through the orbit of a comet
emitting a lot of dust, we can observe a shower of
shooting stars. The correct name for the comet that
causes the Giacobini Meteor Shower is Giacobini-
Zinner. It approaches the Earth once every thirteen
years.

It appears in the north-northwest. As the night
passes, the elevation of the shower decreases, so the
optimal time for viewing is from dusk until the middle
of the night. The shower seems to radiate from the head
of the constellation Draco, the Dragon. In 1933 and
1946, from several thousand to several tens of thousands
of shooting stars appeared per hour. They were said to
have fallen slowly, more like snow than rain.

3 EQUIPMENT TO BRING
Notebook, writing implements, compass, counter,
flashlight (wrapped in red cellophane to lower the light
level), portable lamp, matches, mattress, blanket, hand
warmer, hot drinks, snacks.

4 ADDITIONAL OBSERVERS
Tomoko, Kobayashi-san, Pochiko.

It was unclear where the suggestion had come from, but at
some point we all seemed to agree that Pochiko should come
along.

"She'll make a perfect bodyguard."

"Any bad guys who might be around would be terrified if they saw her coming out of the dark."

"I wonder if we could let her swim in the reservoir while we're there? She must wish for a bigger pond sometimes."

"That's right, and she's nocturnal, so she'll be more active in the middle of the night."

One after another, they kept coming up with more reasons to bring her with us. I worried that Pochiko's stubborn disposition would cause problems, as it had when we'd taken the photograph in the garden, but no one paid attention to my reservations.

〰〰

Unfortunately, October eighth was dark and overcast. From early morning, Mina went back and forth to the terrace, looking up at the sky in search of any break in the clouds. The television played stories of stargazing fanatics who were heading to Hokkaido, the northern part of Honshu, the top of Mount Fuji, Norikura, or even to Irkutsk in the Soviet Union for better viewing conditions.

When it finally came time for the outing, Mina and I were equipped as elaborately as if we were going on an expedition to Mount Everest. Thinking it would be cold in the mountains at night and that we could never be too warmly dressed, Yoneda-san, my aunt, and Grandmother Rosa had wrapped us in every garment they could find. Long-sleeved flannel shirts and sweaters, coats with hoods, woolen underwear, gloves, ski boots, fox-fur mufflers . . . No attention had been paid to the colors or patterns, and Mina ended up looking like a giant marble made of wool.

Not content with just dressing us children, the ladies also

advised Kobayashi-san on his outfit. He listened obediently
and added extra socks and rabbit-fur earmuffs.

"Okay, then, shall we go?"

Kobayashi-san laid a plank on the back and led Pochiko
into the van. He ran a rope from her collar to a hook behind
the seat to make sure she didn't fall out.

We were all excited at the prospect of such a special night,
all except Kobayashi-san, who was as calm and composed as
always. Even though the greatest meteor shower of the century was about to begin, he behaved exactly as he did when
he was accompanying Mina to school or cleaning up after
Pochiko. Without a word, he checked to see whether we had
forgotten anything, whether the cap of the thermos was
screwed on tight, whether the batteries in the flashlight were
working.

As soon as we left the driveway, the van was absorbed into
the darkness. The slope grew steeper and steeper, and we saw
nothing but the signs marking the curves, rising up in the
headlights and then disappearing again. The houses along
the way thinned out and then stopped altogether. The forest grew thicker and darker. The middle-aged gatekeeper at
the Royu Toll Road greeted us cheerfully, asking whether we
were going to see the meteor shower, but his eyes widened
when he noticed Pochiko, and his hand trembled as he passed
us our change without a word.

I stared up at the night sky with my forehead pressed
against the windshield. There was no sign of shooting stars
yet, but I offered a silent prayer then anyway: Please, let us not
meet the Young Man from Wednesday.

35

Mr. Kobayashi stopped the van on the shore of the lake. I immediately looked around for the truck belonging to the Young Man from Wednesday, but the area was completely shrouded in darkness and there was nothing but the faint sound of voices coming from the playground on the far shore.

But then I realized he would never use the Fressy delivery truck for a date, and I had no idea what kind of car he drove when he wasn't at work.

"I think we can watch over there . . . Pochiko, wait, behave yourself." Kobayashi-san gave Pochiko a pat and began unloading our equipment. When he was done, he used the flashlight to point us in the direction of the woods surrounding the lake. Wrapped in our heavy clothes, Mina and I huddled together and followed him.

We were far more likely to encounter the Young Man from Wednesday at the playground, so, as usual, Kobayashi-san was right . . . or so I told myself.

We had not gone far when we came to a grassy clearing. Perhaps he knew the spot and had been leading us here all along, but Kobayashi-san grunted his approval and deposited our gear on the ground. We used the flashlight to check the

compass, and spread out the mattress so we would be facing
north-northwest.

"Kobayashi-san, why don't you take Pochiko for a walk? We'll be fine here," Mina said.

"Are you sure?" he said. "In that case, I'll take her to have a little soak. If anything happens, you just blow on these." Though they hadn't been on the supply list in the notebook, he hung a whistle on a cord around each of our necks.

"I hope they see some stars," he murmured to himself as he repositioned his earmuffs and headed back to Pochiko.

As we stretched out on the mattress, our perspective on the landscape changed completely. The darkness receded, and a deep-blue night sky opened above us. The smell of the earth under our backs calmed and reassured us. As we lay there for a moment, perfectly still, we could hear the trees rustling, hear fish jumping on the surface of the lake. And then, little by little, our bodies seemed to shrink, and we had the feeling the sky was rushing down to meet us.

Mina opened her notebook and held the counter she intended to use to keep track of the shooting stars, ready when the time came. But the sky was less than perfectly clear. A haze covered everything, and only when the wind broke up the clouds for a moment could we glimpse the stars through the gaps.

"Don't worry, there are supposed to be hundreds or thousands of them."

"They'll come right through the clouds," I said, trying to be reassuring.

"Did you know that shooting stars are made when stars die?" Mina asked.

"Really? I thought they were stars going on a trip."

"No, they shine so beautifully because they get pulled in by Earth's gravity and burn up when they reach the atmosphere."

"You're kidding me."

"So, while we're watching them thinking how beautiful they are, they're actually burning up and dying."

"Like matches that look most beautiful the moment before they burn out."

"Did you know that it was comets that brought the elements to Earth that created life? Comets are made of ice, and a gigantic one struck the Earth when it was just forming, and that made the oceans."

"So, does that mean that part of us is in the Giacobini comet? . . . How would we ever know?"

"I learned all this from the library books you borrowed, Tomoko. You're like a comet that brings books. But tell me, what are you going to wish for? When you see the shooting stars."

She turned to look at me, still stretched out on the mattress. The lower half of her face was obscured by the fox muffler. Kobayashi-san's whistle slipped from her chest to the blanket. Even in the dark, her large pupils were clearly visible.

"How about you?" I asked.

"That's a secret. If you tell, the wish won't come true."

"Then don't ask mine. It's secret, too."

"Ah, fine. Whatever."

She pulled the whistle back up on her chest and adjusted her grip on the counter.

⌇⌇⌇⌇

I wonder what Mina wished for as we watched for the Giacobini meteor shower. A cure for her asthma? A closer friend-

ship with the Young Man from Wednesday? A longer life for
Pochiko? For her father to come home?

Or perhaps she had a secret desire that none of us suspected.

In my case, even if it was the best chance in the twentieth century to see a wish come true, I could not figure out what it was I wanted. I had, of course, a few childish desires of my own, but it was the matter of the Young Man from Wednesday that continued to occupy my thoughts.

Each time we heard a car approaching or the sound of footsteps in the grass by the lake, I began to tremble, telling myself that it might be the young man and his girlfriend, worrying about how to prevent Mina from finding out. My nerves were on edge, more from trying to sense their arrival than from looking for shooting stars.

I could almost see the two of them, hand in hand, staring up at the night sky. I blinked hard, trying to dispel the image. If we saw a lot of shooting stars, would we still get only one wish? At any rate, that night I had only one in my heart: that we would not run across the Young Man from Wednesday out on his date.

〰〰〰

"I don't see anything."

"Me either."

As our eyes adjusted to the darkness, we began to see more stars between the breaks in the clouds, and we could even see them twinkling, but there were no shooting stars. The night sky was still, stretching out in every direction.

"I wonder if there's any sign before you see them? The sky getting white, like at dawn, or a whooshing sound?"

I was starting to get tired even though I was lying down.

"I'm not sure, but I think it must start quietly. Even something this important."

Unlike me, Mina seemed to be full of energy. While I was distracted by every little thing, she was totally focused on the sky.

Just then, we heard Pochiko splashing in the lake. But the sound didn't interrupt the expectant atmosphere, rather, it seemed to become part of the watchful calm. The drops streaming down her back, her swelling nostrils, the water flying everywhere as she shakes her short legs—all of it seemed to float up in the darkness and recede again. Even though we couldn't actually see them, we were sure Kobayashi-san and Pochiko were nearby.

"How about a break?" I said, and Mina, agreeing immediately, took the lamp from her backpack and lit it with a match. Needless to say, the matchbox that Mina had in her coat pocket was the one with the picture of a girl gathering shooting stars in a bottle.

The flame flared orange and then faded to blue, illuminating Mina's trembling fingers. They seemed even more delicate than usual in the low light of the match. She waited a moment for the flame to catch and then lit the lamp wick. It was as though a shooting star had fallen into her hand before the real meteor shower had begun.

We drank the hot lemonade Yoneda-san had put in the thermos and ate Bolos. The air was chilly and damp with dew, but we were warm and toasty in our woolen underwear.

We talked quietly, eyes glued to the sky, dissolving Bolos in our mouths, waiting for the meteor shower to begin at any moment.

36

It's still a mystery to me why the Giacobini meteor shower failed to appear in the autumn of 1972.

All sorts of theories were put forward. That there was a discrepancy between the orbit of the comet and the axis of the dust belt; that there was insufficient material in the belt; that the density of the particle belt was inconsistent and a less dense section came in contact with Earth's atmosphere . . . But in the end, even the astronomers seemed at a loss.

That night, meteorites were observed in just a few locations—Hokkaido, Kirigamine in Nagano, Yahikomura in Niigata, and on Mount Nosemyoken in Osaka—but even then, it was just a handful, and those hoping for a "shower" were greatly disappointed.

The amateur astronomers who went all the way to Irkutsk in the Soviet Union saw nothing at all, though the night was perfectly clear.

Some years later, the return of Halley's Comet and the Leonids meteor shower created something of an astronomy boom, and I found myself with a group of girls talking about the events surrounding the Giacobini in 1972. One girl said that was when she'd been given her first telescope. Another girl remembered that she'd screwed up her nerve to tell a boy she had a crush on him but he'd turned her down. Still another girl said she'd never heard about it at all.

I said it was the first time in my life that I'd stayed up all night. Greeting the dawn without ever having gone to sleep, I'd felt that I was no longer a child.

〰〰〰

"Mina, the night's a lot longer than I thought it was."

"I guess Santa Claus doesn't have to hurry to get his rounds done."

"I know what you mean."

"But it makes me a little sad to think that so much time goes by while we're asleep."

Her bath finished, Kobayashi-san had led Pochiko back to our clearing. She plodded along, quite satisfied with herself, then plopped down wearily. Soon, her dark brown body disappeared into the night, and the only proof that she was there was the sound of her tail brushing the grass. Kobayashi-san sat down next to her without a word.

Mina closed her notebook. We knew now. No matter how long we waited, there would be no meteor shower. The morning light was holding its breath, waiting at the edges of the night, and the comet, unseen, was speeding away all alone into the darkness.

"Let's go home," Mina said, and neither Kobayashi-san nor I, nor even Pochiko, disagreed. She clicked nervously at the counter that she'd never had the chance to use. "Look, it's broken," she said. No matter how many times she clicked it, the number stayed at zero.

We could not see the Giacobini Meteor Shower.

∿∿∿

After adding that one line, Mina placed the notebook and the broken counter on the desk in my uncle's study.

We hadn't seen any shooting stars, but still my wish had come true. We had not run into the Young Man from Wednesday.

The next day, Mina spotted a small article among the headlines in the evening newspaper about the meteor shower—CELESTIAL SPECTACLE FIZZLES AND WOULD-BE ASTRONOMERS AREN'T.

"On October 9, at about five-fifty in the morning, Xshima Xo (39), an employee of XX Town in Saitama Prefecture, was discovered in the rocks in a tributary of A River in XXX Village in Niigata Prefecture by the owner of a nearby inn. The cause of death appeared to be head trauma. Xshima-san and a friend had arrived in the area the previous day to go trout-fishing, and he had left the inn alone about eight o'clock at night, saying he was going to observe the Giacobini Meteor Shower. Authorities suspect he slipped and fell while watching for the meteor shower."

Though she was bleary-eyed from lack of sleep, Mina read the article aloud and we all sat down at the table and offered a prayer for this employee, just as we had for the lonely old man who had followed Kawabata in suicide.

∿∿∿

The summer had come up to Ashiya from the sea, but the winter blew down from Mount Rokko. The shape of the clouds changed, the sound of the wind in the trees grew louder, and the sea seemed to gradually recede. At the end of November, we began to light a fire in the hearth in the living room. Of course, the task of setting the kindling ablaze fell to Mina.

The Wednesday after the Giacobini excitement, a different man came to deliver the Fressy. He wore the same uniform, but he was a talkative older man with a paunch who bore no resemblance to his predecessor.

"You're not the usual deliveryman."

"Our new manager reassigned the routes. I'll be making the deliveries from now on."

"I see."

"Do you still want a case? Fressy orders generally go down when the weather turns cold, but sales of hot chocolate and lemon tea go up. The company still makes out either way. It's good business, the winter bonus."

"I'm glad. But here, we take a case of Fressy every week, summer or winter."

"Understood."

The new man and Yoneda-san chatted for a while in the kitchen, seemingly without another thought given to the Young Man from Wednesday.

But Mina stood to the side, crestfallen. She had on a skirt with pockets, ready to receive a new matchbox, but now she just stared vacantly at the door, repeating to herself everything that she'd planned to say about the disappointment of the meteor shower.

I ran out from my hiding place in the ticket booth and called to the driver as he was about to climb into his truck.

"Where is the young man who used to come here?"

"I don't know. Out on another route, I suppose," he said,

clearly uninterested. He tucked his belly under the steering
wheel and drove off without another word. Mina shoved her
hands in her empty pockets and went back to her room. I felt
somehow responsible. I thought that perhaps I'd gone too far,
planning to wish for him to disappear with my falling star.

Mina didn't dare mention him, but every Wednesday she
would show up at the kitchen door to wait for the truck. Perhaps she was hoping that the change was temporary, and
things would soon go back to normal. But she was disappointed each time.

I think the cause was the low-pressure system that came
with the change of seasons and not the shock of the change of
deliverymen, but for whatever reason, Mina soon had another
attack and was admitted to Konan Hospital.

I decided then it was time to go see my uncle's factory.
Nothing was ever solved by waiting around. Maybe if I
went to the factory, I'd be able to find the Young Man from
Wednesday and learn more about him. That was my plan,
anyway.

First, I went to the smoking room and found a pamphlet
for my uncle's company among the mountain of materials my
aunt had gathered in her search for typos. I was sure there
would be information there about visiting the factory. My
aunt had been at the hospital day and night to take care of
Mina, so I could conduct the search at my leisure.

"The Fressy factory opens its doors to the public every second and fourth Sunday of the month. A complimentary van to
the factory leaves at one o'clock from the Hanshin Amagasaki
Station. The tour lasts one hour and includes a free bottle of
Fressy. Come see how Fressy is made! We'll be waiting to
welcome you!"

How could I get to Hanshin Amagasaki Station? Could I go by myself? I headed straight for the library. Mr. Turtleneck was the only one who could help without revealing my secret plan; fortunately, he was at the desk when I got there.

"That's not hard," he said. "Take this with you and you'll have nothing to worry about. It's a map of the railway system with an index of major businesses and institutions." He handed me a document titled "Detailed Map of the Osaka-Kobe Region."

"You have maps in the library?" I asked.

"Of course."

"But I haven't been out in Ashiya by myself yet."

"You'll be fine. A girl like you can go anywhere," he said.

37

The van left Hanshin Amagasaki Station, passed through a residential neighborhood, crossed several bridges, and ran along on the other side of the river. We passed electrical transformers, some warehouses, a water-purification plant, and continued in the direction of Osaka harbor for a while. Eventually, the Fressy factory came into view on the left.

The other passengers were a lively group, mostly parents with children, and I was the only one who'd come alone. Still, I wasn't at all nervous.

As Mr. Turtleneck had said, getting to the station had been relatively easy. You took the same bus that went to the library and got off at Ashiya Station. From there, you simply had to take the train for Umeda. The van from Amagasaki Station ran straight to the factory, so there was no chance of getting lost.

In my bag, I had the "Detailed Map of the Osaka-Kobe Region" that I'd borrowed from Mr. Turtleneck, the brochure from the factory, and two thousand yen that my mother had given me "just in case." The bills were folded up small and tucked into my dictionary. This was the "case" she'd been speaking of, I reasoned, trying to convince myself that my mother wouldn't have been angry.

On my way out the door, I'd told Yoneda-san I was going to the library to study. With Mina in the hospital, the house was in something of an uproar, so my explanation had gone mostly unnoticed.

Passing through a large gate attended by a guard, we came to a sprawling parking lot filled with row after row of trucks identical to the Young Man from Wednesday's, each bearing the Fressy star logo. The bottles stacked in the trucks glittered brilliantly in the early winter light, reflecting all the way to the distant waves on Osaka Bay.

"Oh my!" I exclaimed as we entered the parking lot. None of the other passengers in the van seemed to share my excitement.

〰〰〰

It was an impressive factory, one worthy of having a man like my uncle as its president. The elaborate machines were spotless and worked in perfect rhythm as the employees bent over them in silent concentration. Everything was extraordinarily grand and sophisticated, but at the same time seemed meticulously regulated down to the smallest detail. As though the magnificence of my uncle had taken material shape in this place.

"The Osaka factory here covers an area of one hundred and twenty thousand square meters, approximately the same size as three baseball stadiums. We employ about two hundred workers, and we bottle nine hundred thousand bottles of Fressy a day."

Our guide was a young woman in a blue uniform with a scarf around her neck. She led us along a glass-enclosed tour route above the factory floor, explaining each step of the production process as we went. Our group from the van huddled together to avoid getting lost as we trundled along behind the guide.

"Here we wash and check the bottles. Bottles returned by our customers are cleaned in water heated to eighty degrees and individually checked for imperfections. The machine you see here is the most up-to-date model available and is the only one of its kind in Japan. It is capable of cleaning nine thousand eight hundred bottles simultaneously, and the operator is trained to check two hundred bottles per minute."

The smile never left the young woman's face, and she spoke with perfect confidence, as though she herself had invented the machine and trained the employees who operated it. The adults nodded appreciatively, while the children pressed their faces against the glass or ran along the gallery.

I wanted to tell them that it was not the young woman they should be admiring but my uncle, the director. But I was distracted by my growing realization that I might not ever find the Young Man from Wednesday in such an enormous factory.

"Come this way, please. On the left you'll see three large tanks. Those are where the ingredients for Fressy are mixed. Each tank is two meters in diameter and four meters tall. They contain the raw materials for Fressy, including sugar, flavorings, and sorbic acid, as well as the secret ingredient that gives Fressy its refreshing, delicious flavor. I'm afraid I can't reveal anything more about that, though. I'm terribly sorry."

She retied her scarf, which had slipped back on her neck, and smoothly continued her patter.

I ran my eyes over the employees working at the machines,

wondering whether the delivery people might work here when they weren't on their routes. But it was impossible to tell one worker from another, dressed as they were in white uniforms, white hoods, and white boots.

"Now, it's time to bottle the Fressy," our guide chirped. "The empty bottles are brought by conveyor belt to the filling machine. This machine is the most efficient model currently in use in Japan . . . and, just here, from this angle, you can see it actually filling a bottle with Fressy. Quite a sight, isn't it? By the time one bottle moves into position, it has already been filled and is moving on to make room for the next. And next to the filling machine, we have the capper, for sealing the bottles. After that, each bottle is checked over one last time. Cleanliness and safety are far more important than speed. All of us here at Fressy work each day to ensure that our customers enjoy each and every bottle . . ."

We pressed closer to the window to get a better view of the finished product.

Somehow, it all seemed quite far away to me, though there was just a single pane of glass separating us from the factory. The drops splashing from the bottle washer, the LOW CLEARANCE sign hanging from the ceiling, the attentive expressions of the checkers—they existed in a secret kingdom that I felt I could never reach.

The unending noise of the machines absorbed any quieter sounds, creating an odd sense of calm. The workers spoke little, their attention entirely focused on Fressy; the pistons generated precisely the right force, the gears meshed with perfect precision, and the conveyor belt moved at exactly the right speed. As if in response to this single-mindedness, the bottles themselves lined up in good order, patiently awaiting their turn, and when at last they'd been capped, jostled for-ward almost proudly.

They came along the line, one after another. Production continued, seemingly without end. And yet there was no hint of weariness anywhere. Amid the gray machines, only the pale blue Fressy was bathed in light, as though somehow especially blessed.

For years, I'd been drinking Fressy without giving it much thought. It had never occurred to me that so much time and energy went into producing it, or that there was so much of it being produced. I felt the need to apologize for my negligence, but at the same time I felt an even greater admiration for the lord of the Fressy kingdom, my uncle.

"Now then, ladies and gentlemen," said the guide, her voice even brighter, "we have Fressy and some treats waiting for you in the next room. Please enjoy. The van to the station will be leaving at three o'clock. Please make your way to the front entrance by two-fifty."

Shouting with excitement, the children in the group ran off in the direction of the refreshments. In the reception room, there was a bottle of Fressy for each of us and a paper plate filled with Milk Bolos.

"Okay then," I told myself. The young woman had been more than kind, but I wasn't here to eat Bolos.

〰〰〰

Though I felt quite unsure of what I was doing, I left the little party with the tour group and headed in the direction of the parking lot where I'd seen the delivery trucks. Since I'd had no luck trying to find the young man in the factory, it seemed like the only place left to look for him.

I took the stairs down to the ground floor and walked along a corridor, pretending to be going to the restroom, until I finally found the employees' entrance. I walked through a maze of water tanks, forklifts, and a mountain of empty wooden cases until I ran straight into the parking lot. I encountered some factory employees along the way, but except for a quick glance to confirm that none of them was the Young Man from Wednesday, I kept my eyes lowered to avoid having to speak to anyone.

The parking lot was deserted. I supposed there were no deliveries on Sunday. I hadn't realized when I'd arrived earlier, but in addition to the delivery trucks, there were regular cars, vans like the one that had brought us here, and even motorcycles. They were all lined up neatly, with nothing out of place.

Suddenly, I noticed a little prefabricated hut in one corner of the lot. A simple little house just a bit larger than the ticket booth for the Fressy Zoo.

VEHICLE DISPATCH was written on a sign above the door, which was unlocked and opened quite easily.

Inside, it was dimly lit and sparsely furnished, with nothing more than a desk, two metal chairs, and a filing cabinet. I noticed an old notebook abandoned on the desk: "Dispatch Registry."

I reached out for it, my hand trembling, and just as I started turning the pages, I heard a voice at my ear.

"What are you doing?"

Startled, I let out a cry.

38

"What are you doing?" The question came again, in a tone that sounded even more irritated.

"I'm sorry," I said, hurriedly putting the notebook back on the table. "Forgive me, I'm just here for the tour."

"This place isn't on the tour."

"I know, forgive me. I just got lost." I continued apologizing as earnestly as I could.

The owner of the voice glared at me with increasing suspicion.

Where had he been hiding? The room had been empty when I'd first peeked in, but he must have appeared from behind the filing cabinet, like a bat from the shadows.

He was terribly old. Life with Grandmother Rosa and Yoneda-san had accustomed me to the sight of the elderly, but still I flinched in spite of myself. Thin and no taller than I was, his head was dark and lustrous, and quite bald, except for the spikes of hair growing behind his ears. His uniform was too large, making his movements seem awkward, and a hissing noise escaped from the gaps in his front teeth.

"Can't think what you find so interesting there," he said, flicking his pointy jaw in the direction of the dispatch registry. I could see the words SECTION CHIEF printed on the badge on his chest.

It was clear that he had somehow figured out that his intruder was not simply lost. Otherwise, he would not have been giving me such an icy stare. I racked my brains, trying to decide what to do, to figure out just how honest I could be with him.

"You know . . ." he started in before I'd had a chance to plead my case. "I've been in charge here for over fifty years, since the time of the previous director. You could search the whole company and you wouldn't find anybody who knows as much about this huge parking lot as I do."

He sat down in front of his desk and crossed his short legs with difficulty. I nodded but said nothing.

"I know everything, from the sound of the engine of each truck to the names of the weeds that grow along the fence. Not even a tricycle could come in or out without my knowing about it."

"I'm sure," I murmured, trying to sound duly impressed. He cleared his throat and scratched at the tufts of hair. Flecks of dandruff fluttered down on the registry.

There was no sign of the drivers; the vehicles all huddled silently in their appointed spaces. The van would be leaving soon, but, thinking it would be pointless to have come all this way without trying, I worked up my courage to ask.

"So," I said, "you must know about the drivers as well as the trucks themselves."

"Of course," he sputtered. "I assign the trucks according to each driver's experience, their character, the terms of their contract. The dispatcher's job is to make sure the product gets safely to the customers. Here, look!"

He pushed up his too-long sleeves and pointed at a small blackboard on the wall.

"You see what that says?"

"Yes, 7,281 days accident free."

"That's right. 7,281 days without an accident for any of our trucks. I keep an eye on each and every driver, and they don't dare pass by here without checking in with me."

"We have Fressy delivered to our house every Wednesday," I said. He looked up at me with rheumy, bloodshot eyes. "By a very nice young man, though recently there's been a new driver."

"Where do you live?"

"In Ashiya."

"Ashiya? The Wednesday Nishinomiya-Ashiya route? Ah, you mean that quiet guy? He quit."

"Quit?"

"Got married and moved back home to the country."

"Married?" I repeated stupidly, taken aback by the unexpected turn of events. "There are so many trucks, how could you know that without looking it up?"

"What do you mean, 'look it up'? I told you, I know everything that goes on in this parking lot. It's all right here," he said, tapping his finger against his temple.

Married . . . No doubt to the girl I'd seen on the other side of the Ashiya River. Perhaps he'd proposed at Okuike, the night of the Giacobini meteor shower. The night Mina had clutched the broken counter in her hand . . .

〰〰

I sighed, picturing Mina lying in her hospital bed. At that moment, my eyes fell on the open page of the registry. The

handwriting in the book was extremely neat, in contrast with
the appearance of the section chief. The entry gave the month
and date for a trip by the president's car, from the factory to the
Dojima office and then to the Ezaka Royal Mansion. And another
on a different day, "factory—distribution center—Ezaka Royal
Mansion," and another "Dojima office—International Center—
New Osaka Hotel—Ezaka Royal Mansion."

What was the Ezaka Royal Mansion? And why was my
uncle's car going there so often?

I felt lost, unable to imagine how I had come to be standing
here in this shabby little building. The section chief, clearly
pleased with himself, pulled a cigarette from his uniform
pocket and struck a match to light it.

A match?

I stared at the matchbox in the palm of his hand, as dark
as a bat's wing. The girl on the label was familiar. She was
the same one who I'd seen holding up a jar, trying to capture
shooting stars. Now, on this box, she'd finished her work and
was about to twist the lid shut.

"Sir," I said, "do you think I could have that matchbox?"

∧∧∧∧

I sprinted back to the front entrance and got there just as
the van was ready to depart. I found my seat and caught my
breath a bit, then opened the map and searched for a place
called Ezaka. The map was as useful as Mr. Turtleneck had
promised, and I figured out that I needed to change at Umeda
Station for the Midosuji Line, and get off at the fifth stop.

I had never seen nor heard of this place, and I was already
nervous about having come all the way to Amagasaki. Now

to get on the subway as well . . . I wasn't sure I could manage it. And why was I even going there?

I put my hand in my bag and took hold of the matchbox. The batlike section chief, who had frightened me so much, had given it to me almost without a thought, as though he somehow understood the importance of these little boxes. Perhaps he really did know everything that went on in the parking lot.

Mr. Turtleneck's words—"A girl like you can go anywhere"—echoed in my head. When the van arrived at Amagasaki, I took the train for Umeda, the opposite direction from Ashiya.

〰〰〰

Umeda Station was crowded with people hurrying all about. I asked several of them how to find the subway, and at last a woman took me by the hand and led me all the way to the ticket gate. She must have been worried about me, because she even asked if I had any money.

I continued to ask directions from the passers-by as I made my way toward Ezaka.

"Do you know the Royal Mansion?"

I headed in the direction they indicated, without much thought about what I'd do when I got there. I passed a post office, an orthopedic clinic, a community center. Overhead, the elevated Meishin Expressway blocked out the sky. It all seemed very different from Ashiya. There was no view of the mountains, not even a sliver of sea. No matter which way you turned, everything seemed distant and cold.

The Royal Mansion was on a street behind some restaurants and shops. It wasn't what you'd call a "mansion," much less a royal one. The flowers in the beds at the entrance had begun to wither, and the railings on the balconies were rusting in places. Flies buzzed around the garbage cans out back.

Yet I knew immediately that it was the place I'd seen written in the dispatch register. My uncle's magnificent Mercedes was there in the parking lot.

39

I walked quietly toward the car. I remembered how surprised I'd been at the sight of the Mercedes the first time I'd seen it at Shin-Kobe Station. The image of my uncle leaning against the hood came back to me, his long arms and legs and brown eyes harmonizing perfectly with the elegant lines of the car. The saleslady at the uniform shop, the crêpes Suzette, the beach at Suma—it all seemed to reflect for a moment in the windows of the car and then fade away.

The number on the parking space was 202. Clutching my bag, I made my way into the building and studied the line of mailboxes to the left. A curtain was drawn across the little window of the manager's office. A woman's name was written on the mailbox for No. 202.

I don't remember the name anymore. Unlike Mina or Rosa, it was a perfectly ordinary name of the sort you'd encounter every day, and that was the only time I saw it, on that Sunday afternoon. I certainly never heard it mentioned at the house at Ashiya or anywhere else, and I never spoke it aloud to anyone myself.

Perhaps because I kept this secret for such a long time, at some point I began to believe that the events of that day were all nothing more than a dream. I was thirteen years old, a girl in a skirt her mother had made, standing in the entrance of the Ezaka Royal Mansion. I stared at the mailbox, unable to think of anything else to do. A tattered ad from a saké shop was shoved inside of it.

I remember feeling an extreme aversion toward the number 202. The two 2s seemed to cling cloyingly to the zero between them. There were boxes labeled 203, 301, plenty of other numbers—so why should 202 alone appear so absurd? Why did everything seem soiled now by 202—my uncle, his car, the uniform shop, the crêpes, the beach, even the pride I'd felt just a little while ago at the factory?

〰〰

I'm not sure why I did it, but before I left to go home, I took the brochure from my bag and drew a big circle around the typographical error that my aunt had discovered: "Fleshy." I stuck it under the windshield wiper of the Mercedes.

〰〰

Night was falling on the trip home to Ashiya. The city lights were coming on, and a new moon hung in the sky. I made my way slowly up the hill toward the house. I'd had no idea that a Sunday could be so long, and my legs were exhausted.

As I rounded the last turn, I saw people gathered in front of the gate.

"Tomoko, Tomoko!"

Grandmother Rosa was the first to leave the group and come toward me. Waving her cane and tottering along, she called my name again and again. Behind her, the others appeared one after another, and in a moment, they were all gathered around me.

"Where have you been? Out so late! We've been worried!"

"We went to look for you at the library, but it wasn't open today."

"I was worried sick."

"But you're back safe and sound, and that's all that matters."

My aunt came up to me, almost in tears, and even Kobayashi-san, who was usually so calm, seemed agitated. For some reason, Yoneda-san was holding a plate of sandwiches and seemed to think I needed to eat one immediately to avoid falling down in a faint.

"You must be starved," she was saying, forcing one on me.

As I looked at them, I was taken aback to see how much anxiety I'd caused them and, at a whiff of the ham and bread, realized how hungry I was.

But the thing that surprised me most was the sight of my uncle there with them. He was smiling, as always, but somehow I felt that I was seeing him for the first time, even though I was there among this dear and familiar family.

Clearly, my aunt had no idea that I'd been loitering around the apartment in Ezaka when she'd called my uncle to say I hadn't come home. And my uncle, in the Mercedes, had arrived in Ashiya well before I did, coming by train. All this I learned somewhat later.

"I'm so sorry," I told them. "I didn't mean to cause all this trouble while Mina's in the hospital."

But no one seemed to hear my apology.

"Let's go in."

"It's time for dinner."

"And it's a good thing we didn't call Tokyo and worry your mother for nothing."

"At any rate, you're home."

They seemed unusually talkative, perhaps due to the excitement, and they chattered on, ignoring my excuses.

〰〰

I'm not sure why no one asked me where I'd been. They must have had their suspicions when they found out that the library was closed. I even made up a story, in case I was questioned later. A friend from school had invited me to go shopping at a department store in Umeda, and I had some pocket money that my mother had sent me. Since Mina was away, it had seemed like the perfect chance . . . though I was terribly sorry now for the trouble I'd caused . . . But no one asked, and I avoided telling that particular lie.

Perhaps they thought that I was still just a child who missed her mother and had simply wandered off. Or perhaps, worn out with worry, they found it too much trouble to seek answers now that I was home safely. But it also occurred to me that they knew all too well what I'd been up to. They knew that Tomoko had strayed into that place about which they could never answer her questions.

That night, I peeked into my uncle's study.

"Ah, Tomoko." The house was strangely quiet after all the uproar. The only sound was the crackle of logs in the stove. "Can't sleep?"

My uncle was sitting on the sofa reading a book. I shook my head.

"I'm sorry about today," I said.

"Don't worry about it," was all he said. His legs carelessly crossed, the book resting on his lap, as if he had all the time in the world for me.

The rug under my feet was soft, the lamp cast an amber

light on the walls, and the clock on the shelf was counting out the seconds. Outside the window, the grapevine design on the railing of the veranda stood out in the dark, and, in the distance, Pochiko could be heard chewing on the grass.

I couldn't think of a single thing to say to my uncle. But if I stood there without saying anything, I was afraid my head would be filled with images of the section chief writing "President's car—Ezaka Royal Mansion" in the dispatch registry, of my uncle himself peeking in the mailbox for Apartment 202.

On his desk, I could see Mina's "Record of Observations of the Giacobini Meteor Shower" and the broken counter . . . and the Fressy pamphlet with the circle on the typographical error. I realized he had brought it back to the house rather than ripping it to pieces.

"Good night," I said, nearly whispering.

"Good night," he replied, opening his book again.

As I was leaving the room, I turned back to look at him.

"Please fix Mina's counter," I said. "And then the 'Fleshy' on the pamphlet."

〰〰〰

Soon Mina recovered and came home from the hospital.

"Listen!" I told her. We were sitting in the light-bath room, facing each other. "A lot happened while you were gone." She nodded. "The Young Man from Wednesday came to say good-bye."

The rays of light trembled as the ball clattered above us, warming our backs.

"He said he'd been transferred somewhere far away and wouldn't be coming to make our deliveries anymore, but he said he'd never forget you. He's still delivering Fressy somewhere, and when he finds a matchbox, he'll think of you and how much you loved them. Here, he left this for you."

I passed her a matchbox, the one with the picture of the girl putting the lid on a jar of shooting stars, and she continued to stare at it even after the lamp had gone out and the room had grown dark.

I could hear then a faint rustling in my ears. It must be a message from an angel, I thought. An angel perched on my earlobe, mending her wings.

40

On the day of the ceremony marking the end of the second trimester, I was heading home from school with my report card when I ran into Mina. As I was coming down the hill, she appeared at the bottom turn, riding on Pochiko.

Pochiko came up the steep slope, churning the charming little legs that protruded from her round body. Head down, mouth working to no purpose, she fixed her gaze on a spot in the road and plodded along. Her eyes were tiny and dim, to the point you might wonder if she could see anything at all, but her footing was sure, and her hooves made a sturdy sound striking the pavement. Her dark brown skin was marked with the long years she'd spent making this march.

With a scarf over her mouth to avoid breathing the cold air, Mina relaxed into the roll of Pochiko's back. She hadn't noticed me yet. Her lunch bag, stuffed with her school apron, rested on her lap, and she seemed to be surrounded by an aura of well-being, born of the simple fact that she was with Pochiko.

Kobayashi-san, as always, held the tasseled cord that functioned as a bridle, as he watched for cars and made sure that Pochiko didn't sway too much. His whole manner suggested that he would never butt in where he wasn't wanted or speak out of turn, that anything he could do would be less than insignificant. And yet, he was always there when we needed him, playing a role that only he could play.

Pochiko, Mina, and Kobayashi-san. They were the perfect team, supporting one another, nothing out of balance, nothing lacking.

"Tomoko!"

Mina had spotted me. Kobayashi-san raised his hand in greeting. Pochiko lifted her head, but then looked down again, as if to say they had only a few more steps to go. Hindquarters swaying, she made her way up the last part of the slope.

"Tomoko, how's your report card?" Mina called out to me, her voice full of excitement.

〰〰

Christmas approached. Since the holidays coincided with my mother's vacation from her design school in Tokyo, we had planned to spend the New Year together in Okayama. But then she got the flu and was unable to travel, so I was told I would have to stay in Ashiya. But the sadness at that news was soon swept away by the anticipation of an extraordinary Christmas, beyond anything I could imagine. It's embarrassing to admit, but I was so thrilled that I almost found myself wanting to thank my mother for having come down with the flu.

Soon people from all sorts of shops began showing up at the kitchen door. Many of the things they brought were unfamiliar to me, odd things I couldn't name. Strange-colored powders, branches of plants I didn't recognize, cans with foreign labels, little bottles of liquid that might have come right out of a chemistry lab . . .

Grandmother Rosa would answer me each time I asked

about something, but I could barely remember the strange
names she told me: shallots, spearmint, sherry, powdered
ginger, anchovies, rosemary . . . All for preparing Christmas
dinner, all so exotic and yet somehow perfect for the occasion.

Yes, the maestro wielding the baton this time was Grandmother Rosa rather than Yoneda-san. At the beginning of
Christmas week, she appeared in the kitchen, as if to announce
that her turn had come at last, and, with all the dignity of her
station, began giving instructions to Yoneda-san, Mina, and
me. Grandmother Rosa and Yoneda-san, it seemed, reversed
their roles only for this one holiday.

〰〰〰

The most surprising thing delivered to the house came tied
to the truck from the garden shop: an entire fir tree. It had
apparently been freshly cut and smelled of earth, limbs wet
with dew. At first, I didn't realize it was a Christmas tree.

"Christmas tree?" I wondered aloud. "I thought they were
plastic toys."

In Okayama, we hadn't even had a plastic one.

"Why would you want a plastic tree when there are so
many real ones all around?" Grandmother Rosa asked. The
man from the garden shop, apparently accustomed to the task,
quickly set up the tree next to the piano in the living room.

Not just the food, but every aspect of Christmas required
Grandmother Rosa's supervision: bringing down the decorations for the tree from the storeroom in the attic; getting
out the rarely used silverware, the footed casserole, the red
tablecloth; putting candles in every candlestick in the house;
hanging a holly wreath in the entrance hall. And it was my
uncle who carried out Grandmother Rosa's orders. He had

been home since that Sunday, a record for the time I'd been in Ashiya.

Grandmother seemed to perk up quite suddenly, and it was unclear whether the cause was Christmas or my uncle's return, but her color improved, her voice was livelier, and her cane was used less for support and more to give directions. Everyone in the house was relying on her, and she, in turn, seemed intent that nothing should spoil our perfect Christmas.

〰〰〰

Deviled eggs, roasted chicken, mashed potatoes, cranberry sauce, watercress soup, fruit punch, ginger cookies. We made all these delicacies right there in the kitchen. The stainless-steel pans glittered, the gas range burned, the mixer groaned. Steam swirled, flour flew, aromas savory and sweet wafted together, and we talked and laughed nonstop.

The most exciting moment was when we stuffed the freshly plucked chicken. The dimples where the feathers had been were clearly visible; its legs were trussed up with string, as though it had resigned itself to its fate.

"It's a young bird, so it should be moist," said Grandmother Rosa. "The butcher dressed it, so it's all set." Her instructions were for me, the novice stuffer.

"Like this, Tomoko. Shove it in from the rear."

Mina was used to this, but I was taken aback by her audacious handling of the bird. I was reminded of Pochiko's little trick. Yoneda-san chuckled as she stirred the soup.

The stuffing was made of liver, onions, chestnuts, and herbs, all covered in butter. I gingerly took hold of the chicken by its legs, and, apologizing to it under my breath, pushed in the

stuffing. When it was done, all plump and buttery, Mina ran
her fingers over the breast.

"Looks delicious!" she said.

Mina and I mashed the potatoes, sorted through the cran-
berries, pressed cookie cutters into the dough for the ginger
cookies. We kept careful watch over the oven, peeled hard-
boiled eggs, stripped the leaves from the stalks of mint. We
seemed to sense that only by making them could we know
how delicious these things would be.

Of course, there was a special dish for Pochiko, too: a three-
layer cake of dried grass decorated with nandina berries.

After each dish was finished, Yoneda-san presented it to
Grandmother Rosa, who took her time tasting. She would
bring a spoonful to her mouth and, dentures clattering, sip or
gnaw, muttering to herself.

"Delicious! Excellent! *Ausgezeichnet!*"

〰〰

When I think that 1972 was the last year Grandmother Rosa
would conduct her Christmas symphony, I can only thank the
gods that I was there to witness it. The countless decorations
shimmering on the tree, the light from the candles, the home-
made treats, the modest gifts so full of feeling. Everything
I touched that Christmas Day was filled with Grandmother
Rosa's warmth.

She and Yoneda-san, accompanied by Mina, sang carol
after carol. As always, their beautiful harmonies had us spellbound. From long years of constant companionship, their two
voices had blended together as though joined before birth. I
knew it was impossible, but I found myself hoping that Christmas would never end.

〰〰〰

That night I fell into a deep, deep sleep. My belly was full, my bed warm, and the morning awaited me without a care in the world. No doubt the tree would be just as brilliant in the new light. I dreamed of a breakfast of leftover ginger cookies dipped in milk.

But when I awoke, it was still pitch-black outside. For a moment, I couldn't understand what had roused me, but before long I realized that an alarm was ringing. It was sounding throughout the house, shattering the night and my eardrums and every vestige of Christmas.

41

"Get up!" The first voice I heard was my uncle's. "Mina! Tomoko! Get dressed!"

All the while as he called out to us, the alarm sounded throughout the house. I crawled out of bed and tried to turn on the light, but no matter how many times I flipped the switch, it wouldn't go on. Apparently, the power was out.

"This way, Tomoko, and try to stay calm." I followed the voice, making my way along the wall, and found Mina at the end of the corridor, already in her father's arms. She seemed somehow smaller, and she was trembling slightly.

My uncle brought us down to the entrance hall on the first floor, more or less carrying us the whole way. We found my aunt, Grandmother Rosa, and Yoneda-san there, standing in a tight huddle. They were all in their nightclothes.

"We're probably safe enough, if we're upwind. But you should go outside for a bit, just in case."

"What will you do?"

"I'm going to gather up some things, and then I'll be right along."

"Are you sure? Don't be too long."

"I won't. There isn't much to do. But you all stay together, don't get separated from Mama."

Except for these orders from my uncle, we were all silent. Yoneda-san got out our shoes, and Grandmother Rosa pulled her hairnet tighter around her head. I turned back as we were walking out the door, and I could see the dark form of the Christmas tree, which had been a sparkling wonder just hours ago, sinking into the gloom.

For some reason, it was lighter outside than it had been in the house. Though the light in the entrance was off and there was no moon, the sky in the distance was saturated with a beautiful orange glow. As though all the Giacobini shooting stars had gathered right there.

"There's a fire in the mountains," Mina murmured.

〰〰

We opened the front gate and came out in the road to the north of the garden. People from the neighborhood were standing in the street, looking nervously toward the fire. We heard the alarm from the house for a moment longer, until it was drowned out by the wail of fire engines.

"It won't get all the way here."

"No, but if the wind shifts it could get scary."

"Do you think it could be arson?"

"The fire danger has been so high recently."

We listened quietly as the neighbors gathered to whisper together. I kept my uncle's instructions in mind and stuck close to my aunt, telling myself I mustn't cause any trouble. The fire was burning in the mountains to the northwest, in the opposite direction from my middle school. It seemed to undulate, belching embers and smoke. The rest of the sky was pitch-black, the only light coming from the blaze. The flames ran along the face of the mountains, dancing up, growing gradually denser. The sight seemed dreamlike, and yet I had the sense that the fire could reach the house at any moment.

Mina stared at the mountains, ignoring the sweater that was slipping from her shoulders. Her pupils reflected the orange glow of the flames. They were so much larger and scarier than the ones she lit from her matches; these were capable of engulfing her whole body.

"I hope Papa's okay," my aunt said. "With all these sparks."

"The fire engines are there now. They'll get it put out soon. The fire won't reach the houses. Don't worry." Grandmother Rosa tried to sound reassuring.

"That's right, that's right," Yoneda-san repeated, nodding vigorously.

But no matter how much we tried to calm ourselves, there was no ignoring the fact that the fire was continuing to spread, that the fire engines could do little more than run their sirens. From what we could see, it was difficult to imagine how they were going to extinguish it. The crackle of burning branches blended with the wail of sirens. The wind blew sparks high into the sky.

"I can't imagine what's keeping Papa. There's nothing in the house that important. We should get the car and start down the mountain." My aunt's voice was hoarse. "I'm going to look for him."

But Grandmother Rosa stopped her from going back to the house.

"He won't do anything silly. He's always careful. We promised him we'd wait here, and that's what we should do."

We huddled closer together. My aunt held Grandmother

Rosa's arm, Grandmother put her other arm around Mina's shoulders, Mina clutched the belt to Yoneda-san's nightgown, and Yoneda-san pressed her hand against my back. Though the wind was brisk, we weren't cold at all.

"Sorry I kept you waiting!"

My uncle finally came out of the house. He'd even taken the time to change his clothes and comb his hair. We ran to him and immediately gathered him into our circle. I grabbed hold of his belt.

At that our fears seemed to vanish. If we were all there together, there was nothing to fear. Even my aunt could relax. I told myself I would be fine, as long as I held on to that belt.

"I could see it from the balcony upstairs, but it seems quite far off. I don't think we have to be too worried, but, just in case, I made arrangements for us to go to the dormitory in Fukae." My uncle's tone made it sound as though we were going on a picnic. "Let's get in the car."

"Where? Where are we going? Is it far?" I asked, still clutching his belt.

"Less than ten minutes away. It's where we house the single employees at the company. Nothing to worry about," he said, trying to reassure me.

〰〰〰

Once we were out of sight of the flames, it really was like a picnic. We crowded into the Mercedes for the short drive, and then Mina and I ran around looking at everything in the dormitory. We were so excited we even forgot to thank the manager who had come out in the middle of the night to welcome us.

At any rate, we were delighted to be in such an unexpected place, to sleep together in bunk beds in a spare dorm room. We had completely forgotten the fear we'd just felt. Even after the adults had gone quiet, Mina and I chattered on, as though the Christmas party had never ended. We decided that the fire was actually some sort of strange present from Santa Claus.

The next morning, quite early, when we returned to Ashiya, it became clear that the fire was not as terrible as we'd imagined, despite the uproar it had caused. Just one small area of the mountainside had been burned, and now the summit was shrouded in morning haze. None of the houses in the area had been damaged, and we seemed to be the only ones who had evacuated. Our neighbors were outside sweeping the street or leaving for work, and everything seemed to have returned to normal.

The alarm bell was no longer ringing, and the electricity was back on. Yoneda-san hurried off to start breakfast. The red cloth was still on the table, drips of wax had hardened on the candles, and the star at the top of the Christmas tree glittered in the morning light. My uncle, Mina, and I went out to inspect the garden. Mina was the first to spot her.

"Pochiko!" Her voice echoed through the whole house.

〰〰

Pochiko was floating on her side in the pond. Since her behavior had always been a bit quirky, for one brief moment I thought that she was just swimming a bit oddly. That must be it, I told myself.

"Pochiko!"

This time, Mina called gently, as though trying to coax

her to come out to play. But Pochiko didn't move. Her mouth, which had always been in constant motion, lay half-open, and her tail, her liveliest feature, hung limp.

"What's wrong, Pochiko? Come here."

Mina knelt to splash the surface of the pond, but Pochiko simply bobbed in the ripples.

42

"She had a good long life. They brought her over from Liberia when she was just a year old, and she turned thirty-five this year. If she'd been human, she'd have been a venerable old grandmother. You should know that she died quite peacefully."

As the veterinarian from the Tennoji Zoo spoke, he kept looking back and forth between me and Mina, watching our reactions.

"Was it the fire?" Mina's lips were blue.

"No, that had nothing to do with it. She didn't inhale any smoke, and the heat never reached her. It was pure coincidence that the fire, Christmas, and Pochiko's death all happened on the same day."

"But could she have been frightened by the sirens, run into the pond, and drowned by accident?" Mina wouldn't look up from the ground as she spoke.

"Drowned? That's unlikely. You know better than anyone how at home she was swimming in the pond," the veterinarian said, resting his hand on Mina's shoulder. The stethoscope, which had just been listening to Pochiko's silent heart, hung around his neck. Mina nodded, struggling to hold back tears.

"Did she suffer much?" I asked.

"There were no injuries or wounds on her body, and her

eyes are clear. Look at her. Do you see any sign of suffering? I think she simply didn't wake up this morning and was called away to heaven."

Pochiko lay on the grass at the edge of the pond, legs relaxed, nostrils closed, her face turned toward the morning sun. Her plump body was still slightly damp and glistening. Had she enjoyed her Christmas cake? Her belly was full and round, with little pink nipples visible here and there. That was the first time I realized that Pochiko had nipples—nipples that had never given milk, since she had never had babies.

At that moment, unable to hold back any longer, I started to cry.

〰〰〰

Pochiko's body was cremated at the Tennoji Zoo, and her remains were returned to us. Pochiko, who had once paraded so magnificently with Mina on her back, was reduced to a pile of ashes and bones so small that it fit in Mina's hands.

We gathered around the grave at the base of the myrtle tree, and Kobayashi-san dug a deep hole. Once my uncle had indicated the spot, he worked in silence, his forehead glossy with sweat. We stood listening to the sound of earth flying from his shovel.

Mina knelt and stretched her arms as far down as she could, lowering the urn into the hole. Her skirt was covered with dirt.

"I'll be along shortly. Wait for me," said Grandmother Rosa.

"Yes, me too. We'll see you again soon," Yoneda-san added.

The two leaned against one another as they tossed soil into the grave.

"I'm sorry we left you alone at the end," said my aunt, covering her face with her hands.

"I'm sure you've already seen Saburō the Conductor again. I hope they're all there to welcome you." My uncle tried to force his usual smile, but couldn't. He looked down at his feet and patted my aunt's back.

"Thank you, Pochi," murmured Kobayashi-san, suddenly seeming very old. "Thank you for everything." His hands gripped the shovel, red and swollen.

I had stooped to gather up a handful of dirt, but froze. The sky was clear, the myrtle leaves cast intricate shadows at our feet. With its resident gone, the pond had fallen still, and the nest of grass on the knoll was dark and silent. Mount Rokko looked much as it always had, the horizon seemed far away, not a sound reached us from the outside world. I dropped the dirt, warm now from my hand, into Pochiko's grave.

Mina was the only one who wasn't crying. She was staring into the hole, trembling as though she were furious, her expression filled with annoyance.

"Good-bye, Pochiko," was all she said.

Kobayashi-san filled in the grave with his shovel and replaced the marker.

"'Here Lie Our Friends from the Fressy Zoological Garden.'"

〰〰

Much of the third and shortest trimester was taken up with Pochiko's funeral, and with preparations for my move back to Okayama and changing schools again. After the start of the new year, Pochiko's pond was filled in, and the hut housing the filtration system was taken down. Trucks and backhoes were brought into the garden, and, under Kobayashi-san's careful supervision, the work was completed in just over two days. That marked the final closing of the Fressy Zoo.

I felt a pang as I looked at the patch of freshly turned earth. The sprays of water Pochiko had sent flying, her body floating lazily in the pond—it all seemed like an illusion that was vanishing before my eyes. Though we never mentioned it, Mina and I asked ourselves over and over why we hadn't been more worried about her on the night of the fire. Not only had we forgotten her in our flight from the house, but we'd been excited, thrilled even, about the whole experience. What had it been like for Pochiko that night, all alone, frightened, staring up at a moonless, starless sky? We'd failed to show our gratitude to someone who had given us so much. We were devastated.

Kobayashi-san took to joining his palms and kneeling in front of her grave for a long while every day, as soon as his work was done. He wasn't alone. Every one of us, in our grief, would go spend odd moments with Pochiko, between housework and homework, before leaving for the office, during the lonely hour of dusk. We would take some of the treats she loved so much, and the area around the gravestone was soon littered with apples and pumpkin seeds.

Even my uncle had lost some of his usual energy, which made perfect sense when you considered that Pochiko had been a present for his tenth birthday. But he seemed determined to help us get over our sorrow and focus on our gratitude for Pochiko. He told us amusing stories from her life that even Mina didn't remember.

The counter had been repaired, as had the other broken things that had been left on his desk, but still he came home to

the house in Ashiya every evening. Of course, I had no way of
knowing what had become of the woman in Apartment 202,
but the pamphlet I'd tucked under the windshield wiper on
the Mercedes was still on the desk. It sat there, always opened
to the page where my aunt had circled the typo, like an indict-
ment of his indiscretion and a forthright acknowledgment of
the harm he'd done.

On the morning of the ceremony marking the beginning
of the third trimester, Mina put on her gloves, picked up the
bag containing her school slippers, and walked out the door
with me, under the watchful eyes of the adults. There was no
Pochiko waiting by the palm trees at the entrance, but Mina
turned, looked back at her family, and, in a calm, steady voice,
announced that she'd be back later. They, in turn, refrained
from cautioning her to walk slowly or take it easy, limiting
themselves simply to "See you soon."

Mina set off toward her elementary school, her own, soli-
tary march. I watched her slender figure until she descended
the hill and disappeared around the corner.

〰〰

"I'm returning this," I said, placing my library card on the
circulation desk. Mr. Turtleneck looked at me with a puz-
zled expression. "I'll be leaving in March. I'm going back to
Okayama to be with my mother."

"I see," he said. He was wearing the same turtleneck he'd
worn the first time we'd met, and it was as fresh and white as
it had been that day.

"Thanks for everything," I told him.

"It's a shame, really," he said, looking down at my card.
"I'll miss our talks." The list of titles on the card brought

back every conversation we'd had across the counter, beginning with *The House of Sleeping Beauties*. His smile when he praised my reading habits, the lamplight on his face, the shape of his hand when he pointed out the right aisle—it all came back to me then.

"It's a real loss for the library, to lose the smartest middle schooler in Ashiya. Make sure you keep borrowing lots of books in Okayama."

"I will," I said.

"But there's no need to return this," he added, handing me back the card. "It's a record of the books you've read, of your reading life. It's yours."

I nodded.

"I think a friend of mine will be coming in the spring to get a card. I'm sure you'll recognize her right away. She's petite, with brown hair and eyes, and she's actually the smartest girl in Ashiya. Her name is Mina."

"I understand," he said. "I look forward to meeting her."

43

There was snow on the ground at the end of February. The sleet falling one evening had changed to snow during the night, and when we woke in the morning, the garden was completely transformed. The rails of the little train, Pochiko's hillock, the gravestone in the zoo—everything was covered in white.

Mina and I threw on our coats over our pajamas and ran outside, rushing here and there, making random patterns with our feet in the untouched snow. The wind had died, and the sky was cloudless, the frigid air prickled painfully on our cheeks. Unsatisfied at last with mere footprints, we fell down, stretching out in the snow next to each other. When we moved, ice crystals danced up in the morning sunlight.

Despite the cold, the snow under our backs seemed somehow warm. We suddenly realized that we were lying on the spot where Pochiko's pond had been.

"It's like riding on her back again," Mina said, her eyes squeezing shut with pleasure.

"You're right," I said, imitating her Kansai accent as best I could.

"No, no," she shot back, "your intonation is all wrong. Besides, when did you ever ride on Pochiko?"

"You're right," I tried again.

"Still sounds strange!" She laughed and then rolled in the snow, as if trying to sense Pochiko's presence.

"Look at you girls!" It was Yoneda-san, jogging unsteadily toward us in a scarf, hat, and gloves. "You'll catch your death of cold."

We waved as she approached.

∿∿∿

That winter, despite a severe cold snap and several low-pressure systems, Mina didn't have to go to the hospital even once. She had asthma attacks, bad colds, and the flu, but they were all managed with visits to the doctor.

And then, with the approach of spring, her attacks dropped off sharply. The coughing I'd heard at night through the wall faded into the sound of sleep, and the wheezing in her throat grew so quiet that I wondered whether I was just imagining it.

Spring had come to Ashiya from two directions at once, from the mountains and the sea, enveloping the whole town. The chill air at the summit of Mount Rokko dissipated, the green deepened, and the songs of the birds were somehow different. At the same time, the sea was covered in haze, blurring the horizon, and the number of boats increased.

The season had changed. The date of my return to Okayama had been set for March twenty-fourth, a Saturday.

∿∿∿

"How will you collect matchboxes now?" I asked. Mina gave a noncommittal grunt. The lamps in the light-bath room groaned but continued their reliable revolution.

"If I find any good ones in Okayama, should I send them?" **267**
I asked. But Mina just shook her head without looking up.

"I have enough. If I get any more, they won't fit under the bed."

It was true that the boxes of matchboxes were close to spilling out of their hiding place.

"I start middle school next month, and the Young Man from Wednesday isn't coming back. I think this may be a good time to stop."

Mina's nightgown seemed to be getting a bit small. Her chest was as flat as ever, but the thighs peeking out below the hem seemed fuller. The underpants that had once been so baggy now fit her bottom.

"But you can't get rid of the stories you've written," I said. "You know how much I love them."

"I'll be sure to keep them. I'll put them in a box and write on the lid: 'Here lie stories that had only one reader.' Then I'll store the box in the baby carriage up in the attic."

We heard the adults laughing in the living room. My mother had completed her studies at the fashion design school in Tokyo and now was making her first visit to the house in Ashiya, to bring me home to Okayama. She planned to stay a few days, until the twenty-fourth, since it was the first chance she'd had in a long while to spend time with her sister and her family. It was, of course, my uncle's Mercedes that had brought her from the Shin-Kobe Station, and her response as she'd entered the house had been almost identical to mine a year ago.

"Okayama's not so far, is it?" Mina said. The shadows from the clattering light-bath bulbs wavered on her back.

"Just an hour on the Shinkansen," I told her.

"So, you can come visit anytime. Summer vacation, winter vacation."

"Of course."

There was another burst of laughter from downstairs. No doubt the sisters had a lot to talk about after such a long separation.

Everything that had astonished me about the house—the black marble fireplace, the canopy beds, the chandeliers, the Oriental rugs, the stained-glass windows—apparently had the same effect on my mother, with the single exception of Pochiko, who, of course, was nowhere to be seen. But Mina and I took turns, gesturing wildly in an attempt to describe her appearance, her character, and the wonderful spectacle of her march to school with Mina. My mother could only gasp in amazement.

When she had gotten over her initial awe, she turned to the other adults and bowed her head. "I apologize for all the trouble Tomoko has caused you this past year," she said. But almost before the words were out of her mouth, my aunt and uncle, Grandmother Rosa, and Yoneda-san spoke up one after another.

"Trouble? What trouble?" "She's a wonderful young lady!" "She was a great big sister and friend to Mina!" "We'd love to have her stay with us forever . . ." Yoneda-san was practically in tears.

"Mina can come visit us in Okayama," my mother hastened to say. "Of course, it wouldn't be the same, our place is so small, but we can put a futon in my office and make it work."

The lively atmosphere in the living room was quite different from the silence we'd left in the light-bath room, where our words had slowly dissolved into the orange glow.

"Do you get motion sickness on the Shinkansen?" Mina had wondered aloud.

"Don't worry. There aren't any diesel fumes," I'd told her.

"I suppose not," she'd said, and, apparently reassured, she'd turned to her other side.

As the days passed, we said to each other again and again that Ashiya and Okayama were really quite close, that the Shinkansen was a wonderful way to travel. Neither of us was at all inclined to say good-bye.

But soon the timer had wound down to zero, the light-bath lamps went out, and just the oil lamp was left to illuminate the room.

"I'd like you to have this, as a present," Mina said.

She took something out of her pocket. There was a rustling sound and I knew immediately that it was matchboxes. The outer box that Mina handed me was one that had held one of her inhalers, but when I opened the lid, I could see that now it contained the two matchboxes with the girl catching shooting stars.

"But those are the most important . . ." I started to say, but she cut me off.

"They're yours now."

We sat next to each other on the lounge chair and read the final matchbox story. The adults were busy with their own conversation and didn't notice how long we lingered in the light-bath room—or, perhaps they wanted the children to have as much time alone together as they needed.

〰〰

Once upon a time, there was a little girl who wanted more than anything to know what would become of her after she died. She supposed she might simply disappear, but whenever she imagined what that might be like, she began to feel uneasy.

So, studious girl that she was, she assembled as many dead things as she could find and carefully observed them. The eyes of a fish and the bones from a chicken breast that she'd had for dinner, a dried-up lizard, the shell of a cicada, a withered rose, a rotting clementine, fingernail clippings, and lost baby teeth. She hid them all under her bed, and at night, when the adults had all gone to sleep, she would take them out one by one and try to discover how they would finally disappear.

But no matter how long she waited, the moment never came. Their forms changed, but they never vanished. Some things turned to mush, others crumbled to dust, and still others began to give off terrible odors, but still something of them remained, and eventually, the space under the bed was filled with decay.

Then the girl read in a book that shooting stars were really stars that were dying. So she gathered every bottle she could find and diligently collected shooting stars, carefully stoppering each bottle to keep them from getting away.

"Ahh!" she wondered, holding a bottle up before her eyes. "Do they disappear when they die?" At first, she was convinced they did. She could see right through the bottle. Nothing stirred; there was no odor. But when she shook it, she thought she could see a drop of evening dew at the bottom. And when she looked closer, she saw her own reflection in the dewdrop. Her face, staring straight back at her.

So, she thought, a bit relieved, even when you die, you don't disappear. Matter doesn't vanish, it transforms. She imagined herself becoming an insect shell or a shooting star when she died, and she had a feeling she'd be able to sleep peacefully now. She snuggled into her bed, on top of the many dead things she'd hidden underneath.

44

We could visit whenever we wanted, Ashiya and Okayama were practically next door, and there were no diesel fumes on the Shinkansen. Though we had parted repeating those assurances over and over, in the thirty years since, Mina and I have seen each other only a handful of times.

It's not that we've grown apart or lost track of each other, but simply that time has slipped away much more quickly than we could have imagined when we were young.

And yet, with the passage of time, even as the distance has increased, the memories of the days I spent with Mina in Ashiya have grown more vivid and dense, have taken root deep in my heart. You might even say they've become the very foundation of my memory.

The matchboxes from Mina, my card from the Ashiya Public Library, the family photo taken in the garden—they're always with me. On sleepless nights, I open the matchbox and reread the story of the girl who gathered shooting stars. I remember that Sunday adventure, when I went alone to the Fressy factory, received a matchbox from a batlike man, and found the Ezaka Royal Mansion. And when I recall those things, I feel somehow that the past is still alive, still watching over me.

Once I returned to Okayama, I didn't see Mina again until the winter of 1974, at Yoneda-san's funeral.

It had been a particularly cold night; Yoneda-san had locked up the house and wished everyone a good night before going to bed. She hadn't woken up again the next morning. She'd left on her journey all alone, unwilling to disturb a soul.

There weren't many mourners there—my uncle's family, Kobayashi-san, my mother and me, and a few people from the neighborhood—but everyone was terribly sad . . . and humbled to realize the enormous role Yoneda-san had played in all our lives.

The one consolation was that, by then, Grandmother Rosa's mind was already wandering in a place where she could no longer comprehend Yoneda-san's death. Her body shrunken, she sat smiling all day in her wheelchair. I spoke to her, even traced the character for my name on her palm, but she gave no sign that she knew who I was.

Mina told me she no longer spoke anything but German, though Yoneda-san had been able to communicate with her using a mixture of Japanese and the little German she knew. Their shared language was more proof that they were, in their way, twins.

All sorts of things were placed in Yoneda-san's coffin. Her beloved apron, a can of condensed milk, some contest entry postcards, a pen, photographs, flowers. Grandmother Rosa, smiling all the while, ran her fingers over Yoneda-san's eyelids and then slipped a straw hat and a beret into the coffin.

Mina and I held hands as we watched the smoke from the crematorium rise into the sky. Her arm was no longer as slender as Bambi's leg, no longer the tiny, fragile limb that had seemed on the verge of snapping as she'd stood crying on the beach at Suma, or desperately cheering the volleyball team, or receiving a matchbox from the Young Man from Wednesday. Now it seemed overflowing with life, ready to seize an unknown future.

〰〰〰

The following summer, after Grandmother Rosa had peacefully followed Yoneda-san, Mina left for boarding school in Switzerland without even waiting for the end of middle school. After that, she studied literature at a university in Frankfurt, then worked at a trading company and in the embassy. When she turned thirty-five, she founded a literary agency in Cologne, a company that promoted the exchange of translated literature between Europe and Japan. That was also the year of the Great Hanshin Earthquake.

She didn't return to Japan once during all that time, even when my uncle's company was bought by a giant beverage corporation, or when the house in Ashiya was sold.

The little girl who couldn't get to school without help from Pochiko was marching by herself now, far away in a distant land.

〰〰〰

Dear Tomoko,

It's the most beautiful time of the year here in Cologne. How are things in Okayama? How is your mother?

I grumble a lot about not making any money, but I love my work and put everything I have into it. Being an agent for translated literature isn't exactly glamorous, but

still it brings me small and often quite amazing pleasures.
Today, at a bookstore in town, I saw a young girl buying
a picture book I'd helped publish. She cradled the book
as if it were something precious, heading home holding
hands with her mother, and I found myself watching them
until they were out of sight. It brought back the way I
used to feel, waiting impatiently in the hallway, when
you'd gone off to the library to borrow books for me.

Summer vacation is approaching now—I'd love to have
you finally come visit me here in Cologne, if there's any
way you can. With your youngest one in high school, you
shouldn't be tied to the house quite so much, no?

Actually, the other day, by the strangest chance, I
discovered the apartment in Berlin where Grandmother
and her family used to live. It's in a neighborhood that
used to be in East Berlin. Of course, someone else
lives there now, but somehow the building escaped the
bombing during the war and looks very much as it
would have in their time. When I told Papa, he said he
absolutely had to see it and has decided to come visit
this summer. Mama will come with him, of course. They
plan on visiting the grave where they preserved some of
Grandmother's hair as well, and then spend some time at
their house near Arles.

I thought that maybe you might be able to come with
them. Though I suppose what I should really be asking
is whether you'd be willing to look after two old people
during such a long trip. But it would make me terribly
happy if we could work it out. There are so many things
and places I want to show you here.

Give it some thought at least. I'll wait to hear from

you. Given Papa's age and health, I'm pretty sure this will be the last time they'll be traveling overseas.

Take care of yourself. I'll write again soon.

Much love,

Mina

〰〰〰

Dear Mina,

Thank you for your letter and for the wonderful invitation! Oddly enough, the timing was perfect, since just last week I saw everyone at your father's seventy-seventh birthday party, and I was planning to write to tell you.

I was amazed to think it had been ten years since I'd been to their apartment in Kurakuen. The last time was when I went to help after the earthquake.

With all of Ryūichi's family there, too, it was a very lively party. No catering from the Mount Rokko Hotel, but we had a toast—German wine for the adults, juice for the children—and ate some delicious sushi. Someone pointed out that we would always have had Fressy to drink at an occasion like this before. I wonder how long it's been since they stopped making it?

I was happy to see that your mother and father both seem to be doing well. Your father looks so healthy it's hard to believe he's recovering from heart surgery. His color is excellent, as is his appetite, and he's as much a dandy as ever. Your mother looks after him, and she's clearly fond of her grandchildren, but she talks most about you, and still seems to worry that you live so far away.

It would be wonderful if we could make the summer vacation in Europe work. The library is closed for a week at O-Bon, so I should be able to get the time off, but I'm afraid I'd be more a burden to your parents than a help. At any rate, the first thing I need to do is apply for a passport.

Please take care of yourself. I'm counting the days until I get to see you.

Tomoko

P.S. On the train back from Kurakuen, it suddenly occurred to me that I could get off at Ashiya and go see what's become of your house. I loved that wonderful old place, but I'd been avoiding going back, since I was afraid there might be nothing left of it. But for some reason, that day, as I looked out at Ashiya from the train window, I felt something different. Perhaps I finally really believed that nothing could spoil my memories, even if things were completely different.

As I'd been told, the house has been converted into a dormitory for employees of a chemical company, and they built some apartments as well. Not only has your property been subdivided, but the other houses in the neighborhood are so different that I might have walked right by if I hadn't been paying close attention. Only part of the stone wall is still there.

A man who must have been the manager of the dormitory happened to be sweeping in the entrance hall, and when I explained I'd known the house long ago, he let me go inside. But when I did, it was even more disorienting. The view of the sea from the dining room window seemed impossibly small and far away, the garden was overgrown with weeds, and the parking lot for the apartments was just outside.

But I could still see the myrtle tree out the window on the west side. It's grown enormously tall, but there's no doubt it's the same one that stood watch over the Fressy Zoo gravestone. Scarlet sage was blooming at the base now, lovely red flowers. Maybe the seeds came from Pochiko's native Liberia to bloom on that very spot.

THE LEOPARD

The leopard is one of Harvill's historic colophons and an imprimatur of the highest quality literature from around the world.

When The Harvill Press was founded in 1946 by former Foreign Office colleagues Manya Harari and Marjorie Villiers (hence Harvill), it was with the express intention of rebuilding cultural bridges after the Second World War. As their first catalogue set out: 'The editors believe that by producing translations of important books they are helping to overcome the barriers, which at present are still big, to close interchange of ideas between people who are divided by frontiers.' The press went on to publish from many different languages, with highlights including Giuseppe Tomasi di Lampedusa's *The Leopard*, Boris Pasternak's *Doctor Zhivago*, José Saramago's *Blindness*, W. G. Sebald's *The Rings of Saturn*, Henning Mankell's *Faceless Killers* and Haruki Murakami's *Norwegian Wood*.

In 2005 The Harvill Press joined with Secker & Warburg, a publisher with its own illustrious history of publishing international writers. In 2020, Harvill Secker reintroduced the leopard to launch a new translated series celebrating some of the finest and most exciting voices of the twenty-first century.

Pedro Almodóvar: *The Last Dream*
    trans. Frank Wynne
Laurent Binet: *Civilisations*
    trans. Sam Taylor

Édouard Louis: *A Woman's Battles and Transformations*
  trans. Tash Aw
Édouard Louis: *Change: A Method*
  trans. John Lambert
Geert Mak: *The Dream of Europe: Travels in the Twenty-First Century*
  trans. Liz Waters
Layla Martínez: *Woodworm*
  trans. Sophie Hughes & Annie McDermott
Haruki Murakami: *First Person Singular: Stories*
  trans. Philip Gabriel
Haruki Murakami: *Murakami T: The T-Shirts I Love*
  trans. Philip Gabriel
Haruki Murakami: *Novelist as a Vocation*
  trans. Philip Gabriel & Ted Goossen
Ngũgĩ wa Thiong'o: *The Perfect Nine: The Epic of Gĩkũyũ and Mũmbi*
  trans. the author
Kristín Ómarsdóttir: *Swanfolk*
  trans. Vala Thorodds
Intan Paramaditha: *The Wandering*
  trans. Stephen J. Epstein
Per Petterson: *Men in My Situation*
  trans. Ingvild Burkey
Andrey Platonov: *Chevengur*
  trans. Robert Chandler & Elizabeth Chandler
Mohamed Mbougar Sarr: *The Most Secret Memory of Men*
  trans. Lara Vergnaud
Dima Wannous: *The Frightened Ones*
  trans. Elisabeth Jaquette
Emi Yagi: *Diary of a Void*
  trans. David Boyd & Lucy North